About the Author

Sandhi Smalls Santini grew up on Edisto Island, a remote sea island on coastal South Carolina, USA. She (Sandra L. Smalls) received her BA in Journalism and Theatre Arts from prestigious Howard University in Washington, DC. Subsequent studies were obtained in Human Rights from the Columbia University Graduate School of Arts & Sciences, NYC, NY. The author of "Edisto Island: Seaside Stories From A Geechee Gal", her writings have been published in *The Columbia University Newsletter of the Institute of African Studies; The Charleston Chronicle; The Howard University Hilltop;* and *Routes Magazine.* A member of Screen

Actors Guild/American Federation of Television & Radio Artists (SAG/AFTRA), League of Professional Theatre Women, and Society for the Preservation of Theatrical History; the author-playwright-cabaret performer has headlined worldwide as a vocalist. She currently lives in New York City, and is a correspondent for *Routes Magazine: A Guide To African American Culture*.

SH+AGUAR
The Night Huntress

Sandhi Smalls Santini

SH+AGUAR
The Night Huntress

Vanguard Press

VANGUARD PAPERBACK

A CIP catalogue record for this title is available from the British Library.

ISBN 978 1 80016 666 0

Vanguard Press is an imprint of
Pegasus Elliot Mackenzie Publishers Ltd.
www.pegasuspublishers.com

First Published in 2023

Vanguard Press
Sheraton House Castle Park
Cambridge England

Printed & Bound in Great Britain

In loving memory of my dear parents, Eugenia (Nene) and Samuel (Bandy), who inspired and nurtured my imagination, and my beloved husband, Giancarlo, who introduced me to the glorious world that once was Chelsea Place.

Chapter 1
Ultraviolet Visions

Catapulted into a corridor of light, my weightless body spirals at full velocity, then barrels through a tunnel without walls! It is a mystifying journey somewhere to the ends of the unknown. In this violet-tinted place, there are no boundaries, no terra, no ceiling, no measure of time. I am twirling even more rapidly now. Behind me the tunnel narrows, whipping and slithering like the tail of an angry serpent. Ahead, a hungry, cavernous gape opens, and swallows me whole. All that is left are remnants of my fragmented mind and soul, shredded pieces of the person I once was.

Swish!

Whoosh!

Thump!

In this place, I see no land, no sky. There are no delineations whatsoever. No beginnings, and, seemingly, no endings anywhere. Like the tunnel without walls that transported me here, there are no visible lines drawn between the real, the unreal, and the surreal. All that exists are copious shades of violet and purple layers that blend infinitely. In this world, everything that happens occurs within, around, and about me. I am no doubt baffled by all that I see, smell, and sense. But for reasons unknown, I feel quite at home here. I am neither frightened nor afraid in this otherworldly place.

I hear a cacophony of discordant, deafening sounds. There is a continuous chorus of indistinct, babbling that encircles me. Not the kind of babbling that is normally ascribed to chatty humans, but rather, the kind of imagined menacing howls that would come from some abhorrent creature. In this peculiar place, everything blends seamlessly, and invariably into what appears to be reflections of willowy shadows. The commotion is further compounded by a collage of two twisting figures — phantasmic silhouettes that are intriguingly graceful, and comely. I am haunted deeply by these two, rather seductive images. One is filled with bright, blinding, ultraviolet rays. The other, shrouded in deep, purplish darkness. They seem to dance, then merge into a single, oversized shadow — a towering and powerful penumbra that allures and consumes me. Whatever '*it*' is, I am now a part of it. We are *one*.

I do not know how to aptly describe this fascinating thing, but it leaves the most indelible impression on me. Both seen and unseen, it is neither human, nor beast, but rather something in between. By all accounts, it is a living, breathing, creature. Misshapen and indefinable, it hovers around me, very much alive, changing and morphing so constantly, that I become dizzy and disoriented. Transfixed, I can only observe, as its spirited energy dances lithely around me. *Is it worshiping me? Or is it trying to seduce me?* I am finally rendered dazed and wholly confused. Whatever *it* is, it never leaves me alone, not even for a moment.

Then, without warning, it happens again, a sudden surge of energy! A blinding flash of light! A brilliant wave of violet! And…

Swish!

Whoosh!

Thump!

Huh! Huh! Huh! I'm back! I'm back home! Huh! Huh! Huh! And I'm breathing! Yes! I'm breathing! Which means I'm still alive… I think. Whew! I've found my way back home. But I've completely lost my mind! Where the hell is that place? And why do I keep going back there?

The last thing I remembered… I was in my bedroom. The next thing I knew, I was spinning through that goddamned *tunnel*! And now I'm here at the bottom of the stairs, just as I was yesterday and the day before, in this stalk-and-ambush position — on all fours — scratching the floor with my newly manicured nails!

The roof of my mouth is stimulated by a sensational aroma. I gasp, in pure pleasure, and it suddenly hits me. It is the definable smell of a feline. More specifically, the tantalizing scent that reminded me of the times I'd bury my face in the belly of Queen Sheba, my childhood cat. The smell, so overwhelming, that I spun around, thinking my beloved black beauty was nearby.

Somewhat disheveled after that harrowing journey, and with the smell of cat permeating the air, I hit the bathroom for a quick shower. I needed to reboot, to wash away everything, and start anew. I needed time to rethink *everything,* starting with my outfit for the day. On any other wintry day, the frigid temperature of twenty-seven degrees would have given me goosebumps all over. But instead, this morning, the air felt more like a soft, autumn breeze. I'm not cold. I'm not shivering. And I'm certainly not freezing. As a matter of fact, the weather is perfect for the right cape, the right hat, and the right pair of boots.

The cape I'm wearing? It is by Loro Piana, a luscious shade of burgundy. It's all wool. Suede-trimmed, and yes, certainly understated. I love capes! Capes are a must-have, a necessary outerwear. No one's closet should be without at least two of them. I love the way wearing a cape makes me feel — brave, gallant, and heroic. What can I say? Capes have an empowering effect on me. The hat I'm wearing is a classic, wide-brimmed Borsalino, in charcoal gray. Hats signify a degree of nobility, authority, and power. They add that finishing touch to an outfit. Hats protect the head, and they also help to keep heat in one's body. On my feet, I am wearing a pair of soft-as-butter Stuart Weitzman boots — in a rich, charcoal gray color, with sensible heels, of course. Why these boots? Because, above all,

I'm extremely practical. They're made *really* well. They're comfortable, made for walking, and they will last forever! Finally, the money bag. Today, I'm bringing along my burgundy and gray Ferragamo tote. It's the perfect size, just big enough to hold everything a woman, or a man needs. The overall look reflects the perfect blend of classic, contemporary, and chic — a look my mother would certainly approve of. I'm the first to admit it, I am a die-hard fan of fashion. I've learned that fashion, as with life, comes down to having just the right amount of style, class, good taste, and sensibility. I call it *balance*. And after all that I've been through lately, a good strong dose of balance is exactly what I need.

Now, back to those strange occurrences I've recently encountered. They are vividly realistic, even if they leave me feeling severely separated from what I consider to be my own reality. The only thing that I am completely certain about, is that something profoundly inexplicable is happening to me. I am definitely caught up in some kind of weird twilight zone. Or, God forbid, the unthinkable: *Am I slowly slipping away from the world and losing my grip on life?* In other words… the most plausible explanation for what I've been going through is that I'm simply going mad!

The sudden, invisible waves of energy… the tunnel… the violet haze… and those visions that seem to surge and zoom from… who knows where. These are only some of the unsettling events I've been experiencing recently. What I do remember is that today is the third time I've gone back *there*… to that place… wherever it is. I am left thoroughly bewildered by all that I have seen and felt there. What I find most alluring are those obscured, elusive images — unrecognizable, faceless, and nameless — all shadowed in a mysterious violet-tinted cloud. Where and how are these things happening? Why am I left feeling so discombobulated?

I'm not sure if I ever really fell asleep last night, or the two nights before. A part of me desperately wants to believe that I was dreaming. But the truth is, I could not have been dreaming. I was fully awake, all three nights. And my eyes were wide open. Even now, those mysterious sounds still linger in my ear, those smells still entice my palate.

I can imagine just how Jason, cloaked in arrogance, would attempt to explain all of this unexplainable madness to me: "Mom, those experiences were all enclosed somewhere within the deep, unlimited confines of your head. They were merely thoughts and imaginings nestled between the lobes, folds, and walls of your innermost mind."

Sure! Right! He'd have to come up with a better theory than that. That's barely a stone's throw away from me trying to sell someone the Brooklyn Bridge! Now, since I was in fact, wide-eyed during these odd experiences, chances are that I was probably not dreaming. For lack of a better term, I will call these encounters *ultraviolet visions,* bearing in mind that it all happened suddenly, forcefully, and powerfully, and that everything existed, or co-existed, within a realm of brilliant shades of violet. I think that sounds more or less, appropriate.

The sudden, fierce waves of light directed towards me, the sounds, the smells, and sights, were all from another place, another time, another *somewhere else.* Curiously enough, deep down inside, I was convinced that at least, some part of me, belonged *there,* in that place. What I need right now are plain, simple, rational answers — the kind of answers I always got from Lem. He always said that there was at least one good explanation for *almost* everything that happens. "*Lem! My precious Lem! Seven years ago! No! I can't... I won't go back there! I've got to block that terrifying memory from my mind. It's time Jason and I move on with our lives!*

Considering that I'm functioning on a mere two hours, or less, of sleep, and haven't had my morning brew, I'll just brush those visions off, for now. Besides, believe it or not, in spite of everything that is against me, I am actually brimming with an overabundance of energy — the kind of raw, unquenchable energy that I haven't felt in a very long time. I feel really good! Perhaps this is just pure adrenaline kicking in. Maybe it is my body's way of keeping me awake and moving. If this is out-of-control adrenalin, then bring it on. After all, it feels damned good!

This is actually the kind of energy I need to help me get through what I know will be a heated and highly contentious meeting with Giancarlo Santini and Big Joe D'Amato. The meeting comes at Santini's behest. Were it not for this private, very important meeting, all 115 pounds of my five foot, four inch frame would still be tucked underneath one of my mother's warm, handmade quilts, curled fetal position, in my bed. Instead, I'm making my way down to Chelsea Place, to meet with my general manager and bouncer.

Clang! Clang! Clannnng! The sound of the latching wrought iron door re-echoed across the quiet enclave. A quick pull, or two, on the doorknob, just to make sure it's really locked, because s*ecurity matters.* I've learned that sounds, like people, can be quite deceiving. That done, all of my attention is now focused on the cell phone I'm holding. On the screen, the little red house icon flashes — pulsing and throbbing, much like the rhythm of a human heartbeat. I enter my well-guarded security code, then wait for three neon green check marks to appear. The green check marks, and green house icon, confirm that the ultra-high security surveillance and video system on my townhouse, and all of its immediate surrounding territory, have been properly activated and synchronized with my portable devices.

When the little red house turns green, I'm good to go. This reassures me that I have, in fact, entered the correct code — an unforgettable series of numbers that I will always remember, simply because they are permanently and painfully etched into my memory.

Performing this ritual has become as automatic to me as breathing. No, I am not at all paranoid. Paranoia is the result of distrusting people without reasonable cause. All of my actions are justified — I am *territorial.* That's right... territorial — *"protective of my area, my home, my spot."* In case you've forgotten, allow me to remind you, Manhattan has always been, and still is, a glass and concrete jungle — wild, untamed, and extremely dangerous!

My little townhouse is located on a quiet, tree-lined block. This is my domain. It has my mark on it. Never mind that it is not even half the size of the Riverside Drive brownstone I once shared with my husband Lem, and our son, Jason. And it looks nothing like any of the other heavily renovated, modernized houses on this ritzy row of residences on West Twenty-Second Street, in New York City's Chelsea District. It is not a big house. What it does have is some personality, and a whole lot of security.

It is an elegant structure, with numerous essential attributes. The house sits more than twenty feet away from the sidewalk, sufficiently removed from pedestrians. There's a generous front yard, a gated backyard, and two splendid side yards, totally detached from houses on either side. Yes, one might say that this is social distancing at its very best. It has attic windows, encircled with engraved, ornamental wreaths, wrought iron handrails, towering gates, and a recessed, arched doorway, complete with a heavy, alarmingly loud-sounding wrought iron door. That was the blaring sound you heard earlier.

There is something very comforting about the sound of a heavy door closing. It proves that you are doing your part to keep the unwanted and the uninvited outside — away from your person, away from your loved ones and prized possessions. The house's special amenities were attributes that immediately appealed to me when I bought it almost seven years ago.

Thanks to my high-powered team of lawyers, I was finally given the go-ahead to erect a towering, fortress-like wall around all of my territory. Needless to say that, once completed, this construction was much to the disdain of my nice-but-nosy neighbors, some of whom have publicly labeled my property, 'the Fortress of Twenty-Second Street'. My neighbors can say whatever it is they say. They're neither family nor friends. They are just nosy neighbors. What I do within my territory is my business. Little do they know that I have damned good reasons for all of this madness. Right now, I'm far more concerned about those appalling experiences I've been having lately.

For goodness sake, this is New York City! The wild jungle, remember? The place that never sleeps! But here, on this block, at least, there is not even another soul anywhere in sight. The morning, still too young for anyone in this pampered community to even entertain the thought of getting up, going out, and about. Too early to do anything, that is, other than look forward to, lunching, brunching, and shopping. Yes, it is definitely too early for the lovely ladies who lounge, graze through lunch, and spend their days getting manicured and pedicured. Behind those ornate, gilded facades, waif-like, well-kept moms are having breakfast in bed, while their Eastern European, Filipina, and South American au pairs hurry sleepy-eyed, uniformed kids off to Trinity, Spence, The Chapin School, St. Bernard's, Marymount, and Dalton.

Finding balance in life is essential to one's overall survival. It is a road that must be traveled, along the way, to finding self-discovery. I find balance in life when I position myself squarely between the right side and the left side of my person. Doing so lands me smack in the middle of my *comfort zone*. You know, that place where you are *most* comfortable… that private, little world where you are totally and completely in control of everything — you, your state of mind, your life, your existence, your environment, your weaknesses and strengths, your good, and bad. Finding balance gives me comfort and peace of mind. It is a concept that I can totally wrap my arms around and embrace.

Time, on the other hand, is, in every way, a four-letter word. It is a concept that is altogether different: An indefinite, continued progression of existence, a constant flow of past, present, and future events — all meeting, merging, and connecting — combining to create a beginning, middle, and end. Time is a fleeting, indefinite concept that frightens me. I simply cannot be bothered with it.

A quick glance at my cell phone lets me know that I have more than enough time to get to my meeting with Santini and Big Joe.

So, just who are Giancarlo Santini and Big Joe D'Amato? They are easily two of the most stubborn people I have ever encountered in my entire life, that is, with the exception of my husband, Lem, and our son, Jason.

In short, Santini and Big Joe are two people who are constantly on a collision course, so to speak. They come from different worlds, and very different walks of life. Their backgrounds and histories are eons apart, and tell two distinctly different stories. They clash constantly. But in spite of their differences, they do have certain characteristics in common. For the record, they are both contentious, stubborn, hard-headed, Italian men; both, good, decent, and honest human beings, to a fault.

Giancarlo Antonio Santini comes from old Italian nobility. He was born in Milan, Italy, into an affluent, but greatly fractured aristocratic family. He is European upper-crust at its utmost. Santini and I have known each other for a long time. To be more specific, I've known him for most of my life. He has a habit of finishing my sentences, and equally annoying, I finish his sentences. I know him, the way he knows me — better than we know ourselves. We have quite a history. I've known him longer than anyone else here at Chelsea Place, with the exception of my best friend Eugenia McKelvey. This dignified gentleman once managed my singing career in Europe. Together, his well-placed connections in high places, and my hard work and diligence, paid off handsomely. He is now the trusted and esteemed general manager of Chelsea Place.

Joseph 'Big Joe' D'Amato is our towering and intimidating bouncer. An ex-New York City detective, Big Joe was born in an apartment above his parents' restaurant on Mulberry Street in Manhattan's Little Italy. He grew up between the world of Catholic priests and the domain of the Italian mafia. We met the night my husband, Lem, was violently abducted from our home on Riverside Drive.

Santini and Big Joe are a combination that reminds me of oil and water. They do not mix well. In fact, they do not mix at all. They are extremely civilized, decent, good-hearted human beings who are, unbeknownst to each other, quite similar. These two men have finally found common ground for something they both feel equally as passionate about, their irrepressible detestation and contempt for Vlad. They want him gone from Chelsea Place in a bad way — out of sight, out of mind, and out of their way. ASAP! Forever! If it were up to them, they'd gladly volunteer to accompany Vlad thirteen steps up to the gallows, or, drag him to a guillotine, and happily position his head just so — whichever came first.

Big Joe D'Amato is, by all accounts, a towering and intimidating figure. If he didn't like you, he made sure you knew just how much he disliked you. It was crystal clear that he hated Vlad from the moment he first laid eyes on him. Since then, that volatile relationship has seriously gone downhill, with Big Joe's greeting to Vlad further reduced to a sullen, razor-sharp sneer. They no longer exchange words with each other, only mean, guttural grunts.

Other than their unbridled hostility towards Vlad, Giancarlo Santini and Big Joe D'Amato are truly perfect gentlemen. One might conclude that there's at least a thread of commonality that connects these men. You know, like for instance, their shared Italian heritage. Uh-uh. Not so. They regularly engage in fierce, thankfully, bloodless battles. Between the two of them, they have somehow managed to resurrect The Civil War. There are moments when Chelsea Place becomes their private battlefield. Not wanting to get caught in the crossfires, I've learned how to run for cover, and hit the ground fast, whenever verbal shots are fired between them. What I find most perplexing is that, most of the time, they're in agreement. They say the same things, only differently. The thing is, they both *love* to talk. If only they'd stop talking, and listen to each other, once in a while, they'd be surprised to learn just how much they agree on.

It is safe to say that none of us is even remotely enthusiastic about returning to Chelsea Place so early in the morning, barely five hours after we'd closed for the night. But there is one, big, messy problem that has to be cleaned up immediately — an un-welcomed guest — a foul problem that is offending my exceptional staff, as well as the good patrons of Chelsea Place. That problem comes in the name of one *Vlad, The Caviar Czar,* as he so arrogantly, and annoyingly, introduces himself. So, why are we meeting? We are meeting to discuss, in Santini's words: *"the disturbing, despicable, and totally unacceptable shenanigans of Vlad, that fucking so-called Caviar Czar."*

Vlad, The Caviar Czar, is a rambunctious, ostentatious Russian, an unseemly type who has recently taken a real liking to Chelsea Place. He comes in each and every night. A rotund, bull-necked man with thick sideburns, steely pale-gray eyes, and a full head of transplanted, jet black hair, he's flashy, in a grotesque way. Vlad is a walking billboard who wears head-to-toe designer-logos, oversized, chunky jewelry, and way too much cologne. He overindulges in everything. This proclivity alone is reason enough for Santini to condemn and execute him on the spot.

Now, under normal circumstances, we would all have welcomed him, with arms wide open, into our wonderful little circle known as the Chelsea Place family. The problem is, Vlad has deplorable social habits, one of the many reasons why no one likes him. Not a single person I know likes that man! He repulses everyone, in a sickening kind of way. There's something essentially wrong about someone who is so universally disliked.

Vlad certainly rubs me the wrong way. I find him to be quite off-putting, and that's putting it mildly. My extraordinarily warm and friendly staff, and our gracious, well-behaved clientele, are all offended by his presence and behavior. The man is beyond annoying. He is beginning to get under everyone's skin, to the point where he's even chasing away some of our best customers. I will not stand for this. Santini, Eugenia, and Big Joe despise him. There is no way around it. Vlad, the Caviar Czar, has got to go!

Chapter 2
Chelsea Place

"Tell only your best friends."
~Giancarlo A. Santini

There are so many new and interesting places in Lower Manhattan these days. Soho continues to shine brightly with its famous "A-list" celebrities. The Meat Packing District is, well, packed nightly and tightly with wall-to-wall fashionistas and super skinny runway models. Last, but certainly not least, Alphabet City, no longer a grit and grunge destination, has its very own coveted bohemian allure. Each community is constantly and aggressively changing, improving, vying for its claim to fame and the famous, while flaunting a long list of ritzy hotels, chic, overcrowded lobby bars, restaurants, and nightclubs. But they all pale in comparison to *Chelsea Place*. Much like my extremely-fortressed house on West Twenty-Second Street, Chelsea Place — affectionately referred to as "*the place* in Chelsea," has a unique personality. Simply put, Chelsea Place is in a class all by itself. There is no other place, anywhere in the world, quite like *my place.*

A restaurant-nightclub-speakeasy-piano bar — everything is housed in an enviable three-story Greek Revival Mansion. It is an extraordinary place. A glorious landmarked structure situated almost clandestinely, in a slightly recessed area between Eighth and Ninth Avenues, near the corner of Seventeenth Street. Its cobblestoned colonnade leads to a pair of imposing square pilasters, and an impressive entrance — a facade adorned with ornate cornices, and friezes.

Once inside, you enter through mirrored doors of what look like an oversized antique armoire, then step into an elegant piano lounge with huge fireplaces, brick walls, velvet armchairs, chaise lounges, Tiffany stained lamps, and a majestically winding staircase. It's like stepping back into a perfectly preserved, gloriously wonderful place in time.

In the center of the room, perched on a slightly elevated stage, is a magnificent white concert piano. The piano lounge is where most of the live action takes place. Upstairs is ultra-private. Like the restaurant downstairs, it is strictly by reservation only. Guests in the innermost loop make their reservations far in advance, laying claim to their favorite table and waitperson. Upstairs is in some ways, an uber private club, aptly nicknamed *"The only legal speakeasy in New York."*

Discreetly hidden downstairs is an intimate and very romantic glass-enclosed, candle-lit restaurant with a cascading pond. This slate trimmed pond is home to two highly entertaining white ducks. We have appropriately named them Fettuccine and Alfredo. They are showbiz ducks who love to be seen, and heard. Quiet and motionless until the restaurant is full, they make their grand entrances — swirling and gliding around inside the pond — performing to an adoring audience of diners!

Chelsea Place is its own little universe. It is a world unto itself; a frenzied nighttime playground for international jet-setters, royalty, aristocrats, high-rollers, film stars, moguls, heads-of-states, billionaire athletes, and other assorted beautiful people. It is home to what the uppermost class still calls *"the smart set"* — a gilded microcosm of the world's wealthiest class — a delicious potpourri of power, privilege and prestige, from the oldest aristocracies, to the recently minted, beyond imagination, nouveau riche.

Welcome! I am KITT KOUGAR! Yes, clearly a stage name — given to me by none other than Giancarlo 'The Count' Santini, himself. I've kept the name because it is definitely catchy, and it sounds good. It is the name by which most people know me. It also allows me to keep my original initials. For your information, my name at birth was Kathleen Keels. I was born on Edisto Island, a picturesque, remote sea island on coastal South Carolina. But that, my dear friends, is another place, and, indeed, another story yet to be told.

In any case, I've finally arrived. And here we are! Welcome to CHELSEA PLACE — *the place in Chelsea!* Near its aesthetic entrance, a bronze plaque, befittingly installed, says all one needs to know about what goes on behind that gilded door. Discreetly embedded into the wall, the plaque simply reads: *"Chelsea Place. Tell only your best friends."* — Giancarlo Antonio Santini.

"*Buongiorno. Sei puntuale!*" Santini greeted me, wearily. His voice floated from his favorite chair in the corner of the room. Gazing thoughtfully into the fireplace, his mind was at least a million miles away. He pretended not to notice the imposing man who had just entered his realm.

"Br-r-r-r! Feels like Alaska in the dead of winter!" Big Joe chimed in, slowly peeling out of a long, army green coat. He had arrived just ahead of me.

"Good morning, guys. Looks as if you spent the night here!" I yelled out with a quick wave of my hand. "Glad you're enjoying the fireplace."

Big Joe rubbed his hands briskly, slid into a chair across from Santini, then stared sleepily into the fireplace. "Yep! Feels like I never left. Great idea having these fireplaces done up… you know… re-done… or whatever it is they call it these days," he said under his breath.

No verbal response was forthcoming from Santini, who kept his eyes glued on the orange-red flames.

I was busy digging inside my tote bag for the key card that opens the door to my office, but clearly heard Big Joe's remark. "It's called up-cycled, upgraded, and repurposed for maximum performance," I replied, determined not to start the meeting on a sour note. "In short, that pretty Art Deco fireplace that was once fueled by smokey, sooted logs, now radiates clean and efficient heat."

Santini drew in a long, deep breath, and exhaled. "I must say, I do love the glowing logs and the crackling sounds. Quite dramatic… and very realistic-looking." He paused, closed his eyes, then leaned back into the chair. "This almost reminds me of my real fireplace back home in Milano," he added, talking to himself.

"Sounds as if someone's getting a little homesick," Big Joe said dryly, his gaze fixed firmly on the flickering flames, intentionally not turning to face Santini.

"Only now and then," came the other's slow response, his eyes still closed, as if he were asleep.

"No smoke, no soot, no need to cut any logs; and you can adjust the amount of heat that comes out. Genius!" Big Joe deadpanned.

Neither was even remotely engaged in the conversation. They were accustomed to speaking to each other that way — without ever making any eye contact whatsoever. *Why on earth do people do that?* I wondered to myself. I understand that some people are just extremely timid and shy away from eye-to-eye contact. I get that. And I respect that. But I had been brought up to always look someone straight in the eye when speaking to them. To this day, whenever someone avoids making eye contact with me while we're talking, I feel disconnected and downright uncomfortable.

"Good morning everybody! Your regulars? One cappuccino for Ms Kitt… one espresso for Mr Santini… and one big mug of strong black coffee for Mr Big Joe, yes?"

"Yes, please. Thank you, Javier. We'll have them here in my office."

"*Non problema.* I bring them right away," the custodian replied, sprinting across the room, and downstairs to the kitchen.

Javier returned within moments, the smell of hot fresh coffee filling the room. "Okay, coffee and Danish for everybody," he announced, walking past Santini and Big Joe while pointing the large tray towards the office. "I'll put it inside," he added, placing the tray carefully on Kitt's huge, antique desk. He nodded, smiled, then quickly exited.

Reluctantly the two men rose, and yawned, unapologetically. Neither was quite ready, just yet, to part with the soothing ambience created by the over-sized, glowing fireplace. I was already seated behind my desk when they dragged themselves into the office.

While Santini and Big Joe helped themselves to Danish pastries and coffee, I placed both of my cell phones on the desk, and wrapped my hands around my cup, delighting in the aroma circling from the rich, foamy, cappuccino. I savored a mouthful, closed my eyes, then sank into the softness of my big leather chair. As they reached for their cups, and settled into their leather chairs facing me, Big Joe raised a curious eyebrow. "Isn't that coffee still too hot to drink? My God! There's steam billowing from it!"

"Yes, normally I allow my coffee to temper down just a bit," I replied, looking curiously at the steam rising from my cup. "I guess it's okay. It didn't burn my tongue. In fact, it's actually kind of lukewarm."

A puzzled look covered his face. "No way on earth that kind of steam comes from anything that's lukewarm!" He grunted, shaking his head in disbelief.

Santini was in his own world, adding way too much sugar to his espresso, and oblivious to the fact that Big Joe and I were waiting for him to begin the meeting. It was, after all, he who declared, in no uncertain terms, that "*Vlad's caviar czar's ass should be permanently booted and banned from the premises, subito!*" That announcement was first issued, unabashedly, in fiery, overly dramatized Italian — complete with hand, leg, and bodily gestures. It was later translated into English, in a cooler, less colorful way. Thoroughly entertained by Santini's histrionics, and laughing uncontrollably,

Big Joe and I wholeheartedly agreed that Vlad was far more deserving of the spicier Italian version.

Settled comfortably into our chairs, Big Joe and I turn our attention to Santini and give him our undivided attention. Like two eager students in a classroom, we stare obediently at him, and eagerly wait for the professor to, first of all, deliver his lecture on Vlad, the undesirable, and then, wisely instruct us as to how we can quickly and permanently eradicate this nuisance from Chelsea Place. Instead, Santini pulls a fast one on us. With his sugary sweet espresso in hand, he takes a small sip, then, with an exaggerated nod of his chin, gestures to Big Joe.

"Let's start with what you have," he says, without looking at him. "After all, you are our so-called *gate-keeper*. You're the first person Vlad sees when he arrives at Chelsea Place. If you'd just refuse that ass-hole entrance at the door, you'd be the last person he saw. End of story."

Big Joe's face turned beet red. He took a big gulp of coffee and stared into the dark brew, as if searching for patience. "Easier said than done!" He fumed. He shifted his body in the chair, then directed his attention to me. "For starters, Vlad rubs everyone the wrong way. His vulgarity, especially, makes women feel uncomfortable"

"As does his distasteful habit of bringing in under-aged girls, and unabashedly parading them all night long!" Santini interrupted, finishing his espresso and slamming the empty cup onto the tray.

"Everyone here is on the same page," I said, sternly, folding my arms and leaning into the conversation. "We all agree that Vlad is a repulsive human being, who is not welcomed here. Please… let's focus on that and decide together, how we can best handle him. Go on, Big Joe."

Big Joe rubbed his red eyes and took another gulp of coffee. "Vlad throws around a lot of cash. He never uses credit cards. We've been vigilantly checking for counterfeit bills, and so far, his money has come up clean"

"Clean!" Santini exploded. "I find that hard to believe. There's not a damn thing clean about Vlad! He's a no-good piece of filthy shit! Rude, crude, and obnoxious! He doesn't belong here! Just do your job and keep him out of here! Stop his goddam Russian ass at the door!"

"Whoa! Whoa! Whoa! I don't need you telling me how to do my job, Santini! In case you haven't noticed, Chelsea Place is fucking expensive! I'm sure it looks and feels like one of those uppity private clubs you once owned. Drinks alone cost an arm and a leg! But this is not a private establishment. It's public, which means anyone who can afford these sky-high prices can come in!" He took a deep breath and glanced sheepishly at me. "No offense to you, Kitt, but we all know that the people who come in here spend more money in one night than the average New Yorker pays per month in rent! Talk about disparities!"

It was an awkward moment. I winced, glanced briefly at Santini, then stared silently at Big Joe, who had suddenly come to a full stop.

Indignation radiated from Santini's face, as he shifted in his seat, then stared at Big Joe. "With the exception of Vlad, I see nothing at all wrong with our clientele!" he seethed.

"For the record, most of the people who come into Chelsea Place are good, decent people, who just so happen to be very rich and very powerful." He folded his arms defiantly, and raised his eyes. "Mister D'Amato, I should hope that you do not dislike any of these people simply because they're wealthy."

Big Joe knew he had some explaining to do. He placed his cup on the tray and sat up in his chair. "No… No… No! That's not at all what I'm saying! Listen Santini, I'm sure you Europeans approach it differently. But here in New York, there's a thin green line between kicking someone out of your club and getting sued in civil court for discrimination!"

"Guys! Guys! Listen. I know you don't always see eye-to-eye. (*A blatant understatement!*) But we're all here for the same reason. We need to have a united front if we're going to get rid of this Vlad guy!"

The tension between Santini and Big Joe felt like the repulsive force that exists between two different magnets, both pushing away from each other when they're nearby. What I loathed, were times like this, when they went after each other's jugular, with total disregard for me or any of the staff that might have gotten caught in the crossfires. Eugenia had mastered how to quickly extinguish those fires the two men were known for igniting. Watching them in action is what I would imagine a spectator must have felt like while seated in the audience of an amphitheater in ancient Rome, anxiously looking on as two armed combatants, in the arena, violently confronted and fought each other to the death of one. I do not take well to highly combative sports, and I am certainly not in the mood for any of that this morning. I've already had more than my fair share of drama, far more than either of them would have been able to handle. And it's still morning!

Separately and individually, these two men are extremely good at what they do. Their personalities render them each, perfect for their positions. I admire and respect them both, and I am not about to take either side this morning. I must remain neutral, for the benefit of Chelsea Place, and the sake of all of us. All I want to do is get rid of Vlad! After a moment of heated silence, Santini let out a protracted sigh, threw his arms into the air, and leaned back into his chair, with that wicked little smile plastered on his face. I know him like I know the back of my hands. This is a gesture with a very short lifespan. He's yielding for the moment. But trust me, it is a temporary truce.

Exasperated, Big Joe shot Santini a dagger-look, and sighed. "According to Halo, Vlad targets certain profiles at the bar, you know, single, cocky, men. He buys them just enough drinks to loosen their lips, get them bragging about how important they are, and how fat their bank accounts are. If they pass the litmus test, bam! They get a pretty, young girl on each arm."

I glanced briefly at Santini, then Big Joe, hoping to keep the conversation balanced and civilized. "Poor guys never learn, do they? What about these young girls he's peddling here?"

Santini's voice was filled with contempt. "The man brings in a harem of under-aged, so-called nieces, and puts child prostitution up close, right in everyone's face! This is totally unacceptable!"

Big Joe nodded slightly. "His rainbow family of nieces are mostly Eastern European, Asian, South American types. Those girls are dressed to the nines, and armed with perfectly flawless, fake IDs. Did I mention *flawless?*" he added, sarcastically. "It's my word against their flawless ID's. Damn fake cards are made so well not even I can tell the difference between them and the real ones!"

I was burning inside with anger. "Abhorrent! Child prostitution is disgusting and ugly on every level! People who promote it should be thrown in jail and locked up forever!" I took a deep breath and sighed. "That is the last thing we need here. Having our names associated with child prostitution would be detrimental to Chelsea Place. That's the kind of thing that would get us and our guests a lot of unwanted notoriety."

Big Joe groaned, leaned forward, and folded his long arms on the desk. His deep, piercing eyes were like two arrows. Looking at him, I understood why most people would tread cautiously around him. It wasn't so much his size, as it was the energy he gave off. Big Joe trusted no one. And that was something everyone felt immediately. I rather liked that quality about him. He got instant respect, which always brought out the best in people. Everyone behaved well in Big Joe's presence.

When he spoke, his voice was always firm, and controlled. He cracked his knuckles and exhaled. "Vlad's hands are definitely deep into child prostitution, which usually goes hand-in-hand with child enslavement, child pornography, international slave trade, money laundering, human trafficking, corruption, and other scary things that lurk in the underworld."

They were both as revolted by Vlad as I was. How could two people with so much goodness, honor, and dignity not find a way to get along? Giancarlo 'The Count' Santini, and Joseph 'Big Joe' D'Amato — so different, yet so very much alike.

Here's where my best friend Eugenia McKelvey, Chelsea Place's three-star Michelin chef, comes into the mix. The three of them, Eugenia, Santini, and Big Joe, collectively formed a kind of human pyramid — enduring, unbroken, and unyielding — each of them his own mystery. They're all stubborn by nature, all set in their own ways, and all convinced that their way is the only right way of doing things. They are extremely near and dear to me. All old enough to know just how cruel, unfair, bad, and ugly life can be. Like me, they've had more than their fair share of life's disappointments, heartbreaks, pains, and unkindnesses. Eugenia, Santini and Big Joe are all cut from the same fabric — a little bit of wool, a little bit of silk, and a whole lot of heart. They are salt of the earth people — trustworthy and straightforward human beings of exceptionally good character. I appreciate them, their honesty, loyalty, and most of all, their old-fashioned ways. I know how extremely fortunate I am to have each of them in my life, and on my side.

Chapter 3
Inside Santini's Head

Santini sat quietly, rubbing the day-old beard on his chin, tapping his foot, and staring at the floor. He was completely lost in his thoughts.

What on earth is he thinking about? I wondered.

When he looked up, our eyes met. Suddenly… there it was… again… that invisible wave of energy… the violet-tinged light…! The tunnel…! The whirling!

SWOOSH!

WHISH!

THUMP!

Dear God! I'm inside Santini's head… listening to his *thoughts!* I am clearly reading his mind!

(HIS THOUGHT) Mio Dio! I don't see why this is such an issue for Big Joe. Just tell the jerk he's not allowed in! If that doesn't work, try slapping and kicking him a few times! That will keep him away!

"We've got to get rid of this man quickly and quietly," Santini murmured.

(HIS THOUGHT) Life was simpler and so much sweeter in Europe. Oh, how I miss living in Italia!

"It's an awful shame that we have to handle him with kid gloves."

(HIS THOUGHT) Kitt was the brightest shining star in the cabaret world. I was the happiest man alive. We were such a powerhouse, and there was no Vlad to contend with!

"Some of our best people are already staying away because they do not like Vlad. He's a persona non grata here," Santini said in a low, almost ominous voice.

(HIS THOUGHT) How does she not realize that what we share is so much greater than love? I would give anything to relive those days! They were the best times ever!

For the fourth time during this conversation, while he was saying one thing, he was actually thinking something else. I heard his thoughts the same way I heard his voice. Can he feel my presence inside his head? I wondered. Did he know that I had gotten inside his head? Entered his mind… and invaded his private thoughts? My journey inside Santini's head was interrupted by the buzzing of my cell phone, which I reached for a nanosecond before it vibrated.

BUZZZ! BUZZZ! BUZZZ!

Hurtled from his mind, I exited the same way I had entered — in a sudden flash of light. With a thrust of speed, I was again barreled through that mysterious tunnel!

SWOOSH!

WHISH!

THUMP!

"Hah!" I blurted out, frantically grasping the chair arms. I was thrusted from his head. It had all happened so fast!

"Hey! One crisp Ben Franklin for your thoughts!" Big Joe's baritone voice boomed, jolting me back to our meeting, and prompting me to sit up and collect myself — emotionally, physically, and otherwise. Shell-shocked, my body jerked in such a manner that Santini and Big Joe were both convinced, beyond a doubt, that I had nodded off to sleep in the middle of our meeting.

"Planet Chelsea Place calling Kitt Kougar! Are you still here with us?" Big Joe teased, his thick eyebrows raised, playfully.

My eyes were still fixed firmly on Santini, who seemed to be enjoying the moment.

He leaned his head to one side and mischievously chimed in. "You fell asleep my dear, are we boring you to death? Or are you simply in need of more hours of sleep?"

"No one wants pennies these days," Big Joe chuckled. "I thought I'd up the ante!"

Their eyes were focused on the phone as it wiggled on my desk. Without looking at the caller ID, I knew exactly who was calling.

Eugenia's voice resonated from the phone. "Hi Kitt! Just a quick call. I know you folks are in the middle of a big powwow right now."

"No worries, Eugenia. What's up?"

"It's more like who's up? That would be your son, aka my godson. Where is that boy? I've been trying to reach Jason for two days now and he hasn't gotten back to me. He never ignores my calls. That's not like him!"

"He's been putting tons of overtime in at work. I'm calling him after our meeting. I'll tell him to call you. By the way, how are plans coming along for his birthday bash tomorrow night? Do you need help with anything?"

Eugenia's voice took on the glowing tone that always surfaced whenever she talked about Jason. "Nope! It's a done deal! Everything's taken care of! My godson is going to have the best black and white birthday bash ever! He's earned it! The entire staff has volunteered to pitch in and help. We've got a great bunch here! They remind me of my staff at The Jazzy Joint!"

"They do, don't they? We're lucky to have such a great team of people working here!"

"Don't worry, Kitty! Everything is done! Jason will be stunned. It's going to be a fabulous party! Nothing but the best for my godson!"

"I feel useless. I've done absolutely nothing to help. Nothing!"

Not to my surprise, Eugenia completely ignored what I had said and continued.

"When you speak to Jason, remind him to wear the silk tuxedo I had tailor-made for him."

"Will do. That is one sharp looking tuxedo. Anything else?"

Yes, tell him to please wear that lovely silver and black cummerbund and tie set Santini gave him. They'll be perfect together. My godson is going to look like the dashing prince that he is! That's all! Go back to your meeting. Tell Santini and Big Joe I'll see them later. Ciao!"

"Ciao!" I ended the call and stared curiously at the two men seated in front of me, both of whom were deliberately making no eye contact whatsoever with each other or me. *Dammit how that annoyed me!* Silent, conspiratorial guilt, scrawled in capital letters, covered both faces like masks. This was one of those head-scratching moments. I cleared my throat.

"Why's everyone so secretive about Jason's birthday bash?" I asked, pitifully, hoping to get a half-ass response from at least one of them. What I got was a loud, dead end silence. *Nada! Niente!* Not a damn thing came from either one of them. Just as Eugenia had ignored me, so did Santini and Big Joe. A moment ago, these two men were about to annihilate each other. Now they're in cahoots with Eugenia and each other, no doubt guarding Eugenia's secret plans for Jason's birthday bash. They were all under Eugenia Mckelvey's spell!

Sweeter than southern honey, Eugenia was my dearest and best friend. Shortly after my sweet sixteen birthday party, against their will, and amidst an ocean of tears from them and me, I packed an old trunk that had been in our family for generations, and left the protective shelter of my loving parents and family on Edisto Island. I arrived wide-eyed, naive, and greener-than-grass in the very soul of New York City. Thanks to Eugenia and Santini, I landed softly, on both feet, with my head to the sky — unshaken, unshattered, and unbroken. My first job was as a singing waitress at *The Jazzy Joint*, a small, cozy Harlem eatery that Eugenia once owned. At twenty-seven years old, Eugenia McKelvey was already a savvy businesswoman, and a shining star among Manhattan's most prominent and popular chefs-turned-restaurateurs. She was a go-getter, a successful, self-made, black businesswoman, who was highly respected by her mostly, white, male peers.

From the moment we met, I was in awe of Eugenia. She was originally from Charleston, South Carolina, forty-five miles north of Edisto Island. Tall, slender and vivacious, she was as beautiful inside as she was outside, a talented, intelligent woman with a keen eye for business, paired equally with her exceptional culinary skills. She was witty, with a great sense of humor, and a heart that was twice the size of Texas! Fiercely independent and determined, Eugenia was a lauded graduate of the prestigious Culinary Institute of America. When she could not find work as a chef anywhere in midtown Manhattan, she gathered her talents, gifts and determination, went uptown, and opened her own restaurant in the heart of Harlem. She named it *The Jazzy Joint.*

Eugenia was the chef-owner-hostess. For her house band, she assembled a revolving group of well-known, well-seasoned, legendary jazz luminaries. As for her staff, they were the best of the best singing waiters and waitresses anywhere in the city. From aspiring wannabe Broadway stars to one-time Broadway performers who were currently in between shows, they all wanted to work at The Jazzy Joint, and for good reason: They loved and respected Eugenia McKelvey. She treated them well, fed them well, and paid them well. The generous tips they all made was icing on the cake. It was no secret that everyone who was anyone in the music industry in Manhattan, regularly made their way uptown to The Jazzy Joint. It was *the* uptown destination location, well worth the trip. The Jazzy Joint was a warm, and inviting hangout, a place where people could partake in the most sumptuous and authentic soul food ever, while listening to the best live music and singers found anywhere in the city.

The day I auditioned for her, and told her where I was from, she hired me on the spot. I started working that night. When she learned how much I was paying for a room in a pricey women's hotel near Pennsylvania Station in midtown Manhattan, she immediately offered me the small studio apartment above the restaurant. I paid her a hundred dollars a week for rent, with utilities included. The four hundred and twenty dollars I paid her was less than a third of what that fancy women's hotel cost!

It didn't matter that my studio apartment always smelled like food. At least it was good food. Besides, everything she cooked smelled like sweet heaven to me. The aromas that floated upstairs reminded me so much of home… the way my mother's kitchen smelled. We were South Carolina homies, from the Lowcountry. Eugenia said that instantly made us family. Nine years my senior she was like a big sister. We were both southern girls, with old-fashioned southern ways. We had had similar upbringings, with the same religious beliefs, good manners, and polite, lady-like mannerisms, ingrained into us. We loved laughing, meeting people, and enjoying the company of good friends. More than anything else, we both loved life, zealously, and had a passion for adventure! For the next year and a half, I sang and waitressed at The Jazzy Joint, keeping my eyes on the floor for Eugenia while she was busy in the kitchen.

A regular visitor to The Jazzy Joint was a young Harlem minister named Reverend Edwin T. S. Prentiss, a dashing, silver-tongued pastor of one of the largest congregations in Harlem. The reverend had tragically lost his wife and child in a car accident, two years earlier. He was smitten with Eugenia. After a five-month long engagement, Eugenia and the handsome minister were married at First Savior's Baptist Church. I was thrilled to be one of her maids of honor. Due to the size of Reverend Prentiss' congregation, and Eugenia's popularity, the reception was held at the splendid Riverside Theater in Upper Manhattan. It was an unforgettable wedding.

Reverend Prentiss became a popular televangelist, and his ministry grew into a megachurch. Meanwhile, business at The Jazzy Joint boomed, increasing twofold, as congregants regularly flocked there on a nightly basis. Between the Jazzy Joint's burgeoning on-site business, and its expanding catering services, life was great, and Eugenia was ecstatically happy. Then she discovered that the good reverend had a big, bad problem. He was a gambler, a high-roller, an addict. Reverend Prentiss was known in the gaming world — from Atlantic City to Las Vegas to the Caribbean as a whale, a cheetah — a gambler who consistently wagers large amounts of money; and in his case, he was gambling with other people's money — money from his generous, but hard-working congregants!

Eugenia tried desperately to save her husband and her marriage. But nothing she did could keep Reverend Prentiss away from the casinos, or the long-legged beauties that his big bucks attracted. Choosing to save herself, Eugenia held on to her pride, and walked away from her husband and their marriage. The divorce was messy, costly, embarrassing, and very public. Her heart and bank account had taken a heavy beating, but Eugenia Mckelvey, being the stronger-than-steel southern belle that she is, was left unshaken, unshattered, and unbroken. As for her head? She held it up higher than ever, and never once looked back.

Eugenia had obviously made Santini and Big Joe promise not to say a word about Jason's birthday bash to me. They were doing just that!

"Now, exactly where were we with Vlad?" Santini asked, effectively changing the subject.

Big Joe leaned back into his chair, and cracked his knuckles. "Vlad's got a lot of shit on his hands, for sure. I can smell it a mile away. Everything about him stinks, even his cologne!"

I was listening to Big Joe, but my mind was on everything that had happened to me.

The 'violet visions' I'd had these past few days; this morning's giant leap — traveling inside Santini's head; knowing it was Eugenia calling before I'd even answered the phone. It all left me feeling perplexed, to say the least. There had to be some reasonable explanation for all of this. There were too many unanswered questions swirling around inside my head.

"I'm sorry, guys. Forgive me for drifting away. It's just too early in the morning." I apologized, knowing damn well that I wasn't at all sleepy or tired. I was overflowing with a tremendous amount of energy. It was as clear as daylight to me. The truth is, I had drifted away… telepathically! Santini was sitting in my office, but his mind was elsewhere. While I was bouncing around, inside his head, his thoughts had taken me on a journey, down memory lane, back in time to a place, which he often, nostalgically referred to as the 'good old days'.

I sat up, rolled my chair closer to the desk, and focused on Big Joe. "Go on, Big Joe. What were you saying?" My intention was to fast-forward the conversation to where we would finally, all agree on how, and when, we'd be able to say good-bye to Vlad forever.

Big Joe clasped his hands prayer-style, and cleared his throat. "All I'm saying is that we have to get rid of him the right way, without any repercussions."

"What do you mean by the right way?" Santini interrupted. "Just keep him out of here! Simple!"

"No! It's not simple!" Big Joe fired back. "Remember, this is New York City. Nothing is ever simple here! I'm a New Yorker! I know! New York is where — "

"Where last I heard anything is possible!" Santini interjected with so much sarcasm it made me cringe.

America's second Civil War was brewing before my very eyes. The fireworks were exploding right here in my office. I had to quell it before red, hot Italian blood flowed from Chelsea Place into the mean streets of Manhattan.

"Please, just let him finish!" I pleaded, appealing to Santini's gentler side. "Guys, remember, we're all on the same side in this war! We have one common enemy. If we kill each other, Vlad wins!" I emphasized, hoping to restore some semblance of purpose and sanity to our meeting. I shot Santini with a look of caution. "Where were we, Big Joe?".

Big Joe took in air, and released a long, impatient sigh. "Vlad is the type who wouldn't think twice about slamming a nasty and very public discrimination suit against us… just to get even and disrupt business."

"Listen, what's important to me is keeping Chelsea Place's good name, and of course, protecting the privacy of our guests," I chimed in. "Some of the people who come here are really like family. I certainly don't want fake news stories about their personal lives popping up on Twitter and posted all over social media!"

Santini leaned back into the chair, and planted his eyes squarely on the floor. "The bad press would definitely scare our patrons away. Next to money and power, privacy is their most prized possession," he said, reluctantly coming around to understanding Big Joe's point.

"I don't care how much money he spends. Let's do whatever we have to do to get that awful excuse for a human being out of here," I said, reaching for my cell phone — just before it vibrated. Without looking at the Caller ID, I knew it was Jason calling. When I answered, I tried not to sound too exasperated. "Happy Birthday, honey! How's my favorite…"

"Mom! Is everything okay with you? Is there anything weird happening to you? How do you look? I mean, how are you feeling? Is everything all right?"

His panic-stricken voice interrupted and frightened me all at once. The barrage of rapid-fire questions from Jason left me dumbstruck. I couldn't manage to get a word in edgewise. "Jason… honey… calm down! I'm… well… to be honest… lately I feel as if I've been going through a strange twilight zone episode. Other than that, your mom is brimming over with energy! How are you? I can tell from your voice that you haven't slept in a while."

His voice was heavy and husky, filled with so much anxiety that he was huffing and puffing. He sounded like someone who had been frightened out of his mind.

"I don't like what I'm hearing, Jason. Are you ill? What's going on with you? And why haven't you answered Eugenia's calls? She's worried sick about you?"

He inhaled and cleared his throat. This time, when he spoke, his voice was deeper, but still, noticeably strained. "Mom… I'll call Aunt Genie later. But right now, I need you to get here immediately! As fast as you can! It's crucial that I check… that I see what you look like! I need to explain why you've been experiencing those twilight zone episodes."

"Honey… what are you talking about? What do you mean? Why the urgency? I'm in a meeting at Chelsea Place with Santini and Big Joe right now. Can we meet later?"

"No! we can't, Mom! I need to see you now! This is serious! Please! I need you to leave the meeting now! You've got to meet me here… at the brownstone…

downstairs in the lab! Jason's hoarse voice cracked as he shouted over the phone."

Santini and Big Joe, obviously overhearing Jason's raised voice, glanced nervously at each other.

"What is going on with Jason?" Santini asked, apprehensively.

"Is Jason okay?" Big Joe mumbled, gesturing for an answer with his hands.

I knew there was something dreadfully wrong with my son, and immediately kicked into mother mode. I had to leave and get to Jason right away. I pushed away from my desk, got up, and was reaching for my cape while still trying to get to the bottom of his anxiety.

Santini jumped up and helped me into my cape. "I'll go with you. You might need help."

Overhearing Santini, Jason responded straight away. "Mom… please… come alone! This is something that is highly confidential and private! It has to stay between you and I — just the two of us! Take a cab… now! And please… come alone!"

"Okay. I'll come by myself. See you soon. I'm leaving now." I ended the conversation looking into Santini's concerned eyes. "Jason wants me to come alone. He says it's confidential." I took a deep breath, grabbed my tote, and headed to the door. "Listen, guys, I'm really sorry; but, you know, it's Jason. I'm worried about him. He sounds frightened. I'd appreciate it if you two could together find a way to deal with Vlad while I'm gone."

"Hey, no apologies. He's your son. Family always comes first. We'll take care of Vlad," Big Joe asserted.

Santini placed a hand on my shoulder, and managed to put a thin smile on his face. "No worries, my dear. Consider it done. Call me and let me know that everything's okay. Let me know if you need anything at all," he added, holding a hand like a phone to his ear.

"Hopefully, this won't take too long. While I'm gone, just focus on finding a way to make Vlad disappear."

Big Joe folded his arms and sighed. "I should be getting some dirt on that scumbag from my contact at the precinct later today. I'll fill you in afterwards."

I zoomed in on Big Joe. "If you're talking about that hot redhead you introduced me to awhile back, my guess is Officer Sinead Gallagher will be calling right about… now."

"WARNING! WARNING! WARNING! Big Joe's cellphone blared in an electronic robotic voice that reminded me of G.U.N.T.E.R. M3-B9, the iconic robot character in the television series *Lost In Space*. He reached inside his blazer, glanced at the caller ID on his phone, and grinned. "Yes ma'am… that redhead. I'm impressed," he said, speaking to no one in particular. "She answers Eugenia and Jason's calls *before* the phone rings, and knows exactly when Gallagher would call. Huh! Not bad!" He added, putting the phone to his ear.

"Perhaps she's going psychic on us," Santini added, dryly, turning, and leading the way towards the entrance. "Come, my dear. The least I can do is put you in a cab."

I shot one last glance at Big Joe, and somehow managed to smile. "In case you haven't heard, sir… it's that thing females are naturally born with. They call it women's intuition! We can't avoid it! It's in our DNA!" I called out, walking towards the door."

"Thank you gentlemen," I smiled, knowing that I could trust both of them with their words. As I left, I wagged my pointer and gave each of them a stern look. "One more thing: No more Civil Wars between you two! I mean it. It's going to take team effort and a united front to get rid of that so-called Caviar Czar!"

"Caviar my royal ass!" Santini fired off.

If either of them had the slightest idea about those mysterious visions I'd been experiencing, it wouldn't be quite so funny. How would Santini have dealt with getting inside my head…? invading my mind…? hearing my private thoughts? And Big Joe. Would he have been able to handle traveling through a tunnel, being twisted at lightning speed by a force he could not see or define? Hell no! I can't say a word to either of them about what I've been experiencing. They'd both agree that I was losing control of my faculties. They'd be convinced, beyond a doubt, that I had lost my mind! Hell! *I* think I'm losing my mind!

Until I can figure out what's going on, I won't mention this to anyone. Not even to Eugenia. Knowing her, she'd be dragging me, head first, to a team of high-powered, new-aged psychoanalysts! Oh, God how I miss Lem! If there was anyone who could get to the bottom of this, it would be Lem! He could find an explanation for anything. Maybe I'll run it by Jason and see what he thinks.

Walking towards the curb, Santini rubbed his hands together briskly, and shivered, in an exaggerated manner. "Br-r-r-r!!! *Fa freddo oggi!*" he said, peering down Eighth Avenue in search of an available taxi. "I have a strange feeling this is going to be a long and wicked winter, Kitt. That is never good for the restaurant and nightlife business!"

I closed my eyes, drew in some air, and opened my cape. "Just another one of those things men and women can't seem to agree on — the weather! You say it's freezing. But I'm actually a little too warm!"

Santini narrowed his eyes and shot me a rather curious look. "I think what you're feeling is actually called a fever! We're all worried about Jason. Perhaps you are who we should be concerned about!"

"You're not going to believe this but… I haven't felt this energized in a long time! I actually feel as if I could jog from here all the way uptown to Riverside Drive and back!"

"I'm sure you can do anything you put your mind to. But, do me a favor and let's not demonstrate that today." He moved closer towards me and examined my face, his eyes widening and narrowing as his head shifted slightly from one side to another.

I have no idea what he was looking for, or, might have suspected. Based on the puzzled look that covered his face, I'm convinced not even he knew what he was searching for. He stepped out onto the street and waved the taxi over. "Listen, if the young man's in any kind of trouble, any kind whatsoever, no one else needs to know about it. We'll just keep it between us. *D'accordo?*"

"Si. D'accordo," I responded.

He opened the door and ushered me inside the cab. "Remember, call or text me as soon as you arrive so that I know everything's okay. *Va bene?*"

"*Si. Va bene!*" I called out, nodding my head.

"Good morning! Where would you like to go, ma'am?" the ruddy-faced cab driver asked, staring sleepily into her rear-view mirror.

"Riverside Drive! The Northwest corner of Seventy-Eighth Street, across from the Park. Please take the highway. I'm in a real hurry!"

"Yes, ma'am!" she grunted, promptly stealing the yellow light, and speeding towards the Westside Highway.

Fortunately for me, the cabbie is a *real* New York driver. The kind I like. She knows, instinctively, when a passenger prefers to be left alone. Right now, what I want is to be left to myself. To gaze out onto the murky water. To meditate. To contemplate. To cry. On his twenty-first birthday, Jason was all that I could think about. Poor Jason! Even the nostalgic views of the

Hudson River are muddied by the memories of that horrific day.

The cab driver is wasting no time. Still, the journey uptown to Riverside Drive feels far and distant. My mind is on Jason. His voice sounded heavy and burdened. Not the way one's voice sounds after a night of too much drinking and partying. But the kind of debilitating heaviness that results from too much anxiety, from worrying too much.

Chapter 4
Revelations On Riverside Drive

There was a time, not very long ago, when all it took to calm Jason was a bike ride along the black-green waters of the Hudson River with his father. He and Lem would meander through park after park, on Riverside Drive. Occasionally, Jason, Lem, and I would abandon the quiet, narrow lanes of Riverside Park and venture into those noisy, overcrowded bike trails in Central Park. That would instantly lift his spirits. That was a welcomed challenge. What truly made his day was Lem riding beside him. They were a father and son team made in heaven. I always felt like the third wheel whenever I went riding with them. Those bikes are now mounted on wall racks, gathering dust, in the basement. They've been pushed aside, abandoned, and forgotten, like so many other things that once brought Jason joy.

Like his dad, Jason is exceptionally intelligent. He's brilliant, a handsome geek, a chip right off of his father's stubborn block. I'm doing what all proud mothers do: I'm boasting about my son, and I have good reasons to do so.

After receiving his bachelor's and master's degrees concurrently in biotechnology and zoological sciences from Columbia University, Jason was immediately hired by Gemini Biotech Laboratories Unlimited (GBLU), the same mega corporation that his father had once worked for. Like Lem, before him, Jason was now considered the company's brightest shining star. Having graduated at the top of his class, Jason was vigorously pursued by the world's leading international pharmaceutical and biotechnological conglomerates. GBLU made it difficult for him to even consider working for any of their competitors. They offered him a six-figure salary with perks that were so appealing, it was impossible for him, or anyone in their right mind, to refuse. Moreover, GBLU gave him an opportunity to work in some of the same laboratories that his father had once worked in. That, alone, was more than enough reason for him to sign on with them.

Between the long hours Jason worked at GBLU, and the time he spent playing in his home laboratory, the boy hardly ever slept. With his exceptional intelligence and good looks, any woman would be thrilled to grab the attention of those mysterious dark brown eyes of his. But there was no time whatsoever in his schedule for chasing girls. Knowing Jason, I'm certain he was in that goddamned lab, stirring some foul-smelling brew, well into the wee hours this morning. He's a night person, like I am. The rest of who and what my son is, comes straight from his father. Like

Lem, Jason's favorite place in the house is the basement laboratory.

I love working in the piano bar at Chelsea Place. I love the people, the music, and the energy. I'm there from four p.m. until four a.m. I'm back home, showered, and in my bed by five a.m. I usually sleep until noon, return to Chelsea Place by four p.m., and the cycle repeats. Jason and I are definitely creatures of the night. I must admit that that is the one trait he inherited from me.

It has been seven years since my husband Lem was abducted from our home on Riverside Drive. Sometimes it feels like ancient history. At this moment, it feels like only yesterday. That is the magic and mystery of time. Whoever said that time heals everything could not have lived, or loved, or had their entire life ripped from them within moments. There was a time when I had an almost perfect life. Until… well… until everything changed. I try hard not to remember. But how can I, when it is impossible to forget! Today is Jason's twenty-first birthday. I remind myself just how lucky I am to have him as my son, how fortunate we are to have each other. But it is precisely Jason's birthday that always reminds me of that harrowing night… when our lives took an unexpected twist — leaving me without my husband, and Jason without his father.

As we approach the narrow, park-lined lane of Seventy-Eighth Street, the three-story brownstone where I once lived, rises before me. Perched majestically on a gentle upslope, the house is a Renaissance Revival style home, fronting the Hudson River and Riverside Park. Flaunting huge, inviting bay windows, five wood burning fireplaces, and a mansard roof over dormer windows, it reminds me of a miniature castle. The entire house is wrapped in limestone and brick, with an enviable English basement — one that Lem promptly converted into a state-of-the-art laboratory. I still miss those Riverside Park and Hudson River views that captivated me. There was a time, when, on warm spring mornings, I looked forward to savoring my morning coffee, while sitting out on the Juliet balcony. The views took me and my breath away.

This splendid brownstone was once lived-in, and enjoyed by my almost perfect family — Lem, Jason, and I. This was our *castle*, where Lem was king, I was his queen, and Jason was our little prince.; but that was then. That was seven years ago, another *time*. It all seems so long ago. And now? Well, I keep reminding myself that at least Jason and I have a lot of good memories to cling to. As for me, Jason is the light of my life. He is all that I have left of what we once had!

As we near, Jason comes into view. He's at least two inches taller than he was when I last saw him. Even from a distance, he looks exactly like Lem.

The full-length, navy blue cashmere coat, thrown cape-like around his shoulders, was Lem's favorite coat. It was a Christmas gift to him from Jason. Pacing back-and-forth, on the sidewalk, in front of the house, Jason's head and shoulders are bent, burdened by the weight of life's disappointments, hurt, and pain.

This agony is further complicated by the nagging uncertainty of not knowing if his father is dead or alive. If Lem's body had been found, at least we would know that he is dead. His death would have been real and cruel, but it would have been certain. A lifeless body, or any kind of human remains of him, would have given us some sense of finality. We could have grieved our loss, said our tearful good-byes, and given him a proper burial. But there has been no closure for us, only gut-wrenching, open-ended uncertainty. We have been tasked, if not cursed, with suffering the agony of not knowing.

"Near or far corner, ma'am?" the gravelly-voiced driver called out.

"Far corner, please. And keep the change," I muttered, placing the fare in the money tray. My eyes were glued on Jason's frail appearance. Even underneath the coat, I could see his emaciated frame. As the taxi cab sped away, I called out to Jason. So lost in his thoughts, he didn't even hear me. A couple giant leaps across the street, and before I knew it, I was standing right behind him. I placed my hand gently on his shoulder.

"Mom! You're finally here!" he shrieked, startled, and relieved all at once. His arms encircled me like a child. We hugged and held on to each other for much longer than a moment. Jason finally released himself from my embrace, and stepped away. Narrowing his eyes, laser-like, he zeroed in on my face, studying it so intently that I felt uncomfortable.

What was it with Santini, and now Jason, examining my face so scrupulously! What were they looking for? What were they seeing? I wondered.

"Am I growing a beard on my face?" I asked, facetiously. "Why are you looking at me like that?"

"I… I… I'm sorry, mom. I didn't mean to be rude. How are you *feeling?"*

"I'm fine. The question is: How are you feeling?" I shot back. "You're skin and bones!"

Jason's eyes were still rapidly scanning me. "You look… normal," he said, exhaling a loud sigh of relief. "You look great! I mean… you look like yourself!" he shrieked.

It was my turn, and I let him have it. I lit into him like a torch, returning an even more severe once-over. "What did you expect me to look like? You, however, look like death warmed over! Look at yourself! You're disappearing! When was the last time you ate…? Slept…? Bathed?"

Jason pulled the coat collar up around his neck. He shivered, then wrapped his arms around himself. His voice was flat and hoarse. "I don't know. I really don't remember," he said, lowering his head. "Anyhow, none of that's important. What is important is you. You need to understand what is happening to you and why."

I stared at Jason, and tried to make sense of what he'd just said. I hadn't told him anything yet. But he had mentioned earlier on the phone that he wanted to explain those strange events I'd been experiencing. That sinking feeling was inside my gut. I took a deep breath, then slowly exhaled.

"Yes… Jason… there've been some rather unusual things happening to me lately. I haven't had time to sort it all out. But whatever it is… it's real… and quite disturbing. I had planned to call you after my meeting this morning to talk to you about these strange events."

A sudden gust of cold, damp wind bellowed from the river, causing my cape to balloon and swirl about me.

Jason's entire body trembled, uncontrollably. His shoulders, again, slumped, now with the wind against his back. He raised his head, and looked straight into my eyes. "Mom… I know what's going on? That's why I needed to see you today. There's so much I have to tell you… So much you need to know."

The tone of his voice struck a strange chord with me. Whatever it was he had to tell me was weighing heavily on his mind. He was extremely anxious and frightened.

I briefly hugged him again. "Honey, you're freezing. Come on, let's go inside," I whispered, looping my arm into his, as we headed downstairs to the laboratory.

In his words, Jason had made "a few major, necessary upgrades," in the laboratory, since Lem's abduction. With the exception of the expanded, cozier-looking cage, now hidden behind a newly-installed voice-activated wall, everything else was pretty much the way Lem had left it — stark, brightly lit, clean, and super organized. A purpose for everything, and everything in its proper place. This basement laboratory, hidden perfectly underneath the house, was where Lem and Jason always felt most at home. This was their man cave, a father-and-son Utopia. The lab was their little piece of paradise.

As for me, in the entire house, this lab was the place I liked the least. I still love the house. Even if I can no longer bring myself to live here. Yet, with all of its orderliness, the laboratory was the one place I steered clear off. I've never felt comfortable down here. I still don't. To the disdain of my beloved son, I'm inclined to refer to the lab as a dungeon, a tomb. To me, it always felt like an underground vault. I've never particularly liked the energy down here. Jason is more than acutely aware of my feelings. He takes offense to my dislike of the laboratory. A heavy silence hovered in the air, as I removed my cape and hung it on the coat rack. Reaching inside my tote bag, I retrieved my cell phones and placed them on the table.

Jason peeled out of his coat, and methodically draped it evenly and neatly over a satin covered hanger, brushing the cashmere the way one runs his hand over a favorite pet.

He did this almost ceremoniously. It is exactly what Lem always did. I studied him, and realized just how much every movement, every gesture, every action reminded me of his father. He is filled from head to toe with Lem's DNA! The way he holds his body. The way he walks. The way he sounds when he talks. He has his father's face, eyes, and his beguiling smile. At six feet, he is about an inch shorter than Lem. But, he is still growing. Despite his reed thin body, I marveled at how handsome and grown-up he looked.

"That coat really does become you, Jason. You look as dashing in it as Lem did."

With that heartfelt compliment, his entire being lit up. There was suddenly a sparkle in his eyes. His lips parted into a broad smile, as he ran a hand over the coat and stared reverently at it. He hung the coat on the top hook. When he turned to face me, I saw Lem's eyes staring back at me. "I take excellent care of dad's coat. In many ways, this coat is *my* security blanket. It keeps me connected to dad. It also keeps me warm, focused, and determined."

The words tumbled out of my mouth. "Jason, you look and sound exactly like Lem! It gives me goosebumps to see how much you've become like your father."

Again, that enchanting little smile appeared on his face, as he eyed me, playfully. "This, from the mother who always said that I looked so much like the men on her side of the family?" he mocked, showing me an exaggerated profile of himself.

We both laughed at his impersonation of me. It was dead-on. For a moment, the tension eased. We were enjoying each other's company. We were laughing the way we used to laugh, from the inside out. It felt good. It felt normal. Jason had scored. The ball was in his court, and I needed to respond appropriately.

"When you were younger, you did look more like the men in my family. But, today, on your twenty-first birthday, it's as if you've stepped inside your father. You're a carbon copy of Lem."

Jason's eyes landed on my cell phones, and his smile slowly faded into heavy, almost unbearable sadness. It was as if I had turned off the light inside him.

"Mom, may I please have your phones?" he insisted, already reaching for them.

"Well this is certainly the way to make me feel warm and fuzzy," I chided, sarcastically.

"May I ask why you need my phones?"

He shot back. "To completely power off these little demons. They're addictive and extremely dangerous! I have a love-hate relationship with them!"

"But they're necessary little demons," I countered.

At that moment, Jason unleashed upon me, that dreaded child-to-parent look.

"Mom, how many times have I told you that these cute gadgets are nasty little monsters with eyes, ears, and amazing memories? Not to mention that they have an uncanny way of recording everything you breathe, say, feel, and do, only to then turn around and use that information against you?"

I yielded to him, with very little resistance. "Go on, Jason. Shut the damn things off. I guess I could use a break away from them. Those phones never stop ringing!"

Jason smiled and nodded approvingly. "And they never sleep. These phones have even found ways to infiltrate our dreams and thoughts!"

"I totally agree. God knows, lately I've had some really strange dreams, visions… whatever they were."

With our cell phones powered off, a cloud suddenly came over Jason's face.

"I can't believe it's been…"

"Honey, please don't do this to yourself. Let it go!" I pleaded, trying to put my arms around him. I wanted so badly to comfort him.

"Seven years to the day since I opened that door, and allowed those animals into our home… to beat and abduct Dad… on my birthday!" he blurted out, his voice burning with harbored pain and anger.

"How were you supposed to know? They were dressed like NYPD officers!"

I finally got hold of his eyes, and tried to change the direction of our conversation. "Honey… I worry about you spending so much time in this lab. I want you to have a real life… outside of this… this goddam tomb!"

His eyes were moist when he looked up and spoke. "This tomb is my life. You know that."

"You're young… smart… and handsome! You should be out and about… chasing girls and having fun! Any girl in her right mind would love to be seen with you!"

Jason rolled his eyes and sighed. "Girls are beautiful, and they can be fun, at times. But honestly, most of them are really too demanding. They 're a lot of trouble, and require constant attention. I have neither time nor patience for that right now in my life."

"Now, when you have the energy and stamina, is the right time to get out and meet women. How else will you ever get to know them? That's not something that can be done in a lab, Jason. Spending time with nice, smart, well-bred women is the only way you'll ever be able to appreciate the right woman when you find each other."

"Don't worry, mom. Remember, I'm only twenty-one. There's still time for me to find the right woman before the world ends. Besides, this tomb is my home. It's my world! It's where I grew up… side-by-side… next to dad. Any girl I meet now would have to be far more comfortable down here than you are!" he quipped.

"Good point. But promise that you'll start getting out of here, and go on some dates."

"I promise," he said, dryly, then took my hands and held them between his. Motioning me to sit down, his thin fingers trembled as he knelt down before me on the floor. "Ahem… those strange things that have been happening to you, tell me about them."

I swallowed and prayed that I didn't come across sounding crazy. "Well… in the past three days, I've had these strange encounters… some kind of unexplainable journey that transports me to… somewhere else. There's a sudden flash of light. I find myself spinning rapidly through a tunnel. Then, I end up in a peculiar place… a kind of world where everything is tinged in shades of violet and purple. When I arrive, I land on all fours… on my knees and hands… like an animal."

Jason's head shot up and his entire body stiffened. "Like… what kind of animal?"

I sighed and searched for the right words. "It's difficult to describe exactly what I saw. There were shadows and dancing silhouettes… elusive… misshapen creatures… images, sounds, and smells of which I've never before experienced. But somehow, I felt comfortable there… as if a part of me knew that I belonged there…"

Jason was jumpy as he tried, unsuccessfully, to interrupt me. "That is because…"

"Let me finish, Jason!" I exclaimed, determined to tell him everything. "When I return home… back to this world… I am extremely invigorated. I've had more energy in the past three days than I ever did when I was eighteen, or twenty years old! What I do know for sure, is that these encounters have awakened something deep down inside of me. I don't know what it is. But I can feel it, and I know that whatever it is… it's real… and very powerful."

Jason shuffled nervously and raised his eyes. "Go on, mom. Please… tell me everything."

I took a deep breath and rolled my eyes. "I know things just before they happen. This morning, I knew Eugenia was calling even before the phone rang. I reached for my phone a second before you called… knowing that it was you. I told Big Joe when his friend would be calling. Here's where it really gets crazy. This morning during my meeting with Santini and Big Joe… I took a trip inside Santini's head. Somehow I got inside his mind and read his thoughts. I actually heard what he was thinking." I paused and stared silently at Jason for a while. Realizing that he was either at a great loss for words, or was probably thinking that I had gone mad, I continued. I figured I had already dug myself into a deep hole by telling him everything. Either he believed me or he didn't. "Honey… I hope I'm not losing my grasp on reality. It would be a brutal shame for you to lose me in this way. You've already lost your father."

Jason's eyes twitched and blinked as his clammy hands tightened around mine. "Mom, you're not losing your mind at all! It's quite the contrary. All of these unusual things that you're experiencing… these strange encounters… they are all real. What is happening to you, is that you're actually gaining… ahem… acquiring the life experiences of someone else's. The mind, thoughts, and feelings of another being have been transmitted to you."

Jason cleared his throat and held his head up. He trembled, his voice shaky and uneven when he spoke. "Dad and I did so many things together, here, in this lab. We shared a lot of important things — secrets we kept from you! There are so many things I should have told you a long time ago… secrets you had a right to know."

"What secrets are you talking about?"

"I only hope that you'll forgive us," he mumbled, turning his face away.

Chapter 5
Jaguar People

My eyes followed Jason's gaze to the far corner of the lab. As my vision adjusted, what emerged was apparently, a large black animal, asleep. Startled by its presence, I shrieked.

Then, instinctively, to silence my outburst, I covered my mouth with cupped hands.

Facing the wall, with its back to us, the large, furry head rested gently on top of forelegs that were folded more like arms than legs. Its massive, human-like silhouette rose and fell, as it breathed in and out. The cage, now upgraded and vastly extended, occupied the entire back wall — a major improvement from the basic military-style cage Lem had installed years earlier. This was, by far, the most accommodating cage I had ever seen, especially for an animal.

"Jason! For heaven's sake! Why is that animal here?"

Jason jumped up, looking as guilty as hell. He quickly went over to the cage and peered in, angling his neck to study the animal's face more closely. "Don't worry. I have her heavily sedated," he said, quietly, his eyes still glued to the creature.

"What on God's earth is that thing?" I demanded.

He finally turned to face me. "It's not a thing!" he responded, emphatically. "*She* is an *ENHANCED. BLACK. MELANISTIC. JAGUAR*," he added, articulating and etching each word into my head. "And… she is extremely rare, I might add."

Again, I felt that sinking feeling, plowing down into my gut. My lips were trembling as I struggled to get the words out of my mouth. "She's one of Lem's special jaguars from the Amazon, isn't she?" I asked, already knowing the answer.

"She's actually an offspring from dad's favorite jaguar."

Jason stood still, then shot another glance at the jaguar. "But this jaguar is beyond special," he boasted, his voice dripping with too much pride.

As my gaze shifted to the sleeping jaguar, my entire body was suddenly filled with stomach-churning apprehension. "Okay… now you're scaring me. Explain why she is beyond special."

"*She* is superior in every possible way," he replied, his stance attentively salutatory, and his eyes fixed admiringly on the jaguar. Even the tone of his voice was filled with reverence and respect. A look of child-like wonder and awe blanketed Jason's face. This was all too familiar — a scene straight from the book of Lem! Everything about this moment looked, felt, and sounded exactly like Dr Lemuel Keith Johnson! I couldn't help thinking: *Like father, like son!*

Lem's genetic imprint was all over Jason — defining, molding, and shaping every nuance of who he was. How he stood, and spoke.

But nowhere was Lem's presence more profound, than in his son's countenance. He had all of his father's features. He was a carbon copy of Lem, a direct and natural offspring. Jason had taken on his father's life, voice, image, and passion. In some ways, he had become more Lem, than Lem, himself. Standing before me, I saw a younger, more determined, version of Lem. The thought of that sent an icy cold chill soaring throughout my entire body. Driven by that kind of ambition made him far more daring than his father. *Jason was dangerous!*

Jason crossed to the cage and peered at the jaguar. "She's almost comatose. I gave her a double dose of sedatives. It'll be awhile before she wakes up. Even then, she'll be as docile as a kitten," he added, returning to the sofa and slumping onto it. His hands fell to his knees, tapping them, nervously — another annoying habit he'd inherited from his father.

"Does that animal have anything to do with why you've ordered me here today?" I asked, my eyes still planted on the cage.

"Yes. She has a lot to do with you and what's been happening to you. I just don't know where to begin."

I sat anxiously on the edge of the sofa, took in a deep breath, and tried desperately to remain calm.. "Start from the very beginning. Dot the i's… cross the t's… and leave no question unanswered."

Jason eyed me, thoughtfully, then bobbed his head, signaling that he was ready to spill his guts.

"Remember, when it's all said and done, I will still be your mother, and you will still be my favorite son." I assured him.

He rose slowly, and cleared his throat. My eyes followed him as he paced back-and-forth.

His demeanor was more like that of a university professor addressing a science symposium, than a son speaking to his mother.

He released a long, protracted sigh. "This jaguar… and those odd things that you're experiencing… are all connected."

"How is that possible? Explain it in plain English!"

Jason shook his head and swallowed. "In 1997, The Center for Biological Diversity listed the jaguar as an endangered species. In 2008, the Bush Administration abandoned the jaguar recovery plan…"

"That's true," I interrupted. "But luckily, for Lem, in 2010, the Obama Administration reversed Bush's policy and pledged to protect critical habitat. That's when your father made another trip to the Amazon Rainforest, just before you were born. He represented the U.S. in a bilateral agreement with the Brazilian government to establish a policy to protect and preserve the Amazon's endangered melanistic jaguars."

"Yes, mom. According to Dad, that was when several older, indigenous hunters led him to a lost tribe in the Amazon, far beyond the known jungle. What he saw there was so phenomenal that he rushed back home to begin experimenting, here, privately in his own lab."

Lem had told me the story so many times that I'd remembered every word of it.

"Your father was beyond impressed with the people of that tribe. The village was isolated and uncharted, and the people unknown. Lem said everyone and everything existed in perfect harmony there. The villagers were masters of nature, extraordinary and unparalleled. He called them *the real jaguar people*. They worshiped and paid homage to the melanistic jaguar and it's incredible hunting skills."

"She comes from that special breed of jaguars," he cut in, proudly motioning to the cage with his head.

I took in a deep breath and exhaled. "Those villagers were so in sync with nature that they were able to do incredible things with their minds and bodies. As I recall, Lem made arrangements to have several of those special black jaguars flown back here to his company's zoo and laboratory compound."

"Mom… what I'm telling you are things dad told me confidentially. Really important things that he witnessed. Things that drove him to experiment at a level far beyond anything that had ever been done before." His body stiffened and his voice became strained. "I felt compelled to see Dad's experiments through to completion. I pray that you will understand why I had to finish his work."

"I'm afraid of what I might hear, Jason. But I have no other choice. The floor is all yours."

Jason's pacing came to an abrupt stop. He sat, drew his legs together yoga style, and settled comfortably on the floor. "Dad discovered that the jaguar people were taught from an early age how to survive in nature, and most importantly, how to co-exist harmoniously with all living things — particularly the melanistic jaguar — whom they worshiped and revered."

I rolled my eyes toward the ceiling, recalling how many times Lem had told me about that lost village of jaguar worshippers. "Jason, I know this story by heart. Believe me. Lem made sure of that."

"There is a very good reason why dad wanted you to know that story by heart. He knew that one day you'd need the details to help you put all of the pieces together. What he witnessed in that village was all he needed to prove his 'one-ness' theory. What he found there were human beings, animals, and nature — completely interconnected — proof of dad's *One-ness theory!"*

My lips were trembling as I repeated what I had heard so many times. "According to Lem, the villagers worshiped and paid homage to the melanistic jaguars because they were the most elusive, most imposing, and most powerful animals around."

Jason's gaze shifted towards the caged jaguar, lingering there momentarily. A slight smile parted his lips. He turned to face me. "Black jaguars are such beautiful, stealth creatures. They are, by nature, solitary, territorial animals." Jason paused and shot another look at the sleeping animal. "Imagine being agile, swift, and strong enough to dominate a prey five times your size. Their bite is the strongest of all the big cats — twice as strong as the lion's!" Jason's voice was filled with so much excitement that it drew me in. My attention drifted towards the jaguar. "Lem said the black jaguars were feared, and often likened to ghostly jungle spirits at night."

"Absolutely, Mom. They are silent, nocturnal marauders."

"They are so light footed and swift that most people only get glimpses of them before they pounce. They are appropriately named. The word *jaguar* means 'he who kills in one bound'."

With those words, a heavy silence hovered in the room. For a moment, the only thing that showed any sign of life was the jaguar, delicately snoring, as she slept. I studied her shapely silhouette, and found myself drawn to her, entranced by her powerful presence… her existence… her being. "Lem called them 'majestic, god-like creatures'. He said the natives believed that the black jaguar was able to cross between worlds — from daytime to nighttime — from the living and the earth, represented by day, to the spirit world of the deceased, represented by night."

Jason sat up as straight as an arrow, thoroughly enjoying this moment and savoring every detail of the story — which he, like I, had heard so many times before. "The phenomena dad witnessed in that remote village were at once real and surreal. What he saw pushed him to experiment at a level far beyond anything that had ever been done before!" Jason lowered his voice and brought his hands together into the shape of a pyramid.

"After his… abduction… I felt the least I could do would be to finish what he had so brilliantly started. Those villagers had tapped into regions of the brain that remain dormant in humans — areas defined as unchartered territories of the brain. They used one hundred percent of their brain, ten times more than humans typically use. Their sense of smell, as keen as that of canines', and their night vision, unsurpassed. They ran at inhumanly high speeds, and leapt great distances. Most importantly, they communicate telepathically, at will. They shared what dad called an existence of 'one-ness' with the black jaguar — a phenomenon that enabled them to master and harness energy, allowing them to transform, transmute, transfigure, and shape shift at will. By combining their advanced mental powers along with certain spiritual practices and beliefs, the jaguar people are able to turn themselves into powerful black, melanistic jaguars."

He came to a full stop and stared, hopefully, at me. Was he waiting for me to ask questions? Did he think I was lost and confused… completely ignorant of what he had said? Or was he hoping and praying that I had grasped, clearly understood, and believed all that he had just said? That uncomfortable silence made a loud and deafening reappearance. He finally broke the silence.

"Are you following me, Mom?"

"Yes!" I grimaced. "Every step of the way and then some!" I shifted, uncomfortably, on the sofa, then, with my eyes held to the floor, softened my tone.

"That reminds me of the Geechee Gullah stories my parents told about certain people on Edisto Island… supernatural people who were able to shed their skins, travel outside their bodies, and transfigure into animals." I turned and waited to get his attention. "Honey, you know how much I hate this subject. Talking about these things makes *my* skin crawl!"

Jason raised his eyebrows, the way Lem always did just before declaring whatever it was that he believed to be indisputable law. "Dad loved telling those stories and I enjoyed hearing them! He said some of the Gullah beliefs and practices on Edisto Island were very similar to the things he saw it in the jaguar village." His eyes were dead-on into mine.

"It all comes straight from the Motherland," he added, driving his point home.

I stared at Jason, reflectively, remembering some of the unusual things I'd seen as a child growing up on Edisto. The people, their way of life, practices and beliefs all came back to me.

“The Edisto Gullah Geechees called it ‘roots’. The practitioners were called ‘root doctors’. Growing up there, I certainly saw a lot of strange things that could not be explained. As a child, I always thought it was just well-rehearsed, really good, entertaining magic.”

“Yes. It is nature’s magic,” he said matter-of-factly. “It’s bewildering, complex, and powerful magic. But it is all very, very real magic.”

My eyes darted over to the black jaguar and stayed there. Several times I swallowed, trying unsuccessfully, to get rid of an egg-sized lump in my throat. The imaginary lump was making it difficult for me to breathe and speak. I struggled for a while, and felt uneasy. Finally the words tumbled out of my mouth. “Lem’s story about the seven huntresses was particularly unsettling.”

I turned to face Jason straight on. The look on my face beckoned him to continue the story I had just started and was clearly having issues with.

He sat up, hugged his knees, and stared directly into my eyes.

“Dad wasn’t allowed to videotape the ritual, but he documented as much as he could using a small, well-concealed device. He recorded, in full, the ritual that involved the seven female villagers who were concurrently menstruating. The seven women were ordered to go out and find a black jaguar who’d just given birth. Upon finding the new mother, the women collected the animal’s placenta and cord blood and returned to the village for a big celebration. This offering of the jaguar's afterbirth was shared among the seven huntresses, and followed by a contest of wit, strength, and endurance. The last woman standing — the smartest and strongest — won the coveted honor of becoming…"

"A powerful black jaguar herself." I interjected, totally consumed with a sickening feeling. "How could I have ever forgotten that story which Lem had told so vividly? I think that was just another one of Lem's colorful stories."

Jason's eyes widened with determination and defiance. And the stature of his body suddenly increased, emboldened with overflowing bravado.

"Yes, colorful. But it wasn't at all a bedtime story." he declared. "Dad was never one to waste time on farce and fiction. These were things he saw with two clear eyes and a sober mind. He's the most objective person I know!" Jason's Adam's Apple slid up and down, his eyes shifted from me to the cage. "It's all frighteningly true, mom. Just like everything else I'm about to tell you," he said, breathing, deeply.

The room, filled, once again, with a gut wrenching silence — was interrupted by loud growls that came rumbling from Jason's hungry stomach. They were so fierce that we both burst into laughter.

"Honey, you're starving! Listen… I'll go upstairs and rummage through your refrigerator to see if I can find something for you that's edible." I pinched my nose and shoved him away, playfully. “In the meantime, young man, do me, my nose, and yourself a big favor: Go take a hot, steamy shower! You stink!”

Feigning embarrassment, he sniffed his underarms and frowned. “You’re right. I haven’t had time to eat or bathe. I’ll feel better after a hot shower and some food. Perhaps everything will be clearer…” His voice trailed off, as he hobbled toward the small bathroom next to the lab.

Overwhelmed by our unsettling conversation, my attention went back to the caged jaguar. Curiosity was pushing me to get a closer look at her. But I was far more afraid of what I might see. The truth is, there was something eerily familiar about the jaguar. I was, at once, frightened and fascinated by her. Her shape, the contour of her body, and the energy that radiated from her, even as she slept, intrigued me beyond words. I did not dare look at her face, for fear of what I might see. Adding to my angst was that loud, little voice, deep down inside my gut, telling me that the sleeping jaguar was fully aware of my presence, even as she snored. She was surely communicating with me. We felt each other’s presence. I shuddered at the thought, and tried unsuccessfully to collect myself, as I staggered upstairs.

After staring into Jason’s grossly neglected refrigerator and cabinets, all expired items were promptly tossed into the garbage. Miraculously, I ended up making two of his favorite foods — tuna melts on croissants with a huge bowl of creamy tomato bisque on the side.

I took his food downstairs right away, then went back upstairs to make him a pot of hot cocoa. Like Lem, Jason was never a coffee drinker. Hot Brazilian cocoa with half-and-half only. No marshmallows. No sugar. The stuff ran through his veins like blood.

I washed the kettle, filled it with fresh water, and placed it on a medium flame. Subconsciously, I wandered into the dining room. It was still picture perfect.

With a soaring frescoed ceiling, original picture frame moldings on the walls, ornate pocket doors, and cushioned window seats under twin bay view windows — every aspect of this lovely dining room was formal. This was always my favorite place in the house. It was where, perched in one of the bay windows, with drapes parted, I read, and wrote lyrics to songs.

So many of them are still unrecorded. Through those windows, I could look outside at the world, with all of its good and bad, and feel protected, completely safe, here, inside this room. That was before Lem's abduction. Poor Jason. He still carries that guilt. All he did was open the door for six men whom he believed were New York City police officers. Those intruders came into our home, wrestled Lem away from us, and our lives have never been the same since. How does anyone move beyond something that horrific? Why does Jason insist on living here?

Ever since Lem's abduction, Jason had taken to keeping the curtains closed, drawn completely together, with not even the slightest glint of light coming through.

This made the room look uninviting, and unnaturally dark. I suppose this was his way of closing out the rest of the world, a world that had been terribly cruel to him. My eyes swept over the long, mahogany table, across the hallway, to the living room. That was where it had all happened. Like the curtains, the glass French doors were closed, creating its own message that screamed *keep out!* No matter how hard I tried to forget what happened, the images replayed themselves over and over again, swirling around inside my head, taunting and haunting me like an evil ghost… a ghost that refused to go away.

Chapter 6
Meanwhile… Back At Chelsea Place

"Thanks, Gallagher. I owe you big time. I swear… I'll find a way to repay you one of these days… promise."

Big Joe ended the conversation and threw his cell phone on the table. Collapsing into the plush armchair, he pressed his head against the back of the chair, rubbed his eyes and groaned.

With two cups of espressos in his hands, and a raised eyebrow, Santini joined Big Joe at the table. "Your subtle expression tells me things just went from bad to worse," he said, dryly. He slid an espresso in front of Big Joe. "Drink up. It's *forte*. It will make you feel better for a while."

Big Joe willed himself forward, straddled the cup with his elbows, and buried his face into a pair of massive hands. "Things can't possibly get any worse!" he complained. "Gallagher, my contact in the Midtown Precinct just shared a very comprehensive dossier on our buddy Vlad. The report comes straight from MCNI, and it is beyond disturbing." He lifted the cup to his mouth, downed its contents in one gulp, and frowned.

"Whoa! That is really strong! Did you lace it with arsenic?" he said, brusquely pushing the cup aside.

Santini sipped some of his espresso. "I thought we could both use a double shot of it," he said, staring blankly at Big Joe and waiting for him to expound. "Forgive my limited understanding of police lingo. I'm afraid I do not know what those letters represent."

"MCNI… Multinational Criminal Network Investigations. It's the Special Ops unit I created." He stopped abruptly, shifted in his chair, and spoke under his breath. "Well… I guess none of that really matters any more."

Santini finished his espresso, gingerly slid the cup to the side, and released a tired sigh.

"In life, everything matters much more than we think. Always remember that. Now… about Vlad… give it to me straight-on. The sooner we can figure him out the sooner we can get rid of him.

Big Joe's eyes wandered over to where Javier was busy cleaning the railing on the stairs. Tapping his long fingers on the table, he leaned in, and waited for him to leave.

Once a successful orthodontist in Venezuela, Javier, his wife, and three children had fled to the United States to escape the unbridled violence, political corruption, and daily lack of food, medicine, and other essentials that plagued Venezuela. His business had been targeted too often by drug cartels demanding "protection" money from him. When he refused to give in to their demands, the thugs had destroyed his business and threatened to wipe out his entire family. He packed up his family in the middle of the night, and left Venezuela. A licensed orthodontist with a once thriving practice in Venezuela, Javier was never allowed to work as an orthodontist in the United States. According to him, he couldn't even find a job working as an assistant to an orthodontist in New York! He and his family lived in a two-family house in Astoria, Queens. He was a diligent employee. Reliable, meticulous, and punctual, always arriving to work earlier than scheduled. In the seven years that he'd been employed at Chelsea Place, he'd never missed a single day from work. Not one day. Sensing that Santini and Big Joe were agitated and wanted some privacy, Javier quickly gathered his cleaning items and went downstairs.

Big Joe's finger tapping suddenly stopped. He rubbed his forehead and spoke in a low, conspiratorial voice. "To begin… his name isn't Vlad. He's got at least five aliases. But his real name is Doctor Vadim. Doctor Igor Vadim, a notorious Russian doctor and scientist, of the worst kind."

"A doctor and scientist!" Santini echoed, incredulously. "Are you sure?"

Big Joe nodded. "I'd question this information if it came from any other source. But MCNI always gets it right." He leaned back into the chair.

"Well… at least 99.9% percent of the time," he added.

“Of all things, a doctor! I wouldn’t be caught dead under that man’s care! I’m sure he’s a sleazeball who pushes snake oil!”

“I’m afraid snake oil is the least of our worries! The doctor has a monstrous history… one that’s marked with corruption, illegalities, international criminality, and man’s inhumanity to man.”

“He’s a dirty doctor!” Santini said, sarcastically. “How shocking!”

Big Joe released a long sigh. “In addition to his colorful life-style, the doctor surrounds himself with a nefarious circle of friends — corrupt politicians, drug cartels, multi-national criminals, and other undesirable underground types.”

Santini leaned forward, rested his elbows on the table, and finally, brought his hands together. “I’m assuming the good doctor has ties to the FSB, Bratva, the KGB, and other members of the Russian brotherhood of mayhem and death.”

Big Joe studied Santini’s face. “Hum… sounds as if you’ve crossed paths with that gallant group of boy scouts,” he said, his voice dripping with sarcasm. “They make the Italian mafia look like a group of Catholic choir boys.”

Santini hesitated. “They’re cowards. Every single one of them. I have nothing but contempt for people who destroy and kill others so heartlessly.” He paused, and for a moment, took in the silence. “What other horrors did your friend tell you about Doctor Vadim?”

Big Joe exhaled and stretched out his long legs. "Vlad… ahem… Doctor Vadim started his criminal career as a young medical doctor slash zoologist in St. Petersburg, Russia where he made quite a name for himself hosting human and animal orgies."

"*Mio Dio*!" Santini grimaced. "Do you mean what I think you mean?"

"What I mean is the doctor practiced bestiality, sexual intercourse between humans and animals" Big Joe replied, frowning. "It's downright disgusting!"

Santini shook his head and shuddered. "It's ugly, sick, and unethical! I thought bestiality was universally forbidden and outlawed!"

"Right. Tell that to China, or Russia, or North Korea!" Big Joe fired back. "Those guys think the laws of nature were made to be broken."

Santini clenched his teeth and slammed his fist on the table. "I knew Vlad was a vile, piece of shit! I'd like to put my hands around his neck and slowly squeeze every breath out of his miserable life!"

"My sentiments exactly," Big Joe said, shaking his head. "The piece of shit was affectionately nicknamed 'Doctor Frankenstein' by his colleagues… and for good reasons. Guess who funded all of his lovely experiments in bestiality?"

"The Kremlin, of course!" Santini replied. "Probably used Chechens, Poles, and Ukrainians as human subjects."

"Good guess!" Big Joe exclaimed. "But they were very selective. They made sure their human subjects were orphans and mentally-challenged people."

Santini wrung his hands and narrowed his eyes. "Despicable and cruel! I'd like to give him a well-placed knife or bullet! That heathen doesn't deserve to live in this world!"

"Ditto! That heathen inseminated dozens of women with ape, chimpanzee, and canine sperm. I'd give anything to take that monster out with my bare hands," Big Joe grumbled, squeezing his hands into a tight, angry fist.

Santini shook his head in dismay. "Who does he think he is to wreak such havoc on the world? Wicked and immoral! That beast should be locked up, unfed, and left to die a slow, painful death! Only a sick-minded person does something like that! That is an abomination!"

"It is an abomination." Big Joe hesitated for a moment. "What is really scary about this whole mess is that… well… it is believed that some of his experiments were actually successful."

"Successful? You don't mean that…"

"Yes… according to Gallagher," Big Joe interrupted, "some of the doctor's depraved experiments, unfortunately, resulted in births."

They both sat silently, not wanting to believe what they'd just heard.

Santini finally mustered up some words. "Poor creatures! What are they? They're neither human nor beast," he lamented. "God! How could something like that be allowed to happen?"

Big Joe cracked his knuckles, and cringed. "The World Health Organization (WHO) got wind of those births and finally intervened. The creatures were biologically classified as chimeras."

"I pray to God they were all euthanized. Please tell me that someone with a heart and conscience did the right thing."

"No. They were not euthanized." Big Joe returned. "After WHO lambasted Doctor Vadim and the Kremlin, it is believed that the creatures were covertly gathered up and dropped off in a remote area in the mountains of Siberia and Kazakhstan."

Santini and Big Joe looked at each other and shook their heads. They were both thinking the same thing, and they knew it. Yet neither said what was on his mind. They were sickened beyond words. They hated and despised Vlad. In this moment, they were both thinking that if they could murder him, and get away with it, they'd kill the evil bastard in a heartbeat. The sound of Javier's cell phone chiming downstairs interrupted the silence between Santini and Big Joe.

Santini was smoldering in anger. He ran a hand across his day-old beard, and thought for a while. "Of all the places he could have taken his hideous ass to in this world, why the hell did he land in the middle of

Chelsea Place? Right in our goddam laps! That piece of no-good shit!"

Big Joe's response was straightforward. "After bouncing from Kosovo, to Croatia, to Serbia, the mad man landed in Miami sometime in 1992. He dropped off of the grid for a while… went underground. He resurfaced two years later in Brighton Beach, where he dabbled in human trafficking, prostitution, murder, extortion, racketeering, arms and weapons trafficking, money laundering, fraud, and a host of socially and politically disruptive cyber-crimes."

"I guess that explains why he's had so much cosmetic work done. He doesn't like what he sees when he looks in the mirror." Santini commented, dryly. "I'm afraid to ask what the monster's up to now."

Big Joe swallowed and his demeanor took a turn for the worse. "That would be a good question with a bad answer. The monster is currently specializing in chemical and biological warfare. There is substantial evidence to believe that he is responsible for developing Novichok, the deadliest known nerve agent ever. Its use is forbidden by the United Nations. Novichok is an invisible killer. Clear, colorless, and odorless, it can be released ANYWHERE… at ANYTIME!" he emphasized.

Santini paled, as if life and blood had been drained from him. "*Che casino!*" he exclaimed, running both hands through his wavy mane. "In the wrong hands, something as dangerous as Novichok could be used in a terrorist attack!"

"That is exactly what our secret services fear. Novichok could be the weapon of choice in our next 9/11," Big Joe added, wringing his hands. "The word underground is that Doctor Vadim and the Kremlin jointly control a large stockpile of this deadly chemical. If it gets into the hands of terrorists, they could use it as an aerosol, or release it using bombs, spray tanks, explosives and rockets." He cracked his knuckles. "Thousands of people could be killed!"

Santini was as white as a ghost. He stared at Big Joe, in painful disbelief. "Unleashed Pandemonium! So much for thinking we were dealing with a simple persona non grata. We've got a potential terrorist visiting Chelsea Place, nightly." With his eyes still fixed on Big Joe, he continued. "I'd hate to be the bearer of such bad news, but Kitt needs to know this. She needs to know just what we're up against."

Big Joe sat pensively, then slowly shook his head in agreement.

Santini reached inside his pocket and pulled out an exquisite gold pocket watch, attached to a gold chain, tastefully paired. He glanced quickly at the time, then carefully returned the watch to his pocket, patting it gently, as he customarily did. It was a rare Patek Philippe 18-karat gold skeleton pocket watch — every component skillfully and clearly crafted from gold.

Originally owned by his great-grandfather, it was one of many priceless heirlooms he'd inherited from his family.

Big Joe eyed Santini. "I sure hope you have a lot of insurance on that expensive time machine! I get nervous every time you pull that damn thing out! Even here, that kind of gold attracts eyes like a magnet!"

Santini chuckled. "Yes, I admit. She is quite a treasure. It's been in my family for many generations. No one makes clocks, watches, and knives like the Swiss do." he added. They know what Yep! They sure do," Big Joe concurred, reaching for his cell phone. "They build clocks and watches to last forever."

Javier's sudden, unexpected appearance, along with the sound of the front door opening, startled them. Their eyes were trained in the direction of the entrance, as Javier dashed across the room towards the door.

"It's Miss Eugenia! She's bringing fresh seafood from the market. I'm going to help her now!"

Eugenia's voice floated from the vestibule into the piano bar. "Javier, my dear, we must get these sea creatures into the refrigerator right away!" Her voice rang out as she lowered two large insulated bags to the floor. "Salmon, flounder, and sea bass are in this bag," she said, pointing with the cell phone she held. "Lobster and soft-shell crabs are in that bag… and shrimp and mussels are in the bag in the vestibule. Thanks!"

She glanced at her phone, a look of concern etched across her face. Raising her head, she squinted her eyes and peered to the back of the dim room, where she zoomed in on Santini and Big Joe. "Ciao, guys! Glad to see that you two are still here on Planet Chelsea Place!" She dropped her large tote bag on a nearby chair and strode towards them, stopping at a point where she could best command their full attention. "It seems everyone else has mysteriously disappeared!" she huffed.

Still shell-shocked and reeling from the awful weight of their conversation, they could barely respond to her.

"Ciao!" Santini mumbled.

"Afternoon, Eugenia." Big Joe said with a weak smile.

Eugenia folded her arms in a gesture that screamed: *What the Hell is going on here!* Her eyes darted from Santini to Big Joe. "Well, at least your bodies are still here," she huffed. "As for your minds, well, I'd say they're at least a million miles away!"

That comment was met with total silence.

Eugenia stared curiously at Santini and Big Joe. "How did your high-powered meeting go?" she asked, not waiting at all for a response. "I certainly hope you guys have come up with a way to kick that jerk out of here. He barges into my kitchen uninvited and unannounced as if he owns the place!" she fumed.

"God how I wish I could blink my eyes and make that man disappear," she continued, determined to make her point. "Consider yourselves warned. The next time he wobbles into my kitchen, I'm greeting him with the heaviest cast iron pan I can lift!"

Santini and Big Joe returned Eugenia's stare, and chuckled lightly. The sight of Vlad getting battered by a heavy cast iron pan appealed to both of them.

Santini rose to help Eugenia with her coat. "Oh, how I'd love to just blink him away also," he echoed. "I'd blink him straight to hell!"

"He deserves much more than being blinked away," Big Joe added, half serious and half kidding. "I'm thinking more along the lines of Eugenia whacking him ten… fifteen times with her heavy cast iron pan. Yep! That would suit him just fine."

Eugenia's eyes swept across the room. "And… where's the lady of the house?"

"She's meeting with Jason… uptown on Riverside Drive."

"Is Jason okay? He isn't sick or anything, is he?" she interrupted.

Santini shook his head. "No, he isn't sick. He just wanted to see his mother, privately."

"Jason wanted to have some son-mother time," Big Joe joined in.

"I've called, texted, meditated and prayed on Jason several times. There's no response from him," she complained. "And I haven't been able to reach Kitt since I spoke to her earlier this morning while you guys were having your meeting. Calls go straight to voicemail. I'm worried out of my mind!"

Santini moved in closer, and his hand went to Eugenia's shoulder.

"No need to feel left out, my dear. It's probably just some mother and son thing. You know… matters between the two of them."

"They are entitled to some private mother and son time, don't you think?" Big Joe queried, mischievously eyeing Eugenia.

"What I *think* is I'll feel much better after I've spoken to them!" she fired back, tapping the speed dial on her phone. "I hate leaving voice messages!" she muttered, rolling her eyes and putting her hand akimbo as the call went straight to voicemail. *Hi Jason, it's your god-mom calling again. Please, baby… let me know that you and your mom are okay. Remember… your birthday dinner tomorrow evening is at eight o'clock sharp! P.S. Lemonade. Sweet or sour?"* She ended the call and leaned against a table.

"I don't recall lemonade being on the menu for Jason's party tomorrow," Santini commented, the look of utter confusion scrawled across his face.

Big Joe eyed Eugenia, conspicuously. "That's because it isn't on the menu," he deadpanned. "Sweet or sour… hot or cold. They're code for trouble. Right, Eugenia?"

The blank look on her face was a dead giveaway.

"Anything that comes out of the clear blue like that can't be anything but code."

"Time for an update, Eugenia. That's *really* old school."

"What code?" she asked, coyly.

"The same old school code my parents used with me when I was a kid. That code!" He said, reprimanding her.

Embarrassed, she finally acquiesced. "We agreed to use it after Lem's abduction. It was the perfect code for a kid."

Santini's face softened. "In case you haven't noticed, Jason's no longer a kid. He turns twenty-one today. That means he's officially a young man."

Eugenia shook her head and reminisced. "As a child, whenever Jason got into trouble with Kitt and Lem, he'd call me and say: 'Auntie Genie, the lemonade is sour today! That was his way of letting me know that he wanted me to drop by and take him out for a while."

She paused. "I swear! kids grow up too fast these days!"

Big Joe's eyes met Eugenia's. "Especially when you love them as much as I love my son." His voice was buried in sadness. "It's a shame he hates me so much."

Aware of Big Joe's broken relationship with his teenage son, Eugenia planted her eyes on Big Joe's sorrowful face, and spoke in a tender voice. "Don't worry. He's still young and foolish. Real love is knowing when to let go. Give him space and time to learn from his own mistakes."

Santini bowed his head and smiled. "Well-said, Eugenia. I couldn't have said it any better. The same goes for you, too, my dear."

"Me?"

"Yes. You."

"What do you mean?"

"I mean… you must surely know how much we all love, worship, and adore you… especially Kitt and Jason. But has it occurred to you that every now and then, maybe they need a little space away from us?"

"But, we're family. We're that close!" Eugenia responded, defensively.

"I understand that. I love them, too. But Jason made it clear when he called that he wanted to see his mother, alone." Santini paused. "Let's give them some breathing room."

Eugenia stared wide-eyed at Santini, then looked away. "We go way back, Santini. You, of all people, must understand why I'm so overly-protective of Kitt and Jason."

"Yes. I do understand. But remember, giving them some space and breathing room is a big part of loving them."

She thought for a while, then smiled. "You're right," she agreed, glancing briefly at her cell phone before dropping it inside her tote. "Kitt and Jason have been through so much!"

"All the more reason why we need to give them some space," he countered.

"Amen! Great sermon!" Big Joe exclaimed, breaking the seriousness of the conversation.

Eugenia reached for her coat and tote. "You guys must think I'm a mad woman!" she joked.

"Well, I've always thought that madness gives balance to sanity," Santini quipped.

"Agreed!" Big Joe chimed in. "Quite honestly, I think giving into one's own madness can sometimes be a healthy thing."

They all roared with laughter, totally understanding the raw absurdity of truth, and acknowledging that at some point, they'd all come frighteningly close to that place called insanity.

"Amen to that!" Eugenia called out, walking towards the stairs that led down to the restaurant and kitchen. "Sometimes a little madness does the soul a whole lot of good!" She shouted in her best church voice, her words trailing behind her.

"See you later tonight!" Santini chuckled, gathering his coat and scarf.

"I'll activate the alarm on our way out!" Big Joe's voice resonated, as they walked slowly towards the door.

Santini took a deep breath and spoke without looking at Big Joe. "We're indebted to your friend, Officer Gallagher. She's shared an abundance of valuable information with us. How can we thank her?"

"Gallagher loves her job. It's all about keeping New Yorkers safe, and putting criminals behind bars." Big Joe thought for a moment. "I'm sure she'd really enjoy one of Eugenia's seafood dishes."

"*Perfecto!* Tell her she has an open invitation here for dinner and drinks, anytime!"

Big Joe stopped in the vestibule and pulled out a small remote. “Now that we have all of this information, how do we use it?”

Santini looked up at Big Joe. “I would think that this sort of thing clearly requires your expertise and background. Does it not?”

“I’m afraid, not. My days as an NYPD officer are ancient history.” Big Joe grunted.

Santini stared up at the man towering above him. “It must be impossible to completely separate oneself from such a daring lifestyle. Do you ever miss it?”

Big Joe cocked his head to one side as he buttoned his coat. “It’s impossible not to miss the constant rush of adrenaline that comes from living life on the edge 24/7. It’s in my blood.”

“I don’t mean to pry. But is it true that you left the NYPD on not-so-friendly terms?”

Big Joe drew in a long breath, let it out, and looked Santini directly in the eye. “I walked away from the NYPD because of internal department crimes and a severe lack of principles by a group of so-called honorable men.”

Santini batted, his eyes rapidly. “Well now, that’s a loaded response. I hope I’m not being too intrusive, but, how so, may I ask?”

Big Joe opened his coat demonstrably, with both hands akimbo. “I’m an open book, Santini. I have nothing to hide,” he said, looking dead-on into Santini’s eyes. “I’ve never been big on building walls — blue, brick, or otherwise. But I was always the first to defend my brothers and sisters on the force, when they were right." He paused for a moment. "I was also the first to call them out, when they were wrong."

"That is quite the honorable thing to do. Guts and a strong backbone are required to take such a stance," Santini remarked, reverently. "I can only imagine how many enemies you must have made by doing the right thing. One of life's many tragic ironies!"

Big Joe cracked a half-smile. "Are you kidding? I became a pariah in blue!

I made enemies from the top brass all the way down to the snotty-nosed rookies on the street. When my back was against the wall, the entire force went code blue and they all turned their backs on me."

The expression on Santini's face was as sincere as the words he spoke. "How horribly unjust. That is indeed, unfortunate. It must be very painful."

Big Joe frowned and shook his head. "All of the above and then some. That kind of pain never goes away. It cuts through the heart worse than a knife or a bullet."

"Officer Gallagher seems to be a devoted friend and a lovely lady." Santini offered, hoping to lift the cloud that had all but consumed them. His efforts paid off and brought some light to Big Joe's face. When he spoke, his voice was a bit higher than usual.

"She's got more balls than all of those jerks combined," he nodded. "And she is definitely a lady."

Santini smiled approvingly. "We all need someone in our life whom we can count on."

"I'm glad it was Gallagher who stepped into my position after I left the department."

"What position was that?"

"Head of MCNI." Big Joe proudly responded. "That special Ops unit was my baby. I conceived and created it. Built it from the ground up. MCNI is the most elite unit the NYPD has ever had."

"That must have been some accomplishment!" Santini exclaimed. "What happened?"

"We were an air-tight unit. A group of highly-trained, brilliant field officers. The best of the best. Then a bad seed found its way inside." Big Joe swallowed and took a moment. "One night during a well-planned sting, the table got terribly turned. Within minutes, my entire unit was wiped out, in what was labeled as the worst bloodbath in recent NYPD history."

Big Joe's immense body seemed to shrink under the weight of his words. "I was the lucky one. I was only grazed on the arm. Everyone else, including my car partner, was gunned down." Big Joe lowered his head, and his voice became nearly inaudible. "He was like a brother... my best friend. He was also Gallagher's husband."

Santini gasped, shocked speechless by what he had just learned. He searched desperately for words that did not come easily. After an uncomfortable moment of silence, Santini emerged from his trance. "Please forgive me, Mister D'Amato. It was really not my intention to take you back to that dreadful time. It was quite insensitive of me to pry into your past. Please accept my sincere apologies."

"No worries. It just happens that my private life is one long, hellish nightmare," he grunted, his voice broken by the heavy burden of self-imposed guilt.

For a moment, neither said a word. It was getting late and Santini had a standing appointment with his barber. "Listen, let's hold off on sharing this information with Kitt until after Jason's birthday dinner party. No need to ruin the occasion with such bad news."

"You're right. No need to dump this crap on her tonight." Big Joe flipped open the concealed alarm pad and gestured to Santini to step outside. They waited and listened for the security signal to appear before continuing their conversation.

Santini pulled out his cell phone and started texting. "I'll let her know that we'll fill her in on Vlad tomorrow evening after Jason's dinner party."

Big Joe rubbed his palms together, briskly. "So, how do we slay this monster?"

Santini wrapped a long silk scarf around his neck and half-smiled. "Back home in the old country, the one lesson we've all learned is that the best way to kill a monster, any kind of monster, is with a bigger, stronger, more powerful monster."

Chapter 7
The Bitter Truth

WHIIIIIEEEEE! The sound of the kettle whistling catapulted me back to the present. Still gripped by fiery anger and pain from that dreadful night, I pelted back to the kitchen. There was something else that kept gnawing at me — those disturbing visions. The pieces were all beginning to come together like a mysterious puzzle. The distant village. The violet haze. The ever-changing images. The silhouette that danced for me. My mind was reeling, spinning at high speeds — with sounds, images, and Lem's voice all randomly swirling around inside my head like a windstorm. With so much going on inside my head, the one thing that became crystal clear was the connection between my visions and what Lem had seen in that remote village. Lem's village story was becoming more and more real.

With a pot of frothy hot cocoa in one hand, and two mugs in the other, I returned to the lab, where Jason had already inhaled every bit of his food. I was ready to hear whatever it was he wanted to tell me. "Now that you're clean and nourished, I thought some hot cocoa would be the perfect fuel to get you started with your story." Sensing the tension that had all but consumed him, I filled the mugs and handed one to him.

Jason wrapped his hands around the mug, holding on to it more so for comfort than warmth. He took a big gulp, then hesitated. "Dad came back from that trip much earlier than planned because of the problems you were having with your pregnancy."

This was not one of my favorite subjects. I took in a deep breath and sighed. "I had such a difficult time carrying you. I was always tired and lightheaded. I suffered from insomnia and severe back pains. I was very sick throughout my pregnancy with you. I fainted so frequently that my doctor ordered strict bed rest. Lem came back from Brazil early to take care of me."

Jason's brows furrowed, as he lowered his head. "I'm very sorry that you suffered so much Mom. I've heard Dad's take on what happened the night I was born. But you… you have always avoided talking about it." He paused, got up, refilled our mugs, then settled back onto the floor. "Mom… what do you remember about the night I was born?"

I rested my head against the back of the sofa, closed my eyes, and allowed my mind to drift… back to that time… twenty-one years ago.

Lem came back from Brazil, completely exhausted from working too many long hours, and under really bad conditions. Physically, I was a total wreck. We thought a little rest and relaxation, away from everyone and everything, would do us both some good. So Lem rented a cozy little cabin in Vermont, for a long weekend. It was located not far from the company's zoo and lab compound. He showed me pictures of the place, and I fell in love with it! It was a beautiful old log cabin that sat in a wooded area, along the Appalachian Mountain chain near the U.S.-Canada border. We were so excited about getting away. But we never made it to the cabin. The ice storm… the worst ever in the Northeastern United States.

"Dad called it the storm from hell. A complete whiteout that brought Vermont, Connecticut, New Hampshire, and Maine all to their knees!" Jason broke in.

"Not one, but three back-to-back bomb cyclones! It all happened with no warning. The most devastating ice storm on record."

"A chill coursed through my entire body, as I relived that horrendous night.

"I had never, in my life, seen nature more violent, more tempestuous, than I did on that night in Vermont. We didn't understand how a few pretty snowflakes had suddenly turned into a raging blizzard of rain, sleet, wind and snow. The temperature dipped, and nearly an inch of ice covered the roads. There were accidents with vehicles that were paralyzed. No one saw it coming. No one expected it. Not even the savviest meteorologists. The road we were on was narrow and blanketed in heavy snow, with swirling wind, ice, and debris obliterating all visibility. Seven months into an already difficult pregnancy, I started panicking, and became extremely ill. Lem realized that my condition was worsening, and there was no way to get any kind of help. The weight of the ice caused limbs and entire trees to break, creating roadblocks. Power and telephone lines were brought down, leaving millions of people without power. All medical helicopters and land ambulances were grounded. Locals were told to go home and bunker down. Motorists were ordered to stay off the roads and highways, and to find immediate shelter. Lem and I were in our jeep, only a few miles away from the zoological lab compound that was owned by the company where he frequently worked. Luckily, the compound had its own generator. Lem felt we'd be safe there. By the time we arrived, I was so sick I couldn't even stand on my own."

"Dad said you were gravely ill, and burning up from a high fever," Jason interjected, matter-of-factly.

My mind bounced back and forth — from present to past, then past to present. It raced with so much speed that there seemed to be no separation of place or time. Every moment and memory was fractured and shattered, like broken glass. The pieces were scattered here, and there.

As I spoke, my mind ran ahead, searching furiously for all of the missing pieces. "I remembered being met at the entrance of the compound by a man and a woman who spoke with thick accents. I thought perhaps they were Eastern European. They both knew Lem and greeted him by name. The woman helped Lem carry me into what looked like a small, very neat bedroom. And then…" My voice faded, as my memory did. Everything went blank. Again, my mind raced, teased, and tugged menacingly, at my whitewashed memory.

Jason stood up and gently planted a little kiss on my forehead, the way I always kissed his forehead when he was a child. When he spoke, he sounded more like Lem, than himself. "They were employees of the compound whom dad had previously met while working there in the laboratory." Jason sighed and ran a hand over his face. "The woman was a lab assistant, and the man was the zookeeper. They were Serbians who had come to the compound to work as exchange staff-members." He paused, drew in a long breath, then exhaled. "According to dad, after securing the animals, and heeding the weather warnings, all of the compound's other employees had abandoned the premises and gone to their respective homes. Only the lab assistant and zookeeper stayed on at the compound." His voice seemed to hang on to those last words.

I stared at Jason until our eyes met. "What *really* happened that night, Jason? What story has Lem shared with you that he has never told me? I want to know the whole truth."

Jason's shoulders slumped, giving in to the heaviness of what was about to follow. Even as a child, his body language always spoke louder than his voice. "The fever made you delirious. You were in and out of consciousness. You started hemorrhaging, profusely. And then you went into labor… prematurely."

"And?"

Jason stood up and began pacing. "The lab assistant helped dad deliver me. But by then, you had lost a tremendous amount of blood." He paused, and searched for words. "Dad was afraid you'd bleed out and die."

"Why can't I remember any of this?" I muttered, under my breath, angry at myself because of so much I could not remember.

"Dad saw that you were slipping away. You were dying, mom… and he didn't want to lose you. He knew that only a transfusion would save your life."

"Lem was a hemophiliac. He has never been fit to donate blood. Was it the lab assistant or the zookeeper who donated blood to me?"

Jason swallowed and took a deep breath. "The lab assistant was severely anemic."

"I see. So, the zookeeper was the donor." I said, uneasily.

Jason averted his eyes, glanced briefly at the cage, then turned to me. "No, mom. According to dad, the groundskeeper was extremely intoxicated, uncooperative, and adamantly opposed to donating his blood." Once again, Jason's eyes drifted over to the caged animal.

My eyes followed Jason's and landed squarely on the jaguar whose delicate, feminine snoring fascinated me. There was something eerily intriguing and familiar about that jaguar! What was it about her that kept tugging at me with so much force? Suddenly, I could not breathe! I struggled, desperately gasping for air, but could not breathe!

When I finally caught my breath, I noticed that I was breathing perfectly in sync with the rising and falling of the jaguar's chest. She and I… *we* were breathing together! Then came the gut twisting thought that brought all of the fragmented pieces together. My mind went into a violent spin. Before I knew it, I was on my feet! "Oh, God! No!" I screamed out, shaking uncontrollably. "Lem… did he transfuse blood from a jaguar into my body?"

Jason's entire body trembled as he nodded his head. "Yes, mom… It was the only thing he could do to save your life! It was impossible to get help. There were no other alternatives!"

"The *best* alternative would have been to just let me die! What the hell was Lem thinking! Why? Why did he do that to me? He pumped a jaguar's blood into my body!" I shrieked, pacing back-and-forth like a rabid animal. "He was crazy! That's it! With all of the pressure he was under… he just snapped! He did that to me in a moment of madness!" I mumbled, before dissolving into a mess of tears.

Jason tried to hold me, but I shoved him away. I was too angry, too frightened, and too distraught. I wanted to lash out at Lem…! Hit him…! Yell at him! And I couldn't, because he was nowhere to be found!

He had done this horrific thing to me, had gotten away with it, and now his son was defending him! I was angry and hurt, consumed with fiery rage! Even worse, the fact that I was having a nervous breakdown before his very eyes, neither elicited sympathy, nor encumbered Jason's impassioned oration.

Jason folded his arms, defensively, and raised his head. "Dad was thinking in leaps and bounds, in spite of all of the pressure he was under. He remembered that a melanistic jaguar at the zoo compound had recently given birth, and that her cord blood and placenta fluids had all been cleansed, and bio-cryogenically preserved. Those blood vessels and umbilical fluids were filled with exactly what was needed to keep you alive — rich, hematopoietic stem cells."

"So he filled my body with fluids and God knows what else from a jaguar! What kind of a man does something so heinous to his wife! I hope he enjoyed playing God!"

"He wasn't playing God!" Jason fired back. "He was being the brilliant, forward-thinking biotechnologist that he is!" He paused and unfolded his arms. "Dad used his knowledge and the jaguar to fulfill a good purpose — to keep you alive! Before that night, biologists had been mixing and blending human and nonhuman matter in petri dishes for decades, without any real success." Jason's eyes teared with pride, as he continued. "Dad accomplished the almost impossible using real subjects… based on his own experiments. It was extremely risky, but it was his only option."

"He used his wife as a lab rat! You can't get more repulsive than that!"

"Dad and the lab assistant did a fast cross-match between you and the jaguar, which revealed that, biochemically, there were no extreme incompatibilities between your blood and hers. You were a perfect match."

I stared at him, pensively, before sharing my thoughts:

I've always suspected that Lem wasn't being completely truthful about what really happened the night you were born! Whenever I brought up the subject, he would change it. My gut feeling told me that there was much more to the story than what he had told me. But not in my wildest dream did I ever think he'd do something like that to me! Only a mad man would have done that! All these years… I've been walking around with jaguar blood… flowing through my body.

"Jason… for God's sake, do whatever you have to do… a transfusion or whatever… but please purge that animal's blood from my body! Please! I'm begging you! Just undo it!"

Jason hung his head and sighed. "It can't be undone. I mean… there's no way to safely purge your body now. Everything is completely integrated. In a transgenic procedure, the objective is for the donor cells to penetrate and permanently live in the recipient. It is permanent, mom."

A very loud SILENCE fell over the room.

I was so nauseous I wanted to vomit. "Look at me, Jason. What am I? What has that transgenic experiment turned me into?"

He raised his head, slowly. "You are what is known as a *transgenic being.*"

"In English, dammit!"

"Transgenic simply means that your body contains DNA sequences from a non-human animal. In your case, it's DNA from a jaguar." He cleared his throat. "Dad made sure that he did a highly specific, well-targeted genetic modification before introducing the jaguar's blood and DNA properties into your body."

"Plain and simple, dammit!"

Jason's voice dipped and peaked. The more he talked, the more animated he became.

"This direct introduction of the jaguar's DNA changed the genetic makeup of your cells, causing them to exhibit new properties, some new characteristics, and new behaviors." Jason glanced briefly at the jaguar. "Dad took her best attributes and complimented them with your best attributes. Then he enhanced and augmented your combined traits, greatly improving all of your capabilities."

"Exactly what does that mean?"

"What it means is that he took the best of what it is to be human and combined it with the best of what it is to be a jaguar. He fused all of those extraordinary characteristics together.

Then he transfused the newly enhanced DNA into you and her."

"And?"

"And… the end result is a transgenic creation that is way beyond human — a super being — something that is powerful beyond comprehension. The result is a new kind of entity… a creature that is almost god-like!" Jason enthused.

"Being human is hard enough! I have no need or desire to go beyond that!" I exclaimed. My eyes were transfixed on the jaguar like a magnet. She was in a deep sleep, but I sensed that she felt my presence… that she was somehow communicating with me. That jaguar knew me… knew who I was… and even as she slept, had connected with me. In my mind, I felt as though we'd met somewhere before… somewhere in another place… somewhere other than here, in this miserable laboratory. Then, it hit me! She was the odd, twisting, changing image that had occupied my mind this morning! She was in the midst of all of that violet confusion — the things that were so unnatural and completely out of place. "Oh, my God!" I gasped, startling Jason.

"Mom… are you okay?"

"The hell I'm not okay! How can I possibly be okay after what I've just heard!" I shrieked. My breathing became labored as I forced the words out of my mouth. "That jaguar… she is the image that keeps appearing in those visions I've been having! The shape of her body is the same curvy figure, draped in purple. The silhouette I'm looking at now, is the elusive ballerina-like figure that strutted so effortlessly, as she danced around me! It's her! It was she whom I kept seeing over and over again in those visions! That explains why I feel so connected to her!"

Jason was clearly caught off-guard. He stood paralyzed, his stance and eyes frozen. He swallowed several times. "I came downstairs just before eight this morning to feed her. At first, she was calm and stood silently. Then we locked eyes. That was when it happened."

"What happened?"

Raising his head, he forced himself to look at me. "That's when she smiled… and walked… the way you've just described it… like a woman. She walked, as gracefully as a ballerina." He paused and gathered his thoughts. "What was astonishing was the ease with which she stood upright on her hind legs and walked… so naturally and effortlessly. I believe she got inside my head the way you got inside Santini's head. I felt her presence inside my mind. She was definitely reading my mind. She communicated telepathically with me to let me know what she was doing. That's when I knew I needed to see you right away. I realized then that the process of amalgamation… the transformation to oneness between the two of you had begun. I was thrown off-guard because the process was happening much faster than I'd anticipated!"

"What are we really dealing with, Jason? I want to know everything about her! Do you understand? Tell me everything about that goddam creature!"

Jason was a bundle of raw nerves, but the wheels were set in motion. Shiny beads of sweat covered his forehead. "I'm sure some of what I'm saying is complicated, but I will explain everything so that you can thoroughly grasp and understand what I'm saying. Dad specialized in transgenic biotechnology, but he was also an experienced zoologist — committed above all, to preserving the Amazon's endangered black melanistic jaguars. The best way to achieve that was to make the female jaguars more fertile in order to repopulate the species. This required some creative genetic manipulation as well as cell-based therapies using human stem cells."

"That's called screwing around with nature!" I yelled out angrily.

"Yes… in a way it is screwing around with nature… but under safely controlled conditions. Dad based his theory on the premises that everyone and everything — humans and non-humans — are all connected by a web of energy. More precisely, a web of continuous, unbroken energy." He paused before driving his point home. "Humans and jaguars share ninety-percent of nearly identical protein coding genes with other similar DNA details."

"But human beings are people, and jaguars are cats! We're not talking about blending peaches and plums here! This is different! It is very, very dangerous!" I shouted, hoping to bring him to his senses.

"Yes, humans and jaguars are different, but at the same time, very similar. Jaguars are warm-blooded animals with milk production, like humans. They also have the same vital organs, arranged in a similar body plan."

"And Lem thought that was reason enough to commingle a jaguar's blood and bodily fluids with mine?" I retorted sharply, before sucking in a deep breath and glancing at the jaguar. "How human is she? And just what kind of a goddam freak has Lem turned me into?"

Jason eyed me cautiously. "You are essentially what she is… and she… is what you are. You are one in the same."

I gasped as my entire body shook uncontrollably. I felt unclean. I wanted to spit and vomit… do anything necessary to purge that creature from my body. For a moment, I almost lost it. But I needed to hear every sordid detail of what Lem had done to me.

Unyielding, Jason forged ahead. "During the transfusion, dad used a special bacterial enzyme to isolate the white blood cells — which carries DNA — from the jaguar's placental blood and umbilical cord blood. He saved your life that night with the cross species fusion. That basically laid the groundwork for a successful human/non-human transgenesis. What you share is something that is called a mutualistic symbiotic relationship."

"In plain and simple English, dammit!"

He eyed the jaguar, then turned to me. "You both benefit equally from this association. Dad observed that within minutes after the transfusion, you were showing signs of miraculous improvements."

"What kind of miraculous improvements?"

"You were healing rapidly, and all of your vitals were astonishingly strong... functioning at levels that were above and beyond human!"

"Above and beyond human!" I huffed. "I find that to be so frightening!"

So focused on the subject at hand, Jason showed not even the slightest hint of sympathy for me. "What was even more impressive, was that dad realized this process had created a heightened psychological and neurobiological connection between you and the jaguar."

I glanced nervously at the jaguar. "A telepathic connection?"

"Yes, that's correct."

"That explains why I've been having these strange feelings... thoughts and images in my mind that I can't explain," I whispered. "I assumed I was going through early menopause. I never imagined going through this kind of change!"

Jason reached out and tried to embrace me, but I pulled away, shaking my head, still fiercely angry and hurt. He cleared his throat, and spoke slowly in a low voice. "I'm saying that you're connected to each other emotionally, physiologically, mentally, and even spiritually. You share a soul telepathy enabling you to hear each other's thoughts and visions. You are two beings that are now united into one." He drew in a deep breath. "Obviously, your bodies are different… and for the most part, that will remain unchanged. But… your humanness is no longer exclusively yours, any more than her jaguar-ness is exclusively hers. Although you have separate bodies, you are one. You no longer exist as separate entities. You share a powerful, indivisible sameness and oneness. You have a soul, and so does she — yours."

I stared at him, long and hard, understanding clearly the impact of what he had said. But I was too angry and hurt, too injured by the years of deception, to say anything. I needed to contain my fury!

I was dumbfounded. He took advantage of my numbness and continued. "Dad was so ahead of the curve. A true visionary! He has catapulted transhumanism far into the future!" he boasted, beaming with pride.

I swallowed and unleashed on him. "Lem's brilliance and his talk of transhumanism were the two things that frightened me more than anything else in this world. He was a great husband to me, and an amazing father to you. But he was so hell-bent on pushing things too far. And look, Jason… look at what he's done to me!"

"He's succeeded in pushing the human condition beyond all limitations!" Jason gushed. "As far as I'm concerned, dad did the right thing. I know, because you've survived all of this time. You're living proof of his 'One-ness theory'." Jason's eyes brightened with enthusiasm. "You're very much alive, aren't you? More importantly, you're better than ever. You are nearly perfect — a greatly improved, more enhanced human being."

Overwhelmed by almost unbearable tension, Jason and I stared silently at each other, for what felt like an eternity. Neither of us batted an eye. He knew how uncomfortable Lem's 'oneness theory' made me feel. That didn't matter. He was more than willing and prepared to defend his father's work. I knew that at least one cool head needed to prevail in a situation that was already hot and boiling over. I had been used as a guinea pig by my husband, and our son was compliant, and defending his father.

In this very moment, I understood how intimate family members could, in a fit of raging anger, seriously injure, or even kill each other. I was so numb I could barely breathe. I wanted to cry, scream, and yell for all of the right reasons! I had more than earned the right to be an ANGRY BLACK WOMAN! Two people whom I had loved more than life — people whom I had nurtured, cared for, and fed — had knowingly deceived me for years! It felt as if they'd driven a knife into the middle of my heart and turned it around and around, twisting it deeper and deeper into me until the intense pain made me wish for the mercy of death. I took several deep breaths, and slowly exhaled… letting go of the fire and fury that raged violently inside me.

Chapter 8
Oneness

"How will this transgenesis affect me as a person? Will it change the way I look or feel? Will I think and speak differently? Am I still a woman, Jason?"

His eyes swept vigorously across my face, scrutinizing it from top to bottom. "There are no visible telltale signs," he replied, with a big sigh of relief. "You look the same — beautiful and ageless!" he added, with a slight smile. "How do you *feel*? What changes are you feeling in your body…? your mind…? your sleep pattern?"

Shaking my head in reply, my eyes were fixed squarely on Jason's body language. "I was fine until a few days ago when… I started experiencing extreme surges of energy. Even after those long nights at Chelsea Place, I felt neither tired, nor the urge to rest or sleep."

Jason's head popped up. "Self-regenerating energy, to be exact. That's one of many enhancements you'll experience. They'll be others… mostly internally."

"What other kinds of enhancements?"

"Increased speed… strength… greater tolerance to environmental extremes… greater endurance… and…" He paused and eyed me, thoughtfully. "You'll be more than human. Transhumanists call it *human plus, post human, or H+*."

"H+! That sounds like something from a sci-fi movie!"

"Except that it isn't science fiction. It's all very real!"

"What other changes can I expect?"

"You'll be bio-sonic, with optical zooming and echolocation powers, enabling you to hear and see things from a distance. Your vision will be greatly enhanced!"

"Enhanced vision?"

"Jaguars have eye-shine and night vision that is at least ten times better than humans, and your vision will be even greater!"

"Considering that I've always been allergic to contact lenses and don't particularly like wearing glasses, that would be a welcomed improvement," I acquiesced, forcing a half-smile.

Jason nodded, affirmatively. "Your sense of smell will improve, as well, allowing you to detect scents from miles away."

"Now, that's something I can do without! Who wants to smell unpleasant odors, from a distance?"

He chuckled. "There'll be other changes… some more subtle than others." He paused and his voice became somber. "However, come nightfall, everything will intensify. Like the melanistic jaguar, you are now more of a nocturnal creature. Internally, you're evolving, even as we speak."

"*Evolving*!" I echoed, sarcastically. "Funny you should use it. That has always been one of Lem's favorite words!" The thought of my body evolving and eventually being covered from head-to-toe in thick, furry hair was at the forefront of my greatest fears.

But I had to know what to expect. I took another deep breath. "What physical changes should I prepare myself for as I'm evolving? Will I turn into some hairy creature?"

He shook his head and glanced briefly at the jaguar. "The chances of you becoming a hairy creature are minimal. Not unless you *will* yourself to do so. She looks the way she does because she comes from the rainforests. Her black, melanistic skin makes it easier for her to blend into the dark shadows of the trees."

I released a sigh. "Well, that's good to know."

"Your physiological performances will be maximized, and most changes will be internal, without any extreme physical augmentations. Naturally, you can expect increased agility, a more toned physique, and, as I've said, more speed."

"That explains why I was walking so fast this morning!"

"With a few exceptions, during the day, you will look normal, and function as a normal human being. But come night, if you choose to do so, you will have the ability to evoke all of your newly acquired powers… at will."

The words "*at will*" resonated in my head, and made my body tremble. "What other powers will I have?"

As his excitement grew, Jason became more relaxed. "Don't worry… I'll explain as much of the science to you as I can. Luckily, most of it will come to you instinctively. Your powers and new abilities will literally become second nature to you," he added, reassuringly.

"Go on, continue."

He could hardly contain himself as he spoke. "Heightened senses, overall. By using one hundred percent of your brain capacity, you will also be telepathic."

"Telepathic!" I exclaimed. "That explains why I could read Santini's mind this morning during our meeting! I felt as if I'd gotten inside his head!"

Jason stuck his chest out, and smiled. "That's because you had *truly* gotten inside his head! Your telepathic powers were already at work!"

"What else can I expect?"

"By use of direct microinjection, dad was able to chemically extract and manipulate the gray and white matter of the brain, increase the composition of neurons, and activate the region of the brain that most people never use."

It was my turn to speak. I made it a point to choose my words carefully. "There's nothing I can do to undo what Lem has done to me. His transgenesis experiment did not kill me. It has made me a stronger person. I guess

I can learn to live with that." I paused and looked straight into Jason's eyes. "So far, I can handle what I'm hearing. My guess is you're either saving the best or the worst for last."

Jason sighed. "I'll let you be the judge of that, mom," he began, bringing his eyes to meet mine. His voice was as clear as a whistle. "A super powerful nocturnal being, at night, you will also have the capacity to transfigure… shape shift… and transform yourself into… something else — a natural huntress — a highly-skilled stalk and ambush, nocturnal killer." He stopped for a moment, glanced at the sleeping jaguar, then turned his gaze to me. "You are the super soldier of future battlefields that every major government and military has dreamed of. Your body has been weaponized in every possible way. Dad knew exactly what he was doing!"

"And the jaguar over there? Has her body been weaponized also?"

Jason shook his head. "Yes… she, as well. But you are even more extraordinary," he replied. "Your human-ness gives you a unique edge over her. Being predominantly human will always give you that extra edge. Our humanity must always prevail."

"Thank God Jason! That is the best news I've heard all day long! My human-ness must be protected. Our humanity should always be preserved!"

"Dad made sure of that," Jason said, affirmatively, then continued. "You will become as stealth as she is, virtually invisible at night. Collectively, your combined physicalities will render you a phantasmagoria of abject horror and terror to the human mind and eye."

"That sounds nightmarishly frightening." I uttered.

"Yes, it is the most terrifying thing the human eye and mind can experience!"

What I had just heard bounced around inside my head, reverberating until I could finally say the words aloud: "I am the battlefield weapon of the future!" At that moment, I understood the immensity of it all. My life, as I knew it, and humanity, had been forever changed, upended, altered, and pushed to the brink. I sat quietly, and still, unable to move or breathe.

Jason seemed to be relieved. He had driven home exactly what I needed to know. His controlled demeanor sobered the moment. "I'll have to monitor and observe you closely for the next few days. We'll do it here, in the lab."

"I'll have to give some kind of explanation to Santini… Eugenia… Big Joe… and the rest of the staff. Our patrons will want to know where I am. I can't just suddenly disappear from Chelsea Place!"

Jason rubbed his forehead. "Don't worry. We'll come up with something. But you CANNOT tell anyone a word of what I've shared with you! This has to stay exclusively between the two of us! No one else must ever know about what you've become. Not even Aunt Genie!"

"With all of these changes I'm going through, how on earth am I supposed to keep this a secret!"

“Promise me, Mom!” he ordered, extending his pinky while eyeing me with a threatening look. “This has to be kept between us! No one else. This is our secret!”

We hooked pinkies, and it suddenly dawned on me: *If Lem performed this transgenesis procedure on me twenty-one years ago, why is it just now materializing?* Trying to keep a lid on the wrath that was already bubbling beneath, I calmly turned to face Jason. “Why has it taken so long for this experiment to manifest itself within me? During the past twenty-one years, I’ve never once experienced the sort of things I’m going through now. Why such a long delay? Why now, after twenty-one years?”

Jason averted his eyes, and stared blankly at the floor, unmoving. It was as if his heart had stopped beating. “Dad kept the effects of the transgenesis suppressed by periodically introducing neutralizing agents into your body,” he answered, coyly.

“How did he do that?”

“The old-fashioned way… he slipped them into your drink… your food… and into those deliciously expensive chocolates that he popped into your mouth.”

“That was lowdown and really sneaky!”

A little mischievous smile parted Jason’s lips. “Uh-uh! Careful what you say. Remember… that is *your* husband and *my* father you’re talking about!”

“Don’t remind me!” I fired back, eyeing him suspiciously. “You and Lem were always partners in crime. I suspect that you did more than just cheer him on from the sidelines." I studied him long and hard, intentionally trying to make him feel uncomfortable. "In my heart and gut, I know that you've contributed to this perversion… in one way or another. What hand did you play in this madness?" I had, at last, gotten under his skin, and it felt good!

Jason's entire demeanor changed. His body tensed as he shifted his gaze from me to the jaguar, then back to me. He opened his mouth, and at first, nothing came out. When he was finally able to get his words out, his voice cracked. "After dad's abduction, I prayed every night that he would return. But when weeks turned into months, and months turned into years, I woke up one day and knew it was time for me to finish his work."

My entire body went limp, as I struggled to speak. "What work, pray tell?"

Jason started pacing again. "Dad did an excellent job suppressing all signs of your transgenesis. Physiologically, your body had already been perfectly primed. The framework was there. The cross-species genes inside your body only needed to be stimulated… reactivated."

"So, you decided to play God. You took things into your own hands and stimulated and activated genes from a jaguar that should never have been put inside my body in the first place."

He avoided my eyes. "Yes, Mom. That is what I did. Dad's cross-species genetic fusion was so seamless, that for years, the transgenic genes stayed dormant in you. I reactivated those genes by boosting your body with transgenic stimulants."

I stared at him, too angry to say anything, and too afraid that if I had moved, I would have killed him… I would have killed him!

Sensing my rage, and knowing that he needed to put some distance between us, Jason backed away, nervously. "There were times when you came here to visit me, that I had to tranquilize you… in order to perform certain procedures."

I leapt up so suddenly that it frightened him. "What goddam procedures!" I demanded, yelling into his face.

Jason's Adam's apple slid up and down inside his throat. "Incremental tinctures, dosages of nucleotides, additional jaguar DNA, blended jaguar plasma, fluids, and other reactivation procedures. I had to make sure the metamorphosis was controlled and timed correctly."

I was sick to my stomach! Before I knew it, my hand was in the air, and I had served him two back-hand slaps across his face. It had happened so quickly that it took us both by surprise. My hand stung, briefly, leaving two big red prints on Jason's cheeks. We each needed a moment to digest what had happened… and the speed at which it had all happened. I recovered first, and got right back into his face. "For God's sake! I'm your mother! Not some goddam lab rat! Who the hell are you to mess with my life like that? You're just as demented as Lem was. Even more so! Lem was under a lot of pressure. But you… you had more than enough time to think about what you were doing. Your actions were all premeditated!"

The look of pain and sudden shock filled Jason's eyes. He trembled, still holding his face with both hands. "Not confiding in you made me feel like a rat. Every time I looked at you, I felt like a rat. But it was the only way to prove dad's one-ness theory."

"You'd do anything for him, wouldn't you? Even if it meant putting my life at risk! You're sick! How could you have done those things to me? Why? For god sake, I'm your mother! Why didn't you just leave well enough alone!" I shrieked. "You and Lem think it's okay to interfere with nature! You think messing with God is some kind of game. Well, it's not a game! It's dangerous!"

Jason slumped onto the sofa and rubbed his cheeks with his hands. Recovering, he slowly raised his head, and revealed tear-filled eyes. "It was the most difficult thing I have ever had to do in my life. But I had to do it… for Dad."

I was emotionally and physically spent. All I could do was look at him. How do I come to terms with this and hold on to my sanity? First my husband… then, my son… by hook, crook, and deceit… they had allowed their egos to erase layers of my woman-ness, my humanity, and replaced them with fibers and threads of DNA — not from another human being, but from a jaguar! "I am so angry right now, I could kill you!" I shouted, over and over, pacing back-and-forth like an angry animal, hoping to diffuse the fiery anger burning inside me. "Go on!" I barked at him. "Tell me everything! Get it all off of your chest!"

Jason swallowed hard, and shifted his gaze to the jaguar. "After I was hired by GBLU, one of my first assignments was at the compound. I learned that she was a second generation off-spring from the jaguar whose cord blood had been transfused with yours. From birth, she exhibited certain unusual traits."

I peered, uneasily at the jaguar. "Other than walking, dancing, and acting like a woman, what other unusual traits did she display?"

He hesitated for a moment. "Emotional and psychological traits," he whispered underneath his breath.

I gasped. The thought of such a frightful thing made me tremble. "Please… please don't tell me that she also talks," I pleaded, lowering my voice.

Jason said nothing as his eyes drifted back to the jaguar. "She communicates telepathically. I saw how rapidly she was metamorphosing… with human traits becoming more apparent. That's when I realized that you would, simultaneously, be experiencing some of the same changes. Hence, my panicked call to you this morning."

I was shaking… filled with anger that was rising inside me like a tide of fire. "Telepathically," I echoed, faintly, now afraid to think or speak. "How powerful is she?" I asked, my voice quivering. "Jason... exactly what are we dealing with here?"

Jason stood up, folded his arms, defensively, and resumed the pacing. This time, he went into an all-out dissertation. "In 2005, dad convinced the Center for Biological Diversity (CBD) that black melanistic jaguars in the Amazon were critically endangered. He got major funding for his project to save and protect the species. But he only told the CBD half of the story. He purposely withheld crucial information about the shape shifting, telepathic, and transfiguration activities linked to the black jaguars. He decided to conduct covert experiments and work independently here, at home, in his own laboratory."

"You're preaching to the choir," I quipped. "Lem practically lived down here. He only came up for air to eat and sleep. He got up every day... went to work at the company's lab... came back home... made his way down here into this crypt... and the cycle repeated itself."

Understanding and appreciating Lem's devotion to his work, Jason shook his head and persevered. "In 2010, under the Endangered Species Act, President Barack Obama commissioned and appointed Dad to oversee the newly-formed agency set up expressly for the protection, preservation, and recovery plan for the Amazon's endangered black jaguar. It was a major joint effort between the United States and Brazil that dad created, organized and "led..."

I interrupted him, fondly recalling the event. "No one was prouder than I was when Lem was honored with the Special International Achievements Award by President Obama. That was such a splendid evening! We sat next to Michelle and the girls, Malia and Sasha. Michelle was so warm and engaging. You and the girls got along really well! I felt Lem had finally gotten the recognition he deserved!"

Jason beamed with pride. "Dad deserved all of the accolades and awards he got. He worked extremely hard, and was totally dedicated to saving those jaguars."

I sighed, and finally managed to get a smile out. "Afterwards, I saw even less of Lem. He completely threw himself into his work. It was as if he was trying to prove something."

"He was. He was determined to prove his 'oneness theory'. President Obama's appointment gave dad the license and funding he needed to expand his research. As a result, he discovered that, akin to chimpanzees and apes, jaguars had very human-like personalities."

"You were constantly down here with Lem... shadowing his every move."

Jason perked up. "I looked forward to the times Dad and I spent together down here. He wanted me to see, learn, and understand every aspect of his work — especially when it came to his oneness theory. It was crucial that I knew that project inside and out... just in case." He hesitated, and his eyes filled with tears. "Just in case... anything ever happened to him."

I took a moment to digest what he'd just said. "It scares me to high heaven that you're so much like him," I whined. Based on my observation, those words not only pleased Jason, but clearly gave him the impetus he needed to continue.

"Dad's work was so innovative that it landed him in the middle of the fiercest, most competitive international arms race ever."

"An arms race?"

His body stiffened, and he returned the stare. "Yes, an arms race. The fiercest competition ever among the United States, Russia, China, North Korea, and other international players."

"Okay… now you're taking me into uncharted territory. You'll have to do some explaining."

His voice cracked when he responded. "They're all vying to be the first to create and develop a superior warrior for battlefields of the future — the *super soldier.*"

"The super soldier. I do recall Lem, occasionally talking about that."

Jason joined me on the sofa, held my hand, and looked directly into my eyes.

"Mom… this is highly confidential. But it's something you need to know. Especially now. Please… please keep this between us. Dad was working undercover for DARPA, the Defense Advanced Research Projects Agency. It is the most secretive arm of the U.S. Department of Defense. Since its inception in 1958, DARPA's main focus has been the creation of vast weapons systems. Now, most of its attention is trained on transforming humans into super soldiers, and preparing them for wars of the future. Under DARPA, Dad experimented with cutting edge genetic engineering and brain chemistry to create futuristic soldiers who are biologically and mechanically enhanced with super strength, telepathy, and immunity to pain and injury. Soldiers who can function on no sleep, regenerate wounds, and leap ten feet or more. Dad created the newest, most revolutionary weapon of future warfare. He made all of this a reality, by creating the first truly invincible super soldier — you!"

Jason paused, and gazed silently at me. The silence now was different, as he waited for me to react, to respond, in some way, to the immensity of what he had just shared.

I sensed that my less than enthusiastic response to everything he'd revealed was clearly disappointing to Jason. As much as he might have been relieved, by confiding in me, I was left hanging way out on a limb. There was so much to consider. Everything about me — my person… who, and what I was… had been irrevocably changed into something else. My whole world, as I knew it, had been turned upside down. Coming to terms with this was not going to be an easy task. It was going to take some doing, and a lot of time. I wondered if Jason understood that?

Realizing how much I did not know about Lem, brought my heart and mind to a place neither had ever been before. We were husband and wife! The thought of sharing my bed, sleeping beside, and waking up next to someone whom I had told my deepest fears and weaknesses to, only to discover that he was perhaps the person I knew the least, was unforgivable! It was also scary! What frightened me more, though, was realizing my own vulnerability. Wrestling internally with my emotions, I fumbled miserably as I tried to find my voice. "A super soldier," I repeated, more so to myself, than to Jason. "Lem was destined to reach that finish line first. I'm glad he did... even if it meant sacrificing me."

Jason eyed me, intently, and threw his long, lanky arm around my shoulders. "Everything happens for a reason. There's a good reason why it's you, and not some crazy, irresponsible, fool!"

Things I hadn't previously understood were suddenly becoming as clear as day to me.

"That explains why Lem was so jittery in the days leading up to his abduction... why he insisted on me packing our things and going down to Edisto Island," I murmured.

"Precisely mom! He became every major power's main target. Domestic and foreign operatives — spies from Russia, Japan, Israel, China, North Korea — even our own government — were all eager to get their hands on his lab journal. He knew that at some point, they'd come looking for it... and him."

"Oh, my God! He didn't want us to be here! Lem's way of protecting me was by not telling me anything! Why didn't I see that! How could I have been so blind!"

"Dad did everything he could to protect us. He wanted to make sure that we were safe, even if he wasn't." Jason's voice faded until it was almost inaudible.

I stared at him. I even felt sorry for him. Luckily, the severity of my anger gave way to more powerful motherly inclinations.

"That night when those people came… while they were beating Lem… ransacking the house and lab… you told them where his journal was."

The veins in Jason's neck bulged. "It was set up that way on purpose. Dad wanted them to stumble upon the journal, after searching for it. I was afraid they'd beat him to death. So I told them where to find the lab log, thinking they'd take it and leave us alone. They took a bogus journal. Dad outsmarted them."

"Lem placed his super soldier right in front of their eyes… in plain sight. Little did they know

that I was the weapon they'd come looking for!" I was very slowly beginning to come around, to appreciate more, the brilliant man I had fallen in love with, married, and the amazing son we had created together. I smiled at the young man sitting next to me.

"Jason… my mother always said that understanding is the brightest light ever! Now, it's all beginning to make sense to me. Lem knew exactly what he was doing by not telling me anything. Had he confessed everything to me, that night when those animals came into our home, I would have given in to them. Lem knew that I would have given my own life, in a heartbeat, to save the two of you. The greatest scientific achievement of our time, and your father hid me right there in plain sight!" The thought of that made me laugh out loud — fueled by Lem's kind of humor — so clever, shrewd and savvy that it was funny. I laughed and kept laughing until I cried.

Jason eyed me, suspiciously. I could tell from the expression on his face that, at first, he wasn't sure about my current state of mind. Seeing me laugh uncontrollably and drowning in my own tears had to have made him feel uncomfortable. When he finally realized that I was laughing at what Lem had done, he slowly joined in, eventually laughing as hard as I was.

Grinning boyishly, Jason looked relieved, as he dabbed away tears from the corner of his eyes. "That setup was the classic example of dad's wry sense of humor," he added, still laughing. "There's always that element of utter surprise."

We had just shared a moment of real laughter — pure comedic relief. It was something we both desperately needed. It made us feel better than we had felt all day. Our laughter unwillingly tapered, and faded into a sobered, calmer reality.

Jason fell silent, for a moment, then reached for my hand. "Mom… are you okay…? I mean… how do you really feel about all of this? You have been weaponized! You are the walking, breathing super soldier the world wants — faster, smarter, more powerful than any human or animal!"

"Your mom is a big, strong, super powerful lady, remember? I'll be fine. I just need time to let it all settle in," I said, smiling, and trying to convince myself of what I had just said.

Jason nodded and returned the smile. "I understand."

I sprang from the sofa and stretched my arms upward and outward. "It's just that this whole thing is so ironic. Who'd ever imagine that the first real super soldier would be a woman… a Black woman!" I exclaimed. "For goodness sake… I'm a cabaret singer-turned-nightclub owner.

"You're a cabaret singer who can still bring the house to its feet, mom! I've seen you in action. You either take the audience's breath away, or you leave them breathless. Once a cabaret singer, always a cabaret singer. Too bad I didn't inherit your amazing voice."

"Who said you didn't inherit my voice? I've heard you singing in the shower. You've got some really good pipes. Unlike your dad, you can carry and hold a tune."

It was another tender moment. Again, we laughed, recalling how Lem was always the first to admit that he was tone-deaf. Our laughter quickly gave way to the more serious issues at hand.

I certainly did feel empowered, and more ready than ever to deal with those haunting questions. Without blinking an eye, I stared at Jason and asked: "Which government or organization do you think got to Lem first?

Jason shook his head. "I don't know. It could be any of them. That is the million dollar question. We'll find him. That I promise!"

The jaguar stirred, ever so delicately, her head sliding into what looked like a more comfortable position.

My eyes landed on her and remained there as I spoke. "What about her? What happens when she wakes up… hungry?"

Jason turned, and walked closer to the jaguar. "I'll leave food and water inside the cage. She'll be okay."

"Fresh, bloody meat, I assume?"

He turned to face me. "Jaguars are carnivores. They only eat meat. But remember, this one is special… in many ways." He paused. "Her appetite is different. She's an omnivore. She eats plants and meat… like we do."

My entire body shook as I tried to wrap my mind around the realization that I had just come face-to-face with.

"I AM THE HUNTRESS." I enunciated each word slowly and deliberately, as if I were engraving them into my mind… my own consciousness… into my entire being. Each utterance bore the agonizing pain of a nail being hammered into my flesh… my all too human flesh!

Our eyes locked. There was only SILENCE, for what felt like a lifetime.

"Correction. You are the *victorious* huntress!" Jason exclaimed, valiantly wagging his pointer. "You are the smartest… the fastest… and the strongest!" He reiterated.

"Dad observed you and took notes into the wee hours of the night. He realized that what he had accomplished was the greatest scientific breakthrough of our time!"

"Lem was so brilliant." I whispered.

"He *is* so brilliant." Jason emphasized, extending his pinky. "Always remember the pinky pledge that you and I made: "*As long as his body is not found, there is hope that he is still alive, and we will find him,"* we said, in unison. *"We will find him!"*

Chapter 9
The Hidden Twin

Something wasn't quite right. Curiosity got the best of me. "Jason, where were the lab assistant and zookeeper while Lem was making this enormous scientific breakthrough? What became of them?"

That question clearly struck a bad chord, as he became quite jittery. He folded his arms, and dropped his head. "Ahem… the Serbian couple… well… they disappeared."

It gave me pleasure to see that I had, for the second time, ruffled his stoic, unshakable disposition. "Disappeared? In the middle of the night? During a blizzard?"

"Yes… they disappeared in the blizzard," he said, quietly. "There's something else you need to know."

"There's no better or worse time than now to tell me. Two bitter pills in one day won't kill me."

Jason's eyes blinked wildly. "Please believe me when I tell you that I got down on my knees and begged Dad so many times. I wanted to tell you years ago. But he made me promise not to say a word to you or anyone… about… what else had happened the night I was born."

"Okay… stop. Think about what it is you need to tell me, and spit it out! It might help if you bear in mind that I am the one whose life has been turned upside down." To my surprise, he did exactly as I had ordered.

Jason lowered his eyes. "Every time you call me your favorite son… I ache inside. I feel so guilty… so wrong." He hesitated. "I desperately wanted to confide in you… but Dad…"

"Well, Lem's not here… so confide in me now. Besides, if what you've already told me hasn't killed me, nothing else will. Go on. I'm all ears."

"You had a difficult pregnancy for a very good reason. Mother nature has a way of reminding us that even the best technology has imperfections…"

"Ok. You're scaring me. Why do I feel as if you've left the worst for last?"

Jason drew in the air and released it. "Shortly after the transfusion was done, dad and the lab assistant made a shocking discovery."

"What?"

Tears welled in his eyes. "They realized that I wasn't the only child you were carrying."

There was a long, awkward moment of silence.

"Okay… that's a really bad joke! And considering what you've already dumped on me today… it's in very poor taste… *and* I'm definitely not in the mood for such jokes."

"It's not a joke. It's true. You have another son… my twin brother."

I stopped breathing, and could not move. I tried twice to get up, and failed each time. It felt as though I was being held to the sofa by a giant, unyielding magnet. The entire room spun around me, as I dug my sweaty, trembling fingers into the arm of the sofa. Shaking, I heaved myself up. My eyes were drowning in tears, as I stared, mouth opened, focusing on Jason's drenched face. For a while, I felt absolutely nothing. Then, it was as if the floor beneath my feet had suddenly turned into rough waters, with me, adrift, in a wobbly canoe. My entire body staggered, as my legs got weaker and weaker. Suddenly, a volcano of red, hot emotions erupted, spewing pain and fiery rage into my chest and gut. I screamed… again and again… each time louder and louder… stopping only when I felt my hands around Jason's neck… clutching it so tightly that he had to push me away in order to break free of my more than powerful grip!

Seething, I stood facing Jason. "That's impossible! You're lying! I had an excellent gynecologist / obstetrician! There's no way on earth she could have missed that! My ultrasounds would have shown two…"

"Your ultrasounds were inaccurate! He was much smaller, and I overshadowed him. His little body was parked behind me."

My legs gave out completely, and I fell onto the sofa. "But how? How was this possible? How could I have carried him, undetected?" I muttered, bursting into tears.

Jason moved cautiously towards me. "Mom… you had a mono-amniotic pregnancy. It's called vanishing twin syndrome. It happens in about 10 percent of multiple pregnancies. You fell into that category."

"But the ultrasound should have picked up two heartbeats and…"

"He went undetected because we were located in the same amniotic sac. Mom… we shared the same heartbeat. It is very, very rare that something like this happens, but it does. It happened to you. Due to his small size, he was always just out of view of the ultrasound during your exams."

"Dear God! My next anatomy ultrasound was scheduled for the day after we would have returned home from our weekend getaway. By then, he would have been visible. But we were stuck at the compound because of the ice storm!"

Tears rolled down Jason's face. "Twenty-five minutes after I was born, Dad delivered my twin brother. He thought it was best you never knew." He sniffed, collected himself, and raised his eyes to meet mine. "Please find it in your heart to forgive us for not telling you."

My eyes burned, as a flood of hot, salty tears overflowed, stinging my face and neck. "All of these years, and neither Lem nor you had the heart or conscience to tell me!" I muttered, my mind spinning wildly, a thousand knots choking my stomach. "Was he stillborn?" I asked, weakly. "Lem didn't think I could handle it. Is that why he never told me? Is that why he kept it a secret from me for so many years?"

Jason mopped his tear-soaked face with both hands, and shook his head. "He was born… alive."

"Alive!" I exclaimed, my heart pounding fiercely against my chest. "What happened to him? Did he die… later?"

"No. He was born as strong as an ox. Dad believed the transfusion saved both of you. Like yours, his vitals were extraordinarily enhanced. Remember… he was still attached to you during the transfusion. Everything that flowed through you was transferred to him."

Tiny, fractured, bits-and-pieces of what had actually happened on that awful night, started coming back to me. Slowly, I began realizing that what I had thought… imagined all of these years, to have been a dream, was not a dream after all. It was real! I had, in fact, heard two babies crying. And at some point, they were both lying next to me — one on either side.

"I wasn't completely out of my mind that night! Yes! Now it's all coming back to me. I remember! There were two of you!" I yelled out, staring into Jason's eyes. "Two tiny, warm bodies laid in my arms in that bed! You were both alive! Tell me… what happened to my other son!" I demanded.

Jason fought back tears. "After we were all safely out of the woods, the lab assistant brought Dad some soup and hot tea. He was exhausted. She convinced him to take a nap, promising that she'd stay awake and keep watch over his family. Hours later, my crying woke Dad up. He felt drowsy, and knew immediately that he had been drugged."

Jason's thin body crumbled to the floor. He buried his face into the sofa, and cried like a baby. He lifted his head and wiped away tears, as he spoke. "The Serbian couple was gone… and so was my twin brother!" he cried out. "Dad searched everywhere… throughout the entire compound and outside in the storm. They had all disappeared! Based on what he discovered during his search, dad later concluded that the Serbians were most likely spies for the Russian government."

It was the first time I'd seen Jason cry since the night of Lem's abduction. He was broken, reduced to a weeping child. The mother in me wanted to throw my arms around him, hold and comfort him, tell him it would all be okay. At the same time, I wanted to lash out at him, strike him for being complicit with his father in these surreptitious secrets. I was infuriated with him, and Lem, for all of the days, weeks, and years they had deceived me, and deprived me of knowing and loving my other son.

The pain I felt was too deep to measure. Together, Lem and Jason had kept me away from someone who belonged to me… a child who had been kidnapped within hours after I'd given birth to him. He was as much a part of me as Jason was. And yet, I didn't even know him. The agony of learning about him twenty-one years later, was unimaginable, and almost unbearable! I felt as if my very soul had been mangled, injured, beyond repair.

Lem and I had never used any form of corporal punishment in chastising Jason. Neither of us had ever once laid a hand on him. But in this heated moment, I needed to lash out. I saw nothing but RED! I felt nothing but FIRE! And I SNAPPED! I SCREAMED! YELLED! STOMPED! I SLAPPED Jason so hard the palm of my hand and fingers stung with excruciating pain. I don't know how many times I punched and kicked him before he could no longer bear the fury of my anger-fueled rage. I cried until I had no voice left, no energy, no anything left inside. I collapsed into Jason's arms, as he held and hugged me. We hovered there, together, the two of us, on the floor, in a heap of erupted emotions, and cried together, until we, and our tears, were completely spent.

I hugged Jason until I knew he was okay, then gently pulled away from him. "That explains why I had such a difficult pregnancy," I said, in a broken voice. "The severe cramping and pelvic pains. The constant bleeding. Now I know why Lem never spoke of the couple, saying only that they had returned to Serbia." I turned and looked directly at Jason. "How could your conscience have allowed you to keep this from me, and for so long?" I pleaded, still weak and trembling.

He sniffed and wiped a tear from his cheek. "After Dad confided in me, I was totally destroyed inside. He's my twin, my other half. I miss him more than you or anyone will ever know. I think about him every day." Jason dropped his head. "Every time I look into a mirror, I see Jacob."

"Jacob?"

"Yes. His name is Jacob. Dad named us Jason and Jacob."

A thin smile parted my lips as I repeated the names. "Jason and Jacob." Jason and Jacob are perfect names for twin boys. As angry and disappointed as I am, I have to give it to Lem. He did a great job naming you… and your brother."

"Well… he did get some help from the lab assistant in the naming department," Jason pointed out, returning a far more generous smile. "Dad had had a long, wicked night. His brain was literally fried. After wrestling with names, he came up with 'Jason' for me. In Greek, it means 'to heal'. The lab assistant came up with 'Jacob'. In Hebrew, the name 'Jacob' means 'the heel holder… to follow behind.'"

"Jason and Jacob. Yes… he followed behind you. Perfect names for my perfect twins!"

For a moment, we just sat there. Neither of us said anything. We both knew what the other felt… wanted to say… but neither Jason nor I could find a way to get the words out. I was still trying to make sense out of all of the craziness. Before I realized what was happening,

I had leapt up and was frantically shaking Jason by his shoulders. “We’ve got to find Jacob! No matter what it takes! We’ve got to find him! You owe it to me to find him!”

Jason stood up and shook his head. “We will find Jacob,” he said, extending his right pinky finger towards me. “If it is the last thing I do… I will find him,” he added, locking fingers. “I promise!”

“DONG! DONG! DONG! DONG!” The Westminster chime rang out from the floor standing grandfather clock upstairs in the living room, startling me, and amusing Jason. “Remember, Dad had it set to chime at five p.m.,” Jason reminded me, with a chuckle. “I kept it that way.”

“My God, is it that late? I need to pull myself together… go home… shower… get dressed… and get to Chelsea Place.” I said, trying to sound as normal as possible. “So… should I expect any changes to take place tonight while I’m greeting my patrons at Chelsea Place?” I asked, half-jokingly. “You know… like black spots covering my body as I shake people’s hands… or long whiskers suddenly sprouting from my face while I’m smiling and greeting my guests?”

A seriousness returned to his voice. “To be completely honest, I don’t know what to expect between now and when I see you tomorrow. I can only make an educated guess. But I don’t think there’ll be any drastic physical changes. That’s why I’ll have to monitor you closely for the next few days. However, you should expect some emotional and internal changes. Your mind will be sharper… and your senses keener. But physically, for the most part, you'll look the same."

"Okay. That much I can handle. But I'll have to explain to everyone why I'm making so many trips up here to the lab. They're a curious bunch, you know."

"I know. Aunt Genie is especially curious! But not even she must know about this! Mom… if any of this gets out… we will all be in danger… every single person will be in danger!"

"Honey… trust me. I understand how significant this is. No one else will ever know about this. I promise. But how do we find Jacob if we keep him a secret, also?"

Jason's forehead furrowed. "We'll cross that bridge when we get there. But for now, let's search for Jacob as discreetly as possible. When we find him… we'll have to tell him everything. There's no way he can be kept in the dark," he added, his voice quivering.

"No more secrets between us, Jason. What else do you have to tell me about Jacob?"

He stared at me for a moment. "I mentioned it earlier, but I think it went unheard. Um… well… since Jacob was still intrauterine… and attached to you during the transfusion…"

"Oh God! Oh dear God!" I cried out. "The jaguar's fluid's! I transferred them to him! That means…"

"Yes, everything that flowed through you was actively transferred to Jacob. That means Jacob is probably a transgenic being, as well. To protect him, we must keep that a secret."

"I wonder what has become of him? Do you think he knows what he is?"

"He's twenty-one years old. By now I'm sure he's figured out that he's special."

"That is all the more reason why we need to find him asap. Let's do whatever we have to do to find him and bring him home. Wherever he is, he belongs here, with us. We are his real family."

"I totally agree. Jacob should be here with us. Don't worry, we will find him, mom. I promise." Jason threw his arms around me and gave me a big, long hug. He smiled slightly and looked straight into my eyes. "Will you be all right tonight, mom? Do you need me to ride downtown with you?"

"I'm okay, but I'm concerned about you. I want you to get some sleep tonight… at least eight hours of sleep. I want you to look rested tomorrow evening when you come by for your birthday dinner."

"That's right… my special birthday dinner is tomorrow evening! With all of this going on, I almost forgot!"

"Honey, no matter what, you must show up tomorrow evening. Your god mother has gone overboard preparing all of your favorite foods. You and I have our hands full, but please don't disappoint Eugenia!"

"Of course not. I would never disappoint Aunt Genie. It'll be good to see her. It's been awhile since I've seen her."

Speaking of Eugenia… we'd better give her a call and put her mind to ease."

Jason gathered the phones and looked at me before turning them on. "Ahem… as for why you're making so many trips here… just say that we're going through a pile of legal papers… documents… you know… highly personal and sensitive documents that I need you to help me sort through. That should work."

"I guess that excuse will do. Sounds good to me."

"How early can you get here tomorrow morning, mom?"

"As early as necessary. Will eight a.m. do?"

"Yes. Go light on breakfast. Drink a lot of water between now and when you arrive here in the morning… and refrain from drinking anything alcoholic tonight. I need to get clean blood samples from you tomorrow."

"Okay. Got it!" I said, removing my cape and tote from the rack. "Is there anything else I need to know, Jason?"

"Yes… As soon as possible, I need you to speak privately with Sam…"

"Sam… the piano man? About what?"

"About the exchange student he shared a dormitory suite with at Howard University… the young man whom he said I reminded him of so much. Sam swears we could be twins."

My heart skipped a beat, as I recalled the first time Jason and Sam were introduced to each other. Sam had gone on and on about how Jason was a dead-ringer for a brilliant exchange science student he'd known while he was a student at Howard University. The student had only been there for one semester, and they barely knew each other. The thought of that student perhaps being my kidnapped son made my heart race.

"Jason… do you think that young man might be Jacob? Could that be possible?"

"Anything is possible, mom. Let's leave no stone unturned. Any piece of information might be the missing link we're looking for. What I do know is that the first time Sam saw me, he really thought I was that student."

"I remember. He kept saying the student looked like your twin! It's worth a try. I'll pull Sam aside tonight as soon as I see him. I sure hope he knows how to get in touch with him!"

Jason powered on my phones and handed them to me.

"I knew it. Eugenia's called six times!" I said, speed-dialing her number.

She picked up on the first ring.

I've been worried sick about you two! All of my calls went straight to voicemail… no returned calls… and…"

"Jason and I are fine, Eugenia. I'm sorry for the delay in getting back to you. We've been plowing through piles of… documents and binders… and lost track of the time."

Got you! I know my godson… Mister Meticulous! Every 'I' dotted and every 'T' crossed!"

"You know him well," I said, eyeing Jason who was motioning air kisses to Eugenia. "Jason is blowing air kisses to you!"

Back at him! Now that I know you're safe… I can breathe again.

"See you later." I ended the call, threw my phones into my tote bag, and eyed Jason.

"Ahem… your tuxedo… where is it?" I asked, throwing my cape around my shoulders.

"I took it to the French cleaners last week. The tailor made some minor alterations. The black and silver tie and cummerbund set Santini gave me is perfect with it."

"Great! That will put a smile on both of their faces!" I took one last look at the jaguar.

"Make sure that cage is securely locked before you head upstairs to bed tonight."

Jason glanced briefly at the animal. "That cage is equipped with a state-of-the-art military-style surveillance lock," he said, reaching for his coat. "Mom… I know how close you and Aunt Genie are. But no one, not even she can ever know about the transgenic secret."

"You and Lem aren't the only people in this family who know how to keep a secret under wraps."

"Dad always envisioned these amazing powers being used for the good of humanity. If this secret ever got out, it could potentially turn the whole world upside down." Jason's voice was solemn, as he opened the door. "Come, I'll get you into a cab."

"There's no need for you to come outside," I ordered, guiding him back inside. It's been a long day for both of us." My timing was perfect. A cab had just stopped at the traffic light across the street. "What you need is some good old-fashioned sleep!" I yelled, sprinting cat-like across the street at lightning speed. "Get some rest!"

I hopped into the cab. "West Twenty-Second Street near Ninth Avenue, please," I called out to the driver, then rested my head against the seat. It had been one long, tortuous day for me. For Jason, it had been many long, painful years of keeping those heavy secrets. Having to choose between his mother and father had to have been difficult. It was wrong and unfair of Lem to have put him in such an impossible position. As for Jason, I had to forgive him. There was nothing else I could do. He is still my son, and I am still his mother.

As for me… I realized that my life had changed. It would never be the same again. Short of committing suicide, and taking myself completely out of this world, there was nothing I could do about that. I could spend the rest of my super powerful life being angry at my husband and son. Or, I could accept who and what I was, learn to live with my new conditions and circumstances, make the necessary adjustments, and move forward. Eventually I'd get used to my new body and life. The choice was not nearly as difficult as I thought it would be. As a matter-of-fact, it was downright easy.

On the surface, I was somewhat frightened. But deep down inside, I wanted to embrace those new powers and extraordinary abilities I now possessed. They were, after all, mine to use however I saw fit, and I wasn't about to let them go to waste. I have learned many lessons in life. But the most valuable lesson is that humans are at the mercy of forces that are far more powerful than we are… forces that are perhaps, more important than we'll ever be.

Chapter 10
A Royal Flush

Big Joe placed his hand gently on my shoulder and guided me away from the entrance into the foyer.

"Hey, got a New York minute?" he asked, keeping his eyes trained on revelers who were already streaming in for dinner.

"Of course!" I replied, then stepped aside to clear the way for a party of four. Led by a stately, discrete bodyguard, they were regulars — The Earl and Countess of Wessex, and the Duke and Duchess of Gloucester — members of the extended British royal family. They were also old and dear friends of Santini's. We had barely exchanged pleasantries when the smiling Welsh hostess rushed over, dipped slightly, and ushered them over to their favorite table in the far corner of the room.

Seeing the way clear, Big Joe moved in closer. "So… is everything cool with Jason?" he asked, genuinely concerned.

"Thanks. He's fine," I sighed. "That boy really dumped a lot on me today!"

"Really?"

"Uh uh… ahem… a whole lot of tedious paperwork… documents… you know… stuff that he needed me to sign off on. He just allowed things to get so backed up that it all overwhelmed him!"

Big Joe's face relaxed. "Well… at least you got to spend some good old-fashioned quality time together." He rubbed his forehead and brought his voice down to almost a whisper. "Seven years to the day since I met you and Jason. Can't believe how fast time flies," he added, shaking his head. "It sucks to high heaven that we came up empty handed. Not a single lead!"

"Hey! Enough! Stop beating up on yourself! Jason and I know how hard you worked trying to find Lem."

Big Joe made a fist and clenched his teeth. "But it wasn't enough! I didn't find him, and I didn't find the bastards who abducted him!" he growled. "It's as if he's vanished in thin air."

"But you found us, and Jason and I are grateful for that."

He beamed and patted his chest with a hand. "There's a special place right here in my heart for you and Jason. Don't you ever forget that."

"We won't. Thank you for being there for us then, and now."

He smiled, and turned to see who was entering. More regulars — a mega basketball star, with his way-too-skinny, supermodel girlfriend. Big Joe and the young man chat briefly about his team, while the pretty model and I exchanged niceties. We waited until the smiling hostess greeted them and led them to their table near the piano stage.

The way clear, I turned to Big Joe. "Santini told me your friend, Officer Gallagher delivered quite a comprehensive dossier on you-know-who. So… what's the verdict?"

"Yep! That man's track record is more than an earful. You'll hear all about it after Jason's birthday bash. Besides, this is not the place or time to talk about anyone. Remember, the walls have ears, eyes, and something called memory!"

"You're right. Not to mention that he's my least favorite person. This conversation ends here and now. Listen… why don't you invite Gallagher to Jason's dinner party tomorrow evening. I'd like to thank her personally."

"Sure thing! As much as I brag about Eugenia's dishes, I know she'd love that! I'll text her now. That'll definitely put a smile on her face."

"Great! Text me if anything pressing comes up!" I said, walking away.

My cell phone buzzed just as I entered the piano lounge. Without even glancing at it, I knew it was Santini. His text message read:

Per favore incontrami nel tuo ufficio al più presto.

Looking across the room, I spotted him, standing near the narrow hallway that leads to my office. He's gesturing towards me, his arm, waving wildly above and around a group of men who were standing directly in front of him. Even from a distance, I could see the look of consternation etched across his face. Making a beeline through the room, I smiled and greeted guests as quickly and graciously as possible, tactfully avoiding those who were trying to stop me or engage me in any small talk that might impede my efforts to get to the other side. I succeeded in my endeavor, with lightning speed!

Clean-shaven, with a new haircut, Santini's blue-gray suit all but blended in with the art-deco mural that strategically camouflaged the door to my office. I sensed how worried he was, angst radiating from him like a smoldering fire. His low-key demeanor told me he was annoyed. I was right.

"Ciao!" I said, tapping the magnetic key card against the door, waiting to hear the click that would allow us to enter. "I hope that expression on your face is about Vlad. Please tell me tonight is the last time I'll ever have to see that beady-eyed serpent again!" I huffed.

We were barely inside when Santini quickly closed the door, and leaned against it. He cleared his throat, folded his arms, and crossed his legs. His voice was calm but stern.

"Vlad is a man of unforgivable character. I'm afraid getting rid of him won't be easy. We might have to deal with him in an unorthodox manner. But let's discuss that later," he replied, dismissively. "More importantly, what is going on with Jason… and why didn't I hear from you all day long? Not even a texted message!" he blurted out, eyes piercing straight through me.

It's a good thing that I know Santini as well as I do. This is one of those times when knowing and understanding someone comes in handy. It is his nature to always be the great protector. *The one and only protector!* It all comes from a good place — his heart. I turned towards him, but deliberately avoided making eye contact, afraid he'd disbelieve the lie I was about to tell him.

"Jason's good. Thankfully, he's not sick… or anything like that," I said, glancing up briefly. "Don't worry… he's not in any kind of trouble," I added, forcing out a smile. "That son of mine has allowed a lot of mail, letters, legal documents, and other important papers to accumulate. It was more than he could handle, so… he wanted my help sorting through stuff," I added, with a sigh.

Santini stared blankly at me. He didn't blink an eye, and did not say a word. This was a tactic he employed whenever he thought someone was trying to pull the wool over his eyes. It was his way of silently telling you that he did not believe a word you had said.

After the harrowing day I had had, two thoughts entered and occupied my mind: *Is he trying to get inside my head? Or, is he already inside my mind, reading it?* I'm sure I looked and acted as guilty as sin! Because…

well… I was! I was lying to him. He knew it, and he wasn't buying it.

His body language was loud and clear. He leaned further into the door, punishing me with that godawful condemnatory look — one which he had skillfully mastered! He finally uncrossed his legs, and released himself from the door. Both hands made their way inside his pockets, as he stared silently at the floor, his words deliberately chosen. "I see. I trust that, when the time is right, you will level with me. You know that I am the one person in this world to whom you can tell anything and everything," he emphasized, with a long, hard stare. "I can't help it, Kitt. Old habits die hard. I still feel the need to protect you."

I swallowed the big lump in my throat, and said nothing, too afraid that if I'd opened my mouth… maybe… just maybe… the truth would have slipped out. I'd made a promise to Jason. I had to honor that promise. There was too much at stake. Not even Santini could know.

He cleared his throat. "As far as Vlad is concerned… I'll find a way to handle him."

"Okay," I breathed, relieved that he had changed the subject.

I don't know how, when, or at what point, but, out of the blue, we had moved on from one awkward moment, addressed another subject, and were now leaving my office. A few steps later, we stood at the perfect vantage point, shoulder-to-shoulder, the two of us, taking in the entire room. Captivated and spellbound, we gazed out at Chelsea Place — the crowd, the music, the sounds — this vividly enchanting, magical place — a world unto itself! It was brimming with an abundance of class, power and wealth — from the oldest of old money, to the newest of nouveau riche. The place was packed to the rafters with well-dressed revelers, adorned in heirloom jewels and expensive taste. Tall, model-like servers holding perfectly balanced trays high above their heads, weaved effortlessly through a crowd of beautiful people. The room was abuzz with the sound of lively chatter and clinking glasses.

There was always a generous sprinkling of royalty — from The United Kingdom's House of Windsor to The House of Saud, the ruling family of Saudi Arabia — Chelsea Place was THE nighttime playground for the world's most privileged and pampered. We loved and enjoyed every magical moment of it! In ways that only the two of us could understand and appreciate, this was also our very own private playground!

Pleased with what he'd just taken in, Santini reached inside his jacket, pulled out his watch, and glanced at the time. "The night's still young and the house is already packed," he commented, returning the watch to its pocket.

My eyes drifted over to one of the corner tables. "The Earl and Countess of Wessex look quite happy together," I whispered, knowing how close he was to them.

A smile lit up his face, and he nodded, obviously delighted by my observation. "Yes... I spoke briefly with them downstairs in the restaurant. I'm more than thrilled that they've reconciled and decided to stay together," he said, beaming. "And it's great to see the Duke and Duchess of Gloucester out and about again. Friends were beginning to think they'd become anti-social," he added, mischievously.

I surveyed the room, smiling and waving at several of our regulars. I was delighted that there were so many of the same people who kept returning to Chelsea Place, night after night, bringing their friends, spouses and business partners in.

Santini adjusted his tie and jacket, lifted his chin slightly, then swept his eyes over the room several times, before turning to face me. "We've got a royal flush in the house tonight, my dear!" he remarked, his voice riveting with uncontainable excitement. "Let's see now... there's Albert of Monaco with his lovely wife, Princess Charlene, at the center, rear table. Barron Philip and Baroness Ghislaine are holding court as usual, rear left corner. Upstairs, Roberto Dinaro is holding a closed, private meeting about his upcoming mega movie collaboration. He'll be downstairs later for drinks and dinner. Several members from the Kennedy clan have just come in. They've reserved the middle table for eight. And The Crown Prince Mohammed of

Saudi Arabia has reserved two round tables, on the far right side of the room. He is scheduled to arrive any moment now with his wives and daughters." Santini paused and smiled. "I'd say it's a very good night!"

I turned to him, half-teasingly. "Let's hope we have enough bottles of Montrachet, Veuve Clicquot, and Domaine Romanee Conti Champagne to keep everyone happy!"

"My dear, there's never enough of that stuff to keep these people happy!" he returned, blowing a kiss to a lovely lady in the crowd.

"No, there's never enough," I echoed.

As was customary, we separated, with Santini working one side of the room, while I worked the other.

Standing away from the continuous stream of waiters placing and picking up drink orders, I had a broad view of the room. Busboys were busy placing baskets of bread on tables, and setting up stands for champagne buckets. The fragrant smell of perfume, intermingled with Eugenia's savory dishes, created scents I had become accustomed to. Tonight, those scents were so concentrated, they burned my nostrils! One sniff and a brief sweep of the room, revealed my heightened sense of smell. This was much more than a case of hyperosmia. My olfactory receptors were on steroids! It took less than a minute to realize that by merely looking at someone, and inhaling, I could literally smell what fragrance they were wearing. Moreover, my sense of smell was so keen that I could, as well, detect the various combinations of essential oils, extractions, flowers, and herbs in every fragrance.

I turned my attention to the bar, where Halo was rigorously scrutinizing ID's from the four young ladies Vlad had brought along in tow. Although they had already been carded at the entrance by Big Joe, this was a checks and balances practice that Halo and Big Joe did to allow them an opportunity to get up close, study faces, personal nuances, and listen to voices. This also gave Halo a chance to bust Vlad's chops — something she thoroughly enjoyed doing. There were cameras discreetly hidden throughout Chelsea Place. But nothing compared to being face-to-face with someone.

I was still trying to negotiate my newly enhanced sense of smell, when competing fragrances worn by Halo, the four young ladies, and Vlad, clashed so intensely that my nostrils felt as if they were set aflame! Halo was spritzed with a hint of geranium and violet — definitely *Hermes Equipage*! A glance at the four girls revealed patchouli, vanilla, blackcurrant bud, and opopanax — *Christian Dior, Yves Saint Laurent, Guerlain,* and *Dolce and Gabbana!* Finally, I stole a quick glance at Vlad. He was drenched in *Creed Aventus!* A mere spritz would have sufficed, but he was drowning in the stuff. Yikes!

Halo stood five feet ten inches tall in flat shoes — an inch shorter than Big Joe. Exotic and lively, there was an aura of mystery around her. She had a keen sense of human nature, and a gift for reading people. She remembered names and birthdays, and had a reputation for mixing the best damned cocktails in all of New York. I watched as Halo gave Vlad and his girls 'the look'. There it was: That thing she did with her eyes and voice when she didn't particularly like someone. She was unleashing it on Vlad, in no uncertain terms — even as he slid a crisp one hundred dollar bill towards her. *Uhm...! A bad investment on his part, if he's trying to impress her.* I thought. Halo was statuesque and stunning. She also loved, worshiped, and adored *only* women. The fact that she was a proud and open lesbian, never deterred men from hitting on her — something she handled quite gracefully.

As the night grew older, the sounds of laughter and chatter from the crowds grew louder. And so did Sam's music. Taking in the room, my eyes darted from table to table. It dawned on me that, not only had my sense of smell intensified, but, my sense of hearing had also become extremely acute. Even with the music, and other sounds in the room, by simply resting my eyes on a guest, I could clearly and distinctly hear what that person was saying — all the way from the opposite side of the room! It was as if I could amplify voices, and mute others by merely focusing on that person. To test my increased auditory abilities, I zeroed in on Infanta Daria, the attractive Spanish Duchess. She sat tucked away in the back, in the farthest corner of the room. Yet, I heard her, as plain as day, bemoaning the woes with her troublesome teenage daughters and their bad taste in boyfriends. Then came a sensational tingling in my nostrils, as if every strand of nasal hair was being electrified. It was her perfume, that glorious smell of *Penhaligon's Bluebell!*

The conversation between Halo and Vlad was, at first, inaudible, but as I held my focus on them, their voices became increasingly amplified, until I could hear every word, perfectly! Glancing on top of the bar, my eyes zoomed onto the one hundred dollar bill Vlad had slid to Halo, viewing it as if it was in my hand, only inches away from my eyes! My hearing and vision were sharper than they had ever been! I scanned the entire room, briefly tuning into random conversations. Curiosity led me to the table where the dashingly handsome Oscar-winning actor, Roberto Dinaro sat. I held my gaze on him, as he negotiated the terms for his upcoming blockbuster movie. He was appropriately wearing *Millesime Imperial,* smooth, musky, and manly. I felt guilty, and ashamed for eavesdropping on my guests. This was so unlike me. But at the same time, I was enjoying, and beginning to embrace my newly acquired powers!

I shifted my attention back to Halo. She disliked Vlad as much as I did. We both despised how he exploited young girls. But with each girl armed with an appropriate and so-called 'legitimate' ID, there was nothing we could legally do to stop this creep from merchandising them. Halo topped off several drinks, collected her tips, and dashed over to where I was standing.

"Love, love, love the dress!" she exclaimed, using both hands to draw an exaggerated outline of my figure.

I smiled and spun around. "Thanks! It comes complete with a built-in miracle spanx!"

She let out a loud laugh and high-fived. "Hey, I love anything that has a built-in spanx! That's every woman's dream!"

Our laughter ended abruptly when Vlad beckoned to Halo with his chubby hand. She rolled her eyes in his direction, and sighed. "If I weren't allergic to jails, handcuffs, and neon orange jumpsuits, I would exterminate that vermin with my bare hands."

"Nasty piece of slime," I murmured.

She leaned in and whispered. "I'll text you and Big Joe if anything looks especially weird."

"Please do. Thanks."

With that, she spun around and headed towards Vlad and the girls. "Enjoy wearing that dress!" she called out.

I was trying to make my way back across the room, when Sam spotted me. It was that time of the night when he usually called me to the stage to sing a song, or two. His voice boomed over the microphone:

"And now, ladies and gentlemen… it is with much pleasure that I bring to the stage, the lovely and super talented Kitt Kougar!"

The crowd applauded and cheered me on, as I approached the stage.

Sam stood up, extended a hand to help me up, and gave me the microphone. "What song would you like to sing?" he whispered.

"*This Is My Life,"* I replied, without the slightest thought or hesitation. After the day I had had, it was the kind of song I felt was most appropriate.

Santini made his way over, and stood right in front of the stage, the way he always did whenever I sang. On this particular night, something was slightly different. Maybe it was the way he stood, looked at me, and smiled. Whatever it was, brought back memories, and reminded me of the first time we had met, so many years ago.

Chapter 11
Enter Santini

Flashback to…

A busy Saturday night, when Giancarlo "The Count" Santini dropped by The Jazzy Joint. Charming, generous, and delightfully eccentric, he blazed into my life like a ball of fire! Passionate about everything in life, he changed my name, and my life. Then, proudly introduced me to a whole new world — his.

I was near the end of my first song, a love ballad, when this impeccably dressed, handsome man approached the band area. Extremely dignified and elegant, he wore a cream-colored suit that complimented his coiffed hair and Mediterranean tan. Applauding wildly, he smiled, then placed a crisp one hundred dollar bill in the fishbowl that sat on a small stand near Fast Finger Frankie's piano.

When the song ended, Frankie, appreciative of the generous tip, swept his hand, several times, enthusiastically, over the piano keys, creating the most melodious *glissandos* I'd ever heard! The drummer gave a lively, spontaneous drum roll, and the bassist played a rhythmic walking bass line. "Thank you!" Frankie nodded. "Is there a song you'd like to request?"

"Bravissimi! Bravissimi!" the man yelled, blowing air kisses with both hands, as he moved closer towards the band.

I was beyond thrilled that we had gotten such a generous tip from this stranger. "Thank you so much!" I gushed.

He returned the smile, took my hand, and gently kissed the back of it. "The musicians are magnificent!" he said, with a slight bow of his head. "But you, my dear, are the most exquisite thing I've ever laid eyes on!"

I was fascinated by his vibrant personality. Everything about him seemed to be bigger than life. His melodic Italian accent, perfectly cadenced, made every word he spoke sound lyrical. Even his body language, and smooth hand gestures, complimented the tone of his voice. "You, and this band were not here when I visited last," he said, flashing an infectious smile. "I certainly would have remembered you! My name is Santini. And yours?"

"My name is Kathleen Keats. But everyone calls me Kitty. It's a pleasure to meet you. I've been here now for almost a year and a half. The band has been here longer. I'm so glad you enjoyed us. Your tip is greatly appreciated."

His eyes twinkled like two little stars. "You are welcome. The pleasure is all mine."

Frankie cleared his throat and shifted on the piano bench — a hint urging me to ask the gentleman for his song request.

I took a deep breath, and prayed that he'd request a song that I knew really well. "Would you like to make a request?"

"Mondo Cane is my favorite song of all time," came his response. "It would please me so much, if you would sing that song for me."

In that moment, I died a thousand, painful deaths. Not only did I not know the song, but I had never even *heard* of it before! And guessing from the title, I thought it was most likely an Italian song.

God! Please save me from this horrible death! Or at least allow me to disappear! Now!

My entire body shook. I opened my mouth to speak, and my eyes and nose began twitching. Somehow, I managed to squeeze out an apology. "I am so... so sorry, sir. You'll have to forgive me. But I don't know that song." Disappointed with myself that I could not sing his favorite song, I shifted awkwardly, and stumbled towards Frankie, hoping he'd come to my rescue. There wasn't a song Frankie didn't know, hadn't played, or hadn't heard. Luckily for me, my instincts were on cue! Fast Finger Frankie was right on the money!

At that moment, Fast Finger Frankie, the pianist and bandleader, a living legend who had played the world over with the best of the best in the business, tilted his head, thoughtfully. He willed himself to his feet, raised up the seat of his piano bench, and thumbed methodically through an old binder. A man of very few words, on those rare occasions when he did speak, he said little. Frankie pulled several sheets from the overstuffed binder. He cleared his throat, and whispered something to his band. The musicians hummed a bit of the song and nodded, signaling that it was a go. Satisfied with his musicians' response, Frankie flashed a pearly white smile at Santini. "Yessiree! We do know that song," he beamed. "The English title is *More*. That's a very lovely song! Beautifully composed! It would be our pleasure to play it for you."

Frankie's partially bearded face was expressionless. If he was the least bit concerned, or afraid, that I might destroy this song, he didn't show any sign of it. With a conspiratorial gesture of his head, he motioned me to come closer to him. In a low, husky voice, he gave me whispered instructions:

"Okey dokey, Miss Kitty… this is how we're going to do this. Don't be nervous. You can't be afraid to sing. Listen to the music. Feel the melody. Let me sing the first and second verses of the song, straight through. Hum the melody in your head so that you get the feel of the song. These are very pretty lyrics. Take your time, think about the words, and sing them real pretty. They'll be a bass solo first, then a drum solo. After that, we'll give you a big build-up to the bridge. Listen to the bass… feel those drums. When it's your turn, jump right in. Take it, and run with it. Ad lib. Do whatever comes naturally. Caress those lyrics. Make love to the song. But make it your song. Just keep singing and loving those lyrics. Another thing… look that man straight in the eyes and sing to him like he's the only person here. He has to believe that you're singing to him. And remember… sing from the heart!"

Frankie handed me a sheet of paper. Scrawled across the page, were hastily written lyrics to the song.

I was so nervous, I could hardly breathe. How on earth then, was I ever going to be able to sing! I smiled, nervously, and whispered. "I'll do my best."

As the band played the intro to the song, Santini swayed and hummed, enthusiastically.

The house was packed to the rafters. But the moment Frankie's fingers struck the first chord, the entire place went silent! Frankie knew how to command attention, and he always got it. He opened his mouth, and embraced each and every word of that song, as if he had lived them. He took the lyrics, and told a real story. He showed me how to sing that song. I wasn't about to let him down!

I listened carefully to the lyrics, and how Frankie sang them. I hummed the melody. Then I sang the words in my head. By the time the band was building up to the bridge, the evocative melody and those romantic lyrics had found a place in my head and heart forever. Frankie turned towards me and gave a dramatic bend of his head.

It was magical! I sang that song as if I'd done it a thousand times! Couples eagerly made their way to the dance area, embraced, and slow-danced to the song. Everyone in the Jazzy Joint was swaying and humming to the music. With no room left on the small dance floor, people got up and danced wherever they could find a spot. Taking his cue from the crowded dance floor and the energy in the room, Frankie waved his hand in a big, circular motion. The band and I knew that he was directing us to extend the song. And did we ever! We nursed it!

Our big ending brought cheers, yells, and everyone in the house to their feet! The fishbowl overflowed with tips. This time, Santini gave a $200 dollar tip! The musicians high-fived, and grinned from ear-to-ear. The waiters cheered and whistled! Eugenia was thrilled beyond words! It was a very, very good night! We were, as Frankie put it: "in Hog Heaven!"

Written by Riz Ortolani and Nino Oliviero, *More* was the 1962 theme song for an Italian documentary film named *Mondo Cane*. It was a song that would become one of my favorite, and most requested songs ever.

Most of the singing waiters and waitresses were tight-fisted when it came to divvying up tips with the band. The singers felt they deserved a bigger cut, especially if they sang a requested song. I never fought over tips. The band knew they could always count on getting their fair share from me. That night, we all made a killing!

Eugenia came over, gave high-fives to the band members, and threw an arm around me. "Great show! You guys brought the house down! You'll have to do that song more often!" she added, shouting over the loud chatter that filled the room. She turned slightly and pointed her head towards Santini's table in the corner. "Frankie… why don't you guys take a break now and grab something to eat. Santini's buying anything on the menu your hungry mouths and tummies desire. That includes a bottle of champagne!" she added, excitedly.

With thumbs held up high, the musicians grinned and gave a resounding wave of "thank-yous" to Santini.

Frankie quickly switched on the background muzak, then turned towards me. The broad smile on his face, and the twinkle in his eyes gave me an instant rush of joy and personal relief. I hadn't disappointed him! Thank God!

"Real good work, young lady! You sang that song the way it should always be sung. Yessiree! Made me really proud!" He threw his long arms around me in a way that reminded me of my father's big, bear hugs.

That was quite a feat, especially coming from Fast Finger Frankie, who rarely gave out compliments. As a matter-of-fact, he barely spoke, except when it came to giving pointers to new singers. He was always reserved, even with his own musicians.

Pleasantly shocked, I beamed up at Frankie, relieved, but still, tremendously intimidated by this giant among musicians. I, like so many of the singers, were in awe of this man. We felt thrilled and honored to be in his great presence. Fast Finger Frankie had bestowed his blessings upon me! His compliments left me floating on a cloud for the rest of the night!

"Since the gracious Mister Santini is treating me, I think I will partake in some of those delicious-tasting grilled baby lamb chops tonight!" Frankie said to Eugenia, flashing a big, toothy smile. He dipped his head slightly then swaggered towards the designated band's table in a corner of the room near the kitchen.

"Enjoy them! They will melt in your mouth!" Eugenia called out. She immediately ushered me towards Santini's table. "Don't worry about your tables. They're all covered," she said, leading me through the crowded little room. Eugenia was smiling, but there was sadness in her voice and eyes. "This is far more important." As we approached the table, Santini rose, smiled, and pulled a chair out for Eugenia, and then, me.

"This young lady is fantastic, Eugenia! Look at her! She's a star!" he exclaimed, throwing a hand elegantly, into the air.

Eugenia shook her head in agreement and smiled. "Yes! Kitty is definitely a shining star! She's also my adopted little sister. And now you're going to take her away from me."

Puzzled, I searched Eugenia's face. "Take me away from you? What on earth are you talking about?" I asked, incredulously. The sadness in her voice did something to me inside.

The head waiter came over with a bottle of Dom Perignon, and popped it open with a grand flare. He filled flutes for Eugenia and Santini, placed a glass of sparkling water and lime in front of me, then took our orders. For a moment, neither Eugenia nor Santini said anything. They sat quietly, exchanging quick glances, each seeming to wait for the other one to say something. Earlier, while I was singing, I'd seen them chatting quite a bit, in what appeared to be a very intense conversation. Perhaps he knew something about her sudden mood change.

After the waiter left our table, I thanked Santini again for the generous tips, and for inviting me to dinner. I turned to Eugenia and whispered: "Why do you look so sad? Are you feeling okay?"

She braced herself, smiled, weakly, and placed a hand gently on my shoulder. Tears welled in her eyes, as she spoke. "Santini owns a lot of fancy places in Europe. He thinks that's where you belong... and I agree," she said, blinking back tears. "He wants to take you to Italy. He wants to manage your singing career."

I couldn't believe what I was hearing. I was shocked into silence. I opened my mouth to speak, but nothing came out. I looked at Eugenia, then at Santini. Still nothing. It felt as if my thoughts and words had disappeared. "Italy...! Europe!" were the only words that came out. Without warning, I burst into a flood of tears! When I was finally able to speak, the words rushed out of my mouth. "Italy! Europe! I've always wanted to visit Europe. But never in my wildest dream did I ever think I'd sing there!"

Santini let out a loud sigh of relief. He drew his chair closer, and sat within an earshot of me. "I will be your manager," he said, firmly, then smiled. "Eugenia and I met years ago when I came to New York in search of entertainers for my establishments. She knows me. She will tell you that I can be trusted." He paused, glanced at Eugenia, and continued. "I've hired several musicians from the Jazzy Joint. They're all paid well… they're happy… and they perform in the best cabaret houses in Europe." He took a sip of champagne, and turned to face me. "You are already a star, Kitty. All I want to do is make you shine! I want you to be the biggest and brightest star ever! I want to be the one who gives you that chance. I will manage your career, and, I promise… I will take good care of you." He paused. "But… you'll have to move to Milano… Italy… where I live."

I could hardly believe what I was hearing. It was all happening so fast. It felt dreamlike. I was only seventeen. I had always wanted to travel and see the world. And now when it was being handed to me, on a golden platter, I was so frightened I couldn't think clearly, let alone speak. My eyes darted from Santini to Eugenia, who was crying and laughing at the same time.

"He's legit Kitt. He's the real thing," Eugenia reassured me, still sounding and looking half-sad, half-happy. "He's a good person. The only problem I have with The Count is he comes here and takes my favorite people away!" she teased.

"From the moment I laid eyes on you, tonight, and heard your voice, I told Eugenia that I had finally found what I was looking for!" He refilled their flutes, then, with a small nod, raised his glass towards Eugenia. "Don't worry, Eugenia... no harm will ever come to your little sister. I will protect her with my life. Nothing bad will happen to Kitty under my watch. Mark my words." He nodded his head, affirmatively and looked at me. "The Italians will fall madly in love with you! That I know for sure! Then it will be easy to book you on the best stages in London, Paris, Munich, Athens, Madrid!"

During the course of the evening, Eugenia and Santini laughed and talked like two old friends. Whenever she referred to him as *The Count,* he brushed it off with a chuckle. A round of drinks was purchased for the house, which made Eugenia smile all night long. Santini insisted that she sit, relax, and enjoy dinner with us — which she did without much persuasion. Besides, Mavis, her Sous Chef, was more than capable of handling the kitchen.

The Jazzy Joint ran like well-oiled machinery. It was small, clean, and homey. Eugenia had finally found the perfect band, she had assembled an excellent staff of singing waitpersons, and she served the best food in Harlem. Most importantly, The Jazzy Joint had a loyal crowd. It was a place where everyone knew each other, like family. Eugenia and Santini thoroughly enjoyed the Dom Perignon, as I sipped ever so slowly on one flute, while little, animated bubbles bounced lightly around inside my head.

Eugenia took several sips of champagne back to back, her eyes now, more glazed over than teary. I was concerned about how much champagne she'd consumed. The woman never drank at work. She always said it was a recipe for disaster whenever a club owner drinks while on duty. The last time I'd seen her take down this much champagne in one evening was the day she decided to end her marriage. "I will really miss you, little sis," she said, smiling. "But remember, I'm always just one call away!"

I was starving, and ate quite well. I floated through the rest of the night. Luckily, I had gotten my passport about a month earlier. There were so many things that had to be done. Santini would take care of my work papers, visa, insurance, and so forth. He booked a one-way, first class flight for me on Alitalia. His friends, people in all of the right places, who could, and would, move mountains for him, expedited everything. My mind was spinning, racing back and forth. I was happy, frightened, sad, scared, nervous, and excited, all at once. It was a dream come true. Then it hit me. How on earth was I supposed to tell my parents that I would be moving even further away, more than 4600 miles away — out of the country, to another continent? They still hadn't gotten over me moving to New York City. I'd have to break the news to them gently.

And what about Santini… the Count? This wildly ambitious man, rattling off a million plans as to how he wanted to package, promote, and introduce me to Europe's coveted cabaret world! We'd just met, but, instinctively, I felt safe with him. Somehow I knew, without a doubt, that I was in good hands with him. I trusted him, and he trusted me. From the moment we met, Giancarlo 'The Count' Santini was determined to shape and mold me into the biggest cabaret star in all of Europe, if not the world. He did just that.

Santini was an internationally renowned music impresario. He was sophisticated and gentlemanly, and only twenty-six years old! Born into an affluent, aristocratic Italian family, Giancarlo Antonio 'The Count' Santini came from European royalty, with bloodlines that flowed straight to the British Crown. He grew up in a world financed by old, old money, shaped by birthright privileges, and defined by the elite, upper class. He had grown up among Europe's wealthiest, attending the world's best private schools in Italy and England. It was all reflected in his genteel style, and his polished, refined mannerisms. His family owned a chain of luxury boutique hotels sprinkled across Europe. To his credit, Santini had acquired a number of high-end cabarets and nightclubs throughout Europe — properties that substantially increased the family's wealth. For generations, the family's old estate was located just on the outskirts of Milan, Italy.

Santini delivered well on every promise he ever made to me. First, he changed my humble name from Kathleen Keels to *Kitt Kougar*. He said that way I could retain my initials. But the new name had a certain ring to it, and was a far better stage name. Besides, my eyes, and the way I walked, reminded him of a cat. I found this analogy particularly interesting. As a child, my parents had nicknamed me *Kitty* because of my affection for our big black cat, Queen Sheba. Santini wasted no time creating me in the image he had envisioned. He molded, styled, and fashioned me into an overnight singing sensation. I was dressed by top Italian designers, labeled an iconic fashion influencer, and became the toast of Italy's nightlife. My career took off, taking France, The Netherlands, Switzerland, and the United Kingdom by storm. There were sold-out concerts in Germany, Austria, Greece, Turkey, Australia, Asia, South America, and Africa!

I was his *principessa,* and I saw the world from a golden pedestal! It had all happened so fast. All along, Santini was right there, with me, beside me, protecting and shielding me, every step of the way. He was always there, and I didn't mind it in the least. He kept me on short reins and made sure *his* close circle of friends was the *only* circle of friends I knew, and moved in. We went everywhere together. Everywhere we went, so came the paparazzi photographers. They named Santini *Le Dolce*

Svengali, because of the way he controlled me. All I knew was that I was completely safe with him. He said that we were a force to be reckoned with. That there was nothing the two of us couldn't do together. I trusted him. I believed in him.

The day came when I crossed paths with Doctor Lemuel Johnson, a handsome, young, lauded biotechnologist. Lem was brilliant and talked about things I'd never heard of. He had a swagger, and a way with words. Before I knew it, he had swept me off of my feet, and just like that, my entire life was, again, changed. So was Santini's. *I wonder if he ever really forgave me?*

Chapter 12
Sam-The-One-Man-Band

They were different. But there was something about Sam that reminded me of Fast Fingers Frankie. Maybe it was the way he commanded the room. Chelsea Place was respectfully hushed, when Sam-The-One-Man-Band put fingers to the piano and began his first set of the evening.

Samuel Smalls was a musician extraordinaire, a musical virtuoso who played several instruments. At twenty-five, he had built up a huge repertoire and had a knack for reading the crowd, and always choosing just the right song for the moment. His well-tuned, soulful voice made people happy, brought them to tears, and on some occasions, silenced the room. An honored graduate of Howard University's prestigious School of Music, Sam was strikingly handsome, a natural showman with an abundance of flair. His taste in clothing, flashy and flamboyant, laid somewhere between the styles of Little Richard and Liberace. On top of his piano sat a pair of ornate candelabra, and between them, he had strategically placed an oversized fishbowl. He was the consummate professional — entertaining, warm, friendly, and fun. The clientele loved him, and rewarded him with hefty tips, generously filling his oversized fishbowl with twenty, fifty, and one-hundred-dollar bills.

At the end of his first set, a waiter sashayed over to the stage and told Sam I wanted to speak briefly with him in my office.

Sam rose gracefully from the piano bench, and, as always, bowed his head slightly to an admiring crowd, a round of applause, and an avalanche of air kisses. He extended his neck giraffe-like, searching the room until our eyes met. I motioned him towards my office, taking the lead, as the waiter followed us with a small tray holding two empty glasses and two blue bottles of sparkling water. He placed the tray on the desk and promptly left.

Sam stood, nervously, until I gestured to him to sit.

"Please, have a seat, Sam. This won't take long. And just so you know, your break begins when this meeting ends."

"Thanks, Kitt. I appreciate that." He pulled a crisp white handkerchief from his pocket and blotted sweat from his forehead. There was not the slightest hint of makeup to be found anywhere on the handkerchief, only the revelation of perfectly smooth, unblemished, chocolate brown skin.

"You sound better and better, Sam! Your piano-playing and voice sound like two well-oiled instruments! Everyone loves you!"

"Thanks! That's a relief!" he gushed, reaching for the glass directly in front of him and taking down several gulps. "I was afraid you were going to give me walking papers!"

"Walking papers! Are you kidding? That would be like cutting off my hands! You're perfect for Chelsea Place!"

He emptied the glass, crossed his legs, and settled into the chair. "Thanks. Coming from you, that's quite a compliment. The money is really good... and I can finally afford to have an apartment in Manhattan!" He cocked his head slightly to one side. "You know... my father walked out on my mom and left her with three young kids. Life was really hard for us. Mom worked two and three jobs, so there was never any real family time." He paused, and smiled. "What I'm trying to say is that you, and the staff are like family to me."

"Great! I'm glad you feel that way. As long as you're happy, you'll always have a home here at Chelsea Place."

He nodded and smiled. "So... to what do I owe this honor?"

"The exchange student you knew at Howard University... the one you said was Jason's look-alike... are you still in touch with him?"

"No… we haven't been in touch. But it shouldn't be too difficult to reconnect via the HU Alumni Association and social media." A bemused look fell over Sam's face. "May I ask why the interest in him now?"

"Jason's determined to trace our family tree. He thinks the uncanny resemblance might be more than coincidental. He believes there's a possibility that that student might be related to us."

Sam looked away and nodded. "Yes… bloodlines and family ties are important," he said, in a sad voice. "I wish my old man felt that way."

I knew Sam's pain and anger. Life had broken his heart, and left it in a weakened state. I felt sorry for him, the way I felt sorry for Jason and myself. "Family is the most important institution there is," I said, as gently as possible. "We should let nothing stop us from connecting with our relatives."

Recovering from his moment of unhappiness, Sam quickly collected himself. "That guy was definitely a dead ringer for Jason!" he exclaimed. "I mean… they have the same body type… same walk… same kind of energy… they even have the same voice quality and intonation!" He shook his head and chuckled. "If I didn't know any better, I'd swear he and Jason were twins!"

I held my gaze on him and thought: from your lips to God's ear… please… please… let that student be my son!

"What was his name?"

"I believe it was *Yanovich...* or maybe *Yacovich,*" Sam said, rubbing his forehead. He had a strange name for a Black dude. The guys on our floor just nicknamed him 'Genius'. The kid was super smart! We're talking Neil deGrasse Tyson smart!"

"The kid?"

"Yeah. He was about four years younger than the rest of us in the suite. He was really an accelerated student — brilliant!"

"That would make him Jason's age," I said, underneath my breath, barely able to contain the hope and excitement I felt, as I scribbled on a notepad. "Do you remember where he's from?"

Sam narrowed his eyes, and tried to remember. Then suddenly…

SWOOSH!

WHISH!

THUMP!

I was inside Sam's head… listening to his voice… *and* reading his mind!

"Ahem… He was from one of those countries near Russia."

(HIS THOUGHT): That geek spoke Russian the way I speak English! Why the hell can't I remember where he was from?

"Do you have his phone number…? email… his mailing address?" I asked, trying desperately to make the most of this opportunity.

Sam shifted nervously in his seat.

(HIS THOUGHT): This is intense! Sounds as if she's as much into tracing their family tree as Jason is!

"We never really hung out together, and he was only at Howard for one semester on a special exchange program."

"Did he ever talk about his… his parents?" This was something I had to know. I was determined to stay inside Sam's head until I found out.

(HIS THOUGHT): He was just a poor Black kid who was adopted by some kind hearted foreigners!

"I remember one of the guys saying he'd been adopted, at birth, by a couple from…"

"Serbia," I interjected.

(HIS THOUGHT): Wow! She took the word right out of my mouth!

Sam eyed me oddly. "Yes… Serbia."

"Can you contact him for us?"

(HIS THOUGHT): Is she asking me or ordering me to find that nerd? Uhm… Looks like I have some work to do. Better jump on this right away!

"I'm sorry… I don't have his contact info… but, like I said, I'll definitely put the word out on social media, and reach out to Howard's alumni association."

Exactly what I wanted him to do--jump on it! And without warning…

SWOOSH!

WHISH!

THUMP!

I was outside his head! As scary as this whole telepathic thing is, I think I'm beginning to appreciate it… and all of its amazing possibilities!

"Thanks so much, Sam. I've kept you long enough. Jason and I would appreciate anything you can do to help us find Ja… the student."

Sam hoisted himself from the chair, and made a beeline to the door. "I'll post a search for him on social media asap. Hopefully, I'll have some good news for Jason when he comes in tomorrow for his birthday bash!"

I speed-dialed Jason no sooner than Sam had left my office, and he answered on the first ring.

The sound of his voice told me that I had awakened him from a deep sleep.

Mom… is everything okay with you?

"Yes, I'm okay," I replied, overflowing with hope. "I wanted to let you know that there'll be plenty of sweet lemonade tomorrow evening!"

The sleepy sound in his voice was replaced with excitement.

Great! I love sweet lemonade! Have a good night! I'll see you in the morning!"

"Bright and early. I'll bring breakfast."

I ended the call, and made my way across the room, stopping here and there, to chat with some of our regulars. I landed near the service area of the bar, just in time to get a good glimpse of Vlad and his caravan of young girls. I'd seen how some of our guests reacted to

Vlad… the disapproving stares and glances directed towards him, and then towards *me,* as if I were somehow responsible for his despicable behavior. For that reason and too many others, I had, by design, limited all head-on encounters with him. Our face-to-face collisions were brief, few, and far between. I avoided that repulsive human being like the plague. And only on the rare occasion, when he had rudely inserted himself into one of my conversations, rather than being forced to exchange polite niceties with him, I had simply excused myself, and moved on to other guests. He's obnoxious, pushy, loud, and overly aggressive… an unseemly type who is creating an uncomfortable environment for some of our best and most loyal visitors. Even worse, and from what I've seen, he's probably pimping young girls! The thought of that made me sick to my stomach! It made me want to vomit — all over Vlad! Chelsea Place had a fine and upright reputation. It was not a place of ill-repute, and it was certainly not going to become known as a place where children were being paraded for the purpose of prostitution.

In the nightlife business, simple mathematics always come into play. Contented customers and a happy environment, equals a prosperous establishment. Contrary to that, when patrons feel ill at ease in a place, not only do *they* stay away, but so do their friends, and their friends' friends — subtracting money and status from the business. Because of Vlad, some of my favorite guests are staying away from Chelsea Place. That is definitely bad news!

The singer in me sees and hears things in terms of music — musical notes, pitches, sounds, and tones. The sight of Vlad always strikes a bad note with me — a sound of foreboding danger and tension. And do I know a bad note when I hear one! A bad note makes me cringe, squint my eyes, and frown. It makes me shake my head, in total exasperation. A bad note sends a shiver down my spine, and makes my entire soul shudder. The sight of Vlad does to me, internally, what a *D Minor chord* does: It immediately sends me to a dark place of dread, distress, and deep despair. And then, there's his voice, which has a quality that evokes grim, ghastly emotions. He speaks in a rather ghoulish-like manner, something akin to what one would expect to emanate from the mouth of a ghost. Yes, I know, this is all quite subjective and reactive, especially coming from the eyes of a dramatic, cabaret performer. But in the case of *Vlad, The Caviar Czar*, everything about his existence gives instant rise to dramatics — dangerous dramatics. So, whenever I feel his cold stare, or sense his proximity, I instinctively look away, or simply detour. I can handle Vlad. What I will not tolerate is Vlad making my guests feel uncomfortable. And I most certainly won't allow him to hawk young girls at Chelsea Place!

I intentionally avoided looking at Vlad, afraid that he would misinterpret the attention as an invitation to come over. Instead, I watched him from the corner of my eye, zeroed in, and focused. I desperately wanted to get inside his head and hear his thoughts. Try as I might, I could not read his mind! I could not read Vlad's mind! There was a wall of some sort, blocking me, preventing me from getting inside his head. This wall was made of neither bricks, steel, nor iron. It was an invisible wall — made of an impenetrable, untraversable force — a force that gave me the most excruciating headache I had ever experienced. The pains inside my head were so violent that I closed my eyes as tightly as possible, and quickly averted my attention away from Vlad. To my surprise, and great relief, the headaches immediately vanished! I avoided Vlad for the duration of the night.

As always, I had more than my share of small talk, sweet talk, and fast-talk. During the course of the evening, I had become privy to, and survived, a laundry list of information — newly-engaged couples, marriages that were on the brink, civilized and uncivilized divorces, reconciliations, mergers, buyouts, and hostile take-overs. Four a.m. finally arrived. Sam slowed his music down to the final good-night ballad. The lights were turned all the way up. And the last, inebriated guests, urged on by their chauffeurs and body guards, reluctantly left.

Big Joe and the waitstaff cleared and closed upstairs and downstairs. It was time to go home. The remaining staff was ushered out along with Sam and Halo. Eugenia and Santini's car service pulled up to the entrance. The alarm was turned on, and as always, Big

Joe drove me home. He escorted me inside, and did a quick detective's scan of the house. Satisfied, and certain that all was safe, he said good-night, and drove away.

Chapter 13
SH+AGUAR,
The Beginning…

I was safely inside, looking forward to a hot, steamy shower. I stepped out of my pumps and headed upstairs to the master bedroom. But, I never reached it. There was a sudden flash of light, followed by an astonishing shot of energy. My heart began pumping… faster and faster… louder… and louder! I felt the heat of blood rushing through my body with the force of a storm surge! My mind and senses were frenzied, as they spun out of control! I was overwhelmed by an onslaught of confusion… sounds… smells… noises… colors… images. My skin… first hot… then cold! Something was happening to me and I did not know how to control it!

I was changing… rapidly! My weightless body shifted, swirled, and twisted… around and around. My body, no longer mine, morphed and stretched in impossible ways! My fingers and toes throbbed and pulsated… extended and retracted… then extended again, this time, with sharp, protruding claws! My entire being was completely reshaped, reconstructed, and redefined. Then, I found myself suspended in a place of violet colored haze. I was somewhere between reality and surreality! Out of nowhere, a silhouette appeared. Moving with unbelievable speed, she stood in front of me…! behind me…! on both sides of me! And then, in one leap…

SWOOSH!

WHISH!

THUMP!

She consumed me, and I, her! The black jaguar and I were ONE! I inhaled, and breathed out, a low, guttural, growl. Before me, in a dark, gritty area, an old, abandoned factory sat. It was situated underneath Manhattan Bridge, at the end of some godforsaken block. Dangling above, a rusty, bent, street sign read: *Terminal Street.* There were three nefarious types inside. A slimy photographer was busily setting up cameras and equipment. Seated nearby, at a table, two hoodlums played a game of cards. I smelled trouble… and it stunk!

In a back room, I heard the wailing and cries of unhappy children. They were being held captive in this horrible place! I felt, smelled, and sensed nothing but danger for them. I had to get to them! I had to save the children! I leapt!

SWOOSH!

WHISH!

THUMP!

A voice inside tells me that the children have all been kidnapped within the last week — lured away from playgrounds, and snatched from bus stops, after school. The three perverts holding them are members of a depraved ring of criminals who make money in the dirty business of child pornography, child enslavement, and child prostitution. *Despicable! Not over my dead body!* These men must be stopped in their tracks.

I must reach out to one of the children, telepathically and give instructions! There are six of them, all crying, except for the girl who is trying to comfort the others. There is a certain aura about her. She is an old soul, enchanting, with eyes that look like two big windows. Her mind is open. She's a crystal child, and senses me immediately. She looks around the room, searching for me, knowing that someone… something … has come to help them. She feels my presence.

"You cannot see me, I tell her. Can you hear me?"

The little girl looks up, around, and nods her head, meekly. "Yes, I can hear you," she replies.

"I can also feel you. But I cannot see you," she adds.

"There is no need to see me. Don't be afraid of me. I'm here to help you. Just do as I say. The bad men who brought you here will be punished. Please… do as I say, and move swiftly. You must call the police immediately! They have been looking for you. They will come to rescue you. When you see a cell phone under the door, grab it quickly and dial 9-1-1. Say that you have been kidnapped and can be found in an old white abandoned warehouse at the end of Terminal Street, underneath the Manhattan Bridge."

With that, the crystal child shook her head, turned her eyes towards the door, and waited for the cell phone.

It was now time to introduce myself to the three monsters in the next room! I leapt stealthily, from beam to beam, across the high ceiling, completely unseen, and unheard by them. The slimy photographer was first. I needed to get his cell phone to the child on the other side of the door. In one fell swoop, I pounced, startled him, and with precision, sent his cell phone sliding underneath the door! I watched, relieved, as little, innocent fingers retrieved the phone. While his shocked partners in crime screamed, cursed, and crouched down in fear, the photographer, not believing what his frightened eyes were seeing, had the audacity to reach for his camera. Amidst fear and fright, in a fruitless attempt to capture what was perhaps, a once-in-a-lifetime photo op, he trained his camera on me. With a single thought, and a snap of my head, I slammed him against the wall, over and over again, and watched as his broken, bloodied body slid down the wall, slime-like, into a crumpled mess on the floor.

By now, the two degenerates, cowering with fear and horror underneath the table, had drawn guns on me… firing silent bullets… shot after shot… then reloading… to no avail. Terrified and hysterical, the cowards grabbed military-grade automatic weapons and unleashed them on me. Nothing they did slowed or stopped me. I was invincible! The bullets stung like mosquito bites, which I found to be quite annoying. When the thugs finally realized that they were in mortal danger, they resorted to kneeling, pleading, and begging for their miserable lives. They squirmed and begged God for mercy.

Why do so many evil, wicked people beg God for mercy? I wondered. What has God to do with this?

"What the hell is that monstrous thing!" one of the deviants cried out, burying his face into his arm.

"I can't tell! Fucking thing won't die!" screamed the other, shuddering with horror.

It was then that I caught a glimpse of myself in the tri-fold mirror that stood in one corner of the dreary room. The horrifically twisted and deformed image reflected, left me petrified! The mirror revealed a hideously imposing creature, a half-woman, half-jaguar, phantasmal beast. Its long, hairy tail coiled, then uncoiled, slithering reptile-like, before extending more than nine feet long! My nude body was covered in neither flesh nor hair, but something unidentifiable. Standing upright on hind legs, my head was less than an inch from the ten-foot ceiling. My hands, though padded in the palms, did not have fingers, but rather, long, sharp, retractable claws. I realized that I was not one figure. I was, instead, an entity that morphed, changed, disappeared, and reappeared, continuously. I was a shadowy, nightmarish apparition, a monstrous beast!

The screams and cries for help from the heathens, brought me back to the issue at hand. I growled at the cowering deviants on the floor, one of whom had shitted all over himself. He was now wallowing in the recycled sausage, pepperoni, and garlic pizza he had eaten earlier in the evening. The room reeked of the foul smell of his feces, and the odor stung my nostrils! How appropriate I thought. *Shit begets shit!*

The NYPD squads were nearby. The children were safe and would soon be reunited with their families. I wondered what Lem would have done in this situation. How would he have handled these pathetic excuses for men? A part of me wanted them brought to justice and thrown behind bars forever. Another part of me, however, wanted to kill them! Why waste taxpayers' money on these worthless animals! Whatever I did, had to be done for the greater good of humanity. Children deserved to be protected from the likes of such depraved predators! At first, I struggled, and fought the urge. But it was no use. I finally gave in. These licentious humans who preyed on innocent children, had to be put out of their misery… once and for all! With eyes shining towards my trapped prey, I quietly and slowly lower my body into a deadly crouching position. In a single leap, I pounce and attack with a bite so ferocious that their skulls are at once, pierced and pulverized!

With justice swiftly accomplished here, my work has been done. Suddenly, without warning…

SWOOSH!

WHISH!

THUMP!

The tunnel… the ferocious speed… the violet haze! I found myself back home, upstairs on the floor, curled into a fetal position. My nerves were racked, as I unfolded, stumbled to my feet, and slowly approached the floor mirror, afraid of what I might see. I exhaled! Relieved, that with the exception of my hair looking a little windblown, and a broken fingernail, everything else looked normal! I looked like myself! Felt fine, and gradually, my body felt normal. I finally climbed into the tub and took a long, hot, steamy shower!

In one day, I had been to hell and back — several times, and then some. I am still in shock of how the fabric of my life has been ripped apart, thread by thread, by Lem and Jason. I feel numb, angry, and disappointed beyond words, by their years of deception. The pain of learning what they did to me feels like a deep, open wound — the kind that oozes blood and pus inside… and never completely heals. I am human. I am supposed to hurt and feel pain. At the same time, I feel empowered… born-again… regenerated… and changed. Strangely, I also feel exceedingly lucky. I have been changed, and, perhaps, for the better. I've been beaten by life. But still, I am a woman, unbroken.

I had to get to Jason right away and let him know what had happened.

"BRRRRRRRING…!

BRRRRRRRING…!

BRRRRRRRING!"

"Dammit! Answer your phone, Jason!"

"BRRRRRRRING…!

BRRRRRRRING!"

Jason was out of breath when he finally answered his phone. *Hi mom…! I was in the shower. Are you nearby?*

"Get dressed. I need to tell you what happened last night! I swear, I didn't mean to do what I did! I… I…"

Please, calm down! Don't say another word until you're here. How far away are you?

"I'm a few blocks away. I'm bringing breakfast for you."

Okay. I'm starving. I'll meet you downstairs.

"No! Not in the lab! Upstairs in the kitchen nook. I need to talk to you… away from her."

All right. If that makes you feel better. He paused. I could actually use a little break away from the lab.

"Great. See you soon!"

Moments later, I grabbed the big bag of food, hopped out of the town car, and ran up the steps — two at a time. It had been quite a while since I'd entered this house from its main door, and doing so made me feel good. There was something very normal about entering a home through its front door, as opposed to entering by way of a basement laboratory. I was already on the top step of the staircase when Jason flung the door wide open and greeted me on the stoop.

"It looks as if someone's overflowing with an abundance of energy this morning," he commented, relieving me of the bags. I stepped inside, turned quickly around, and closed the door. Considering the horrific night I had had, I was no worse for wear. In fact, I was filled with raw energy. My conscience, on the other hand, was a different story. I was wracked with guilt over what had happened.

"I am brimming with energy!" I replied, removing my cape and hat, and hanging them on the coat rack in the entryway. "But no one has Eugenia's energy! Your godmother has the entire wait staff buzzing like a beehive. Everyone's helping her decorate the place as we speak. She ordered me to stay away. Said she had everything under control."

Jason gave me a quick cheek-to-cheek kiss, and a rapid head-to-toe inspection. "That shouldn't surprise you," he chuckled. "Aunt Genie can't help herself. She's a control freak!"

I stood at attention, wondering if there were any telltale signs of last night's ordeal. "I'm glad someone still has control over their actions. I've apparently lost all control of mine!"

He took a step back and continued studying me. "You can tell me what happened over breakfast." Satisfied with his inspection, he turned and headed towards the kitchen.

I wasted no time reheating the food in the microwave and placing everything on the table. Jason was definitely hungry. But he seemed to be preoccupied with something, as well.

"I hope you're ready for your big birthday bash tonight! Eugenia... Santini... Big Joe... they all want this to be a memorable night for you. They've pretty much taken the reins on planning everything."

"I know. I miss them all. They're family. I can't wait to see what they've planned!"

"Neither can I. They've kept me completely in the dark. I'll be as surprised as you are!" I was so traumatized by what had happened the night before, that, needless to say, I had no appetite whatsoever.

Jason turned on the television, surfed to his favorite local news channel, and dived into his pancakes. About halfway through his breakfast, he finally came up for air. "Mom... Since I have no idea what to expect... you know... with your transformation underway... I went ahead and called out sick for the rest of the week. Just in case. I mean... anything could happen."

I shot him a look. "Did you say anything could happen? Well... you should know that I went out on a prowl last night." I paused and averted my eyes. "I was completely transformed into her!"

Jason swallowed a mouthful of hot cocoa and slowly raised his eyes. "Are you sure you experienced a complete transmutation?"

Staring directly at him, I fired back. "It was as complete as it can be! Call it whatever you like... I was completely changed! She took over. That jaguar was in control!"

He picked up his cup, and without drinking from it, slowly returned it to the table. His entire body stiffened. "What did you look like?" he asked, his voice cracking. "I mean… there was no way of me knowing for sure what you might actually look like."

"I was mortified!" I blurted out. "I did not look at all human! There was a mirror in the far corner of the room. I saw my reflection. I was a ghastly, fearful-looking creature that kept changing. I looked like a monstrous abomination… horribly twisted and contorted! My image kept changing, constantly. I looked like something from another world. I was neither a woman, nor a jaguar!"

He swallowed, and his eating came to an abrupt stop. "You said you were out on a prowl." He hesitated. "Did you find prey?"

"I guess you could say that I was out on a prowl for criminals." I turned to face him. "Yes… I did find prey."

Jason gasped. "Oh, my God!"

"It all happened so fast! One minute I was getting ready to jump into the shower… and the next thing, I knew, I was spinning through a tunnel…"

"A tunnel?"

"Yes! A twisting tunnel!" I snapped. "This was not a figment of my imagination. It was all real! I landed, completely changed… transformed… into that creature… near an abandoned warehouse on a deserted street. There were three men… holding six kidnapped children captive."

"What!"

"Those despicable leeches were running a child enslavement and pornography ring!" I blurted out, still angry from what I'd witnessed.

Jason's eyes widened. Riveted by what he was hearing, he sat spellbound and motionless, unable to say anything.

"There was one girl… an unusual child, whom I communicated with, telepathically. Using telekinesis, I seized the photographer's cell phone, slid it underneath the door, and told the girl what to do."

When Jason finally spoke, his voice was filled with trepidation. "What did you do to those three worthless deviants?"

It was not my initial intention to kill those worthless heathens. I only wanted to terrorize them the way they had terrorized the children. I shuddered at the thought of having to tell my son about the violent and merciless savagery I'd inflicted upon those men. It would surely frighten him, as much as it had frightened me. But he needed to know everything. How, in spite of struggling against it, I had been overcome by a strong desire to permanently eradicate those ruffians. He needed to know the ugly truth, and it had to come from me. "I slammed the photographer against the wall so many times, he finally passed out, and fell to the floor, bloodied, mangled, and unconscious."

Jason turned and looked away, without saying a word.

"As for the other two thugs," I continued, "they were terror-stricken by my hideously gruesome image! Their automatic weapons were no match for me. With a single thought, they were flung against the table, tied, and bound tightly with rings of rope! There was no possible way they would have escaped before the NYPD arrived." My plan was to leave them there at the crime scene. I had every intention of leaving them alive! I wanted the bastards brought to justice and imprisoned. But…"

"What else did you do, Mom?" he asked, still avoiding my eyes.

I placed a hand gently on his shoulder, and waited for him to face me. "I wanted to do the right thing. And deep down inside, I knew what had to be done. But I was filled with so much rage, that I eventually gave in to a force that was far stronger than…"

Just as I was about to continue, I was interrupted by a loud news jingle.

BREAKING NEWS! BREAKING NEWS! BREAKING NEWS! flashed across the screen. Big, red, bold, letters in caps, startled us, and seized our attention. We sat silently, attentively staring at the screen. Jason reached for the remote, and turned up the volume.

In an instance, the photos of six children appeared on the screen, and took my breath away. I went numb, listening to the news reporter:

Six children who were victims of random kidnappings last week, have been found, alive and well! The children have all been reunited with their parents. One of the girls said a friendly voice inside her head saved and rescued them by sliding a cell phone under the door, and telling her what to do. The culprits — three well-known felons with long criminal records were found dead at the scene. According to the coroner, forensics show that the three career criminals were all frightened to death. Yes, you heard me correctly. The criminals were frightened to death! In a mysterious twist, the letter "S" was found scratched onto the men's palms. An in-depth investigation confirms that the marks were made by paws belonging to an over-sized jaguar! We are living in strange and unusual times! More to come, as this story develops!

Jason's hands fell clumsily to the table, causing his fork, knife, and plate to go crashing to the floor. The sound echoed throughout the kitchen. For a long moment, it looked as if he'd stopped breathing. Not a word came from him as he turned slowly and silently towards me.

My heart sank deeper and deeper into my being. My eyes were frozen on the screen. I did not move. Did not react. I said nothing. I opened my mouth to try and explain, but nothing came out. This isn't how I wanted Jason to find out. I wanted him to hear it from me first. I needed to explain how it had all happened so suddenly… and without warning. Now, it was too late.

Staring at the broken nail, I lifted my hand and held it up in front of him. "This is all that I have to show for what happened there," I uttered, raising my eyes to meet his. "It all happened so fast!" I blurted out. "After Big Joe dropped me off at home, I felt the change coming on. I knew it was happening… but it couldn't be stopped! Before I knew it… she had entered my body!" I paused and tried to calm down. "Jason… what are we going to do?"

He got up from the table, and stared pensively at the floor. My eyes followed him as he walked over to the counter, and leaned against it. "We'll get through this together, Mom," he said in a low, solemn voice. "Dad and I did this to you. That makes us far more responsible for your actions than you are." He raised his head and stared at me. "As far as I'm concerned, you did the right thing. You saved those children, and got rid of ugly, useless, menaces to society. By doing so, you used your powers for the greater good of humanity."

A huge feeling of relief fell over me. In a way, I felt vindicated knowing that he felt the same way I did. It was one thing to see myself transformed into an ugly, terrifying monster that killed, but another thing to be seen through the eyes of my son, as such. "You do understand then, just how conflicted I was."

"Yes, I do." He paused and scratched his head. "Uhm… I'm curious."

"About what?"

"Why the letter 'S'? That's an interesting choice. Why not 'K'? The letter 'S' is nowhere in your name."

I flashed a big, bold smile, thrilled that I had one-upped him. "Yes, it is… now that I know who I am, and what I am. The jaguar and I share one name. That name is *SH+AGUAR, The Night Huntress*!"

Jason thought for a moment. A smile softened his face, and his entire body perked up. "SH+AGUAR…! SH+AGUAR!" he repeated, as his smile broadened. "A portmanteau for *SHE + JAGUAR*! How brilliant!" he exclaimed. "Well done, Mom! Well done!"

Jason and I cleared the table, mostly in silence. Neither of us knew what to expect, and we were both extremely apprehensive.

Jason looked at me and sighed. "Mom… let's head downstairs. We've got a lot to do today. I'll be observing you, checking your vitals, taking blood and urine samples, and testing your senses."

"Why don't you go ahead and get set up. I'll make a big pot of hot cocoa for you and join you, shortly."

"That works!" he said, smiling weakly, as he headed downstairs.

With the water heating, I stepped away from the kitchen and ended up in the dining room. I peered through the glass French doors into the living room… where it had all happened… Lem's abduction. Before I knew it… it was back — that menacing, inescapable specter — reminding me that what had happened here, wasn't just a frightening nightmare. It was real. And I would never be allowed to forget that.

The doors squeaked as I opened them and stepped inside. A film of dust carpeted the once glossy hardwood floor. My nostrils burned, inhaling the musky smell of stagnant, un-lived-in air. My heart pounded furiously against my chest. I closed my eyes, hoping to shut out the ugly memory. But it all came flooding back as if it had happened yesterday.

Chapter 14
Losing Lem

Flashback to December 12, 2014…

The Christmas tree was sweet and fragrant. A Balsam fir with dense, dark-green leaves, and thick needles, towered between the twin windows in the living room, overlooking the courtyard.

This was the tree that Jason had settled on — after a tireless search, and one that had gone on much too long. When a forage of tree vendors in Manhattan failed to present the perfect fir tree, Jason talked Lem into driving for nearly two hours to a family-owned tree farm where he found *the* perfect Christmas Tree!

Lem and I were dancing to the tune of Donny Hathaway's song, *"This Christmas"*. Jason sat on the floor, surrounded by bags of ornaments and decorations. He was focused on detangling strings of lights, discarding burned-out bulbs, and replacing them with fancier, energy-saving bulbs. We were waiting for his godmother to arrive.

Eugenia had called earlier and said she was picking up a few last-minute items. The stores were packed with local holiday shoppers and tourists. She was already in the checkout line, but there were about twenty-five people in front of her. She'd be about half an hour late. No doubt, Eugenia and Jason had gone behind my back, and against my orders, and added items to his wish list. This wish list was kept strictly confidential between him and Eugenia. It never failed. The two of them always found ways to connect around me, and without my knowledge. She enjoyed spoiling Jason, and he appreciated every act of overindulgence showered upon him. As his 'god-mom/aunt', she was determined to get everything Jason wanted. As far as she was concerned, her godson was worth every painful minute she spent waiting in line. It was always all about making Jason happy.

Moments earlier, Jason had answered a call on the landline from someone who'd identified herself as an NYPD detective. None of us even questioned how, or from where, she'd gotten our landline telephone number. I couldn't recall the last time the house phone had rung. It was a number we never gave out, and very few people knew it. With the exception of my parents and relatives in South Carolina, no one else ever called our house on that landline. Sometimes I didn't remember we still had it! Lem always insisted on keeping it as a backup, just in case there was ever a major grid outage that rendered cell phones and cordless phones inoperative. To appease Lem, I kept the cordless phone easily accessible, while the 'corded' phone was tucked safely on top of our kitchen cabinet. Oddly, Jason was somewhat intrigued by both relics — the corded and cordless phones.

Among other inquiries, the female caller had questioned Jason if his parents were home, claiming that police officers were in the area investigating a series of recent burglaries on Riverside Drive. Jason's response to the caller was that we had had no burglary, and that he wasn't aware of any of our neighbors who had been burglarized recently. I overheard him telling the caller that we actually lived in a very safe neighborhood. He boasted that our vigilant neighborhood crime watch group was one of the best in all of Manhattan. Shortly after he hung up from the caller, the doorbell chimed. Assuming that it was Eugenia, Jason sprinted to the door, looked through the peephole, and saw several New York Police Department (NYPD) officers standing on the top stoop. He let out a sigh of disappointment, opened the door, and greeted them warmly. There was no need to get his parents involved. Besides, they were having so much fun dancing, enjoying each other, the music, and the joys of family life. He was not about to interrupt any of this. He would handle this situation right there in the doorway. There was no need to even let the officers in. I remember hearing Jason's voice, as it floated from the foyer to the living room.

"Thanks for checking in on us, officers, but..."

Jason's voice was abruptly interrupted as the imposters quickly shoved him inside, donned black ski masks, and covered Jason's mouth with duct tape. A gun was held to his head as the men rushed him inside the living room, where Lem and I stood in a moment of shock and disbelief. Startled, we ran towards Jason, but were stopped by men who grabbed us, while others held guns, pointed directly into our faces. Lem pleaded and begged the men to take him. He told them to do whatever they wanted to do with him, but to please, please let his wife and son go.

Duct tape was promptly slapped over our mouths, and our hands tied behind us with a combination of tape and rope.

Lem was led to a chair that had been dragged a distance away from the table. Two other chairs were placed side-by-side, opposite him. Jason and I were then shoved forcefully into those chairs, so that we got a clear view of Lem. While one of the imposters crossed our legs at the ankles, another tightly wrapped duct tape and ropes around them, knotting the rope multiple times. This was all done, it seemed, within seconds, without a word spoken between or among them. They never said anything to us.

"I know what you want! Take me! Take me! Just don't hurt them!" Lem muttered, his words distorted from the tape covering his mouth.

The guy, who appeared to be the leader of the pack, stepped in front of Lem and began slapping and punching him unmercifully in the face.

"Please stop! You're killing him!" I struggled to get out, my voice severely muffled by the duct tape. "Who are you, and what do you want from us?" With that, my mouth was met with a second layer of tape.

They all whispered among themselves, literally speaking into each other's ear. Not any of them spoke loudly enough for me to hear what they were saying. The guy punching Lem, suddenly stopped, then hurriedly scribbled something on a notepad. He held it up to Lem's beaten face, making sure Jason and I could not read what he had written.

Struggling to keep his eyes open, Lem read the note, then shook his head, negatively.

With that, the leader of the pack suddenly snatched the tape off of Lem's mouth, whipped out a large, shiny, box cutter, and pointed it to Lem's throat.

As blood streamed from his nose and mouth, Lem's breathing became increasingly labored. "If that's... what... you want... it's not... here!"

Again, the leader and beater scribbled something on the pad and pulled Lem's head back, forcing him to read it.

Lem's eyes were swollen to two narrow slits, and his face was completely covered in blood. He could barely open his mouth when he tried to speak. With his eyes, bloodied, and swollen nearly shut, there was no way on earth he was able to see, let alone read anything. Realizing that they had probably beaten Lem into a state of near unconsciousness, and obviously growing impatient, the leader of the gang nodded his head vigorously. This immediately sent two of the men running downstairs to the lab. I heard them shoving, throwing, and moving things about, as they tore up the lab. Two of them ransacked the house, tossing things from shelves, looking underneath, above, and behind every piece of movable furniture and appliance.

The leader turned his angry gaze towards me. Even behind his black ski mask, I felt the chill of a cold, heartless stare. Our eyes locked, momentarily, before he abruptly looked away.

I watched helplessly as Lem's head rolled slowly from one side to the next. Occasionally, some unintelligible gibberish escaped from his bloodied mouth. His beaten body suddenly went limp. Almost simultaneously, Jason and I gasped, then struggled, unsuccessfully to get up.

Pacing impatiently, the gang leader noticed that Lem hadn't moved in quite some time. His body was frighteningly limp, with his head hung to one side. He grabbed Lem's wrist, felt for his pulse, then quickly plunged his hands over and over again, into Lem's chest, finally resuscitating him. Lem's eyes flickered, weakly. His body jerked and convulsed, several times. Suddenly, a rush of bloody vomit spewed forth from his mouth, and landed on top of the thug's shiny shoes. The ruffian leapt away, and let out an angry yelp, sending one of the men in search of a towel. He returned, stooped, and began cleaning the boss' shoes. His shoes cleaned, he nodded to the man and whispered something into his ear. At that point, Lem was pulled out of the chair, and stretched out on the floor.

Jason and I looked helplessly at each other, then shifted our attention to Lem, lying on the floor. Beaten into a state of unconsciousness, he was still alive, if only barely. Jason took one long look at Lem, grunted until he got the leader's attention, then gestured wildly towards the notepad. His right hand was freed and a pen quickly shoved into it, as the hideous gang leader held the box cutter to my face.

From where I sat, I had a clear view of what Jason had written:

My father's lab log/journal is at the bottom of a metal safe box on the top shelf of the kitchen cabinet.

With that, the leader, who moved with a slight limp, rounded up his gang, whispered into their ears, and sent them running into the kitchen. He moved over to where Lem laid on the floor and pressed the box cutter against Lem's neck, all along, glaring at us.

The men returned jubilantly, waving Lem's laboratory log, and handed it to the man in charge. He leafed quickly through the pages. When he was done, again, he whispered separately, and directly into each man's ear. Then he placed the log underneath his arm and gestured towards Lem. It was then that he finally let out an evil little laugh.

Lem looked like someone who had drunken himself into an intoxicated stupor, and was knocked out cold.

Don't die Lem...! You can't die...! Please don't leave us! I prayed, silently, but ferociously. Please, God... please don't let them kill my husband and son! Take me, if you must take someone. But let Jason and Lem live!

It took three men to bring Lem to his feet, and four of them to prop him up into a standing position, which gave the impression that Lem was too drunk to stand on his own. The imposters rushed out of the house as quickly, and as violently, as they had entered. Within moments of finding what they had come for, they were all gone. Jason and I were unharmed. But they took Lem.

It felt like an eternity before we heard the sound of sirens. Eugenia and the real police officers finally arrived. When she could neither reach us on any of our cellphones, nor the landline, her gut instinct told her something was wrong. She called 911.

The imposter NYPD officers had staged the perfect crime scene. In front of the house, as a deterrent, they had blockaded the street to keep the neighbors at bay. By the time the real NYPD officers had figured everything out, it was too late. The imposters had gotten away — with Lem.

That night, the house was filled with beat cops, officers, forensic types, and other officials, roaming throughout the place, operating on run-of-the-mill auto-pilot. It felt like one big, unhappy, miserable circus. Detective Sergeant Joseph D'Amato was not the first *real* police officer to arrive at our home, but he was the only one who could get a word, or any kind of reaction out of Jason. Like me, Jason was still in shock. Detective D'Amato came across as being sincere, and a lot more human than the other officers. He showed genuine concern. From the way the house and the lab were turned upside-down, his immediate assessment was that the intruders were looking for something… something of extreme value.

His eyes went back and forth, from me, to Jason. He was studying us… trying to decide which one would be the easier nut to crack. Finally, he made his way over to me. "I'm very sorry about your husband, ma'am," he said, scratching his head. He glanced briefly at Jason, and lowered his voice, taking care not to let Jason overhear what he was saying. "Doctor Johnson was quite prominent in his field… as well as a very controversial figure. I'm sure he had his share of friends and enemies." He paused, glanced at Jason, and continued. "Would you happen to know who his frenemies were?"

My mind was as blank as my body was numb. I couldn't think of anything or anyone. "No… I don't know anyone who would hate him enough to do what those animals did ."

D'Amato's eyes shifted and blinked rapidly. "Other than Dr Johnson's unfortunate abduction, did the intruders find what they were looking for?" he asked, matter-of-factly, surveying the disarray of the house.

Unsure of what to say, I turned to look at Jason.

D'Amato's eyes shifted again to Jason. "From the look of this place, they were determined to get whatever it was they came looking for," he whispered.

Like his eyes, the question was straight-as-an-arrow, and to the point. Ruggedly handsome, with chiseled features, Detective D'Amato had a polished, pulled-together look. With an imposing appearance, he towered easily over everyone. While NYPD officers and others were sniffing mechanically and loudly throughout the messy crime scene, his carriage — aimed and purposeful — brought a sense of calm authority to the house. He quickly picked up on how Jason had moved protectively and closer to an ornate chess table. A magnificent work of art, it was beautiful and eye-catching. Constructed from three different types of inlaid, polished wood, it had inlaid florets, and interlocking cubes, which Jason and Lem had diligently carved and stained. The table was Jason's most prized possession, second only to Lem's blue cashmere coat. Jason did not budge, as he quietly observed the detective.

Detective D'Amato glanced admiringly at the craftsmanship reflected in the table. He studied the intricately laid pieces of wood and shook his head, appreciatively. A chess master himself, he assumed Jason played the game, and struck up a conversation with him. "I bet your dad taught you how to play chess," he said, waiting for Jason to respond. "You're probably as good a player as he is."

That broke the ice, and got a response from Jason. "I play a good game. But no one is as good at chess as my dad is."

Detective D'Amato was later able to get enough information from Jason to start the investigation, and move forward, without further traumatizing my then fourteen-year-old son. Aptly nicknamed "Big Joe" by the other police officers, this giant of a man, with surprisingly gentle ways, soon became just "Big Joe" to Jason and me. He and Jason took an instant liking to each other. I later learned that the detective also had a son, whom he had taught the game of chess to.

In the days that followed, Lem's abduction was touted by all of the city's news outlets as "Breaking News", while, in big, bold, black letters, the newspapers headlined their front pages with variations of: *Acclaimed Scientist Violently Abducted From Riverside Drive Home!* All of this came to an abrupt end when Lem's abduction was no longer considered news. The story was downgraded from front-page headlines, then, eventually, disappeared completely from the media.

Big Joe continued working on the case, as long as he could. But with one brick wall leading to another brick wall, he soon came under pressure from top brass at the Midtown Precinct to close the case. Other than estimated heights and weights, there wasn't much more Jason or I could offer in terms of descriptions of the culprits--other than the fact that the head thug walked with a slight limp--at least on that night. And since we never heard any of their voices, we couldn't even describe what they sounded like. That one, ugly laugh, and an angry yelp from the evil boss were the only audible utterances made.

Eventually, Lem's abduction became another one of the thousands upon thousands of unsolved crimes. As disappointed as we were, neither Jason nor I was surprised when Big Joe came in person, and told us that the case had gone cold. He apologized, profusely, and made it a point to check in on us, periodically calling, to make sure we were coping as best we could. With Jason's help, he even saw to it that a new, high-tech security system was immediately installed on our house — by the same reputable surveillance company he used for his own home. Big Joe went above and beyond the call of duty making sure Jason and I were safe. Once in a while, on his day off, he and Jason would play a game of chess.

Lem was abducted thirteen days before Christmas, on what was Jason's fourteenth birthday.

Were we cursed? Or did God just not like us?

Our house no longer felt like a home. It felt more and more like a vaulted tomb. Those first months following Lem's abduction left us in a nightmarish limbo, as we grieved, both separately, and together. Jason and I were still breathing, but barely existing. In our own way, both of us had withdrawn from the world... from life. We were now faced with the dreadful task of coming to terms with living without Lem. I think we found it far less arduous to simply withdraw from everything. Little by little, we began moving away from everyone--limiting contact with relatives and friends, and then, finally, ignoring phone calls, and refusing visits. At some point, we even started avoiding each other.

We were zombies, the living dead. We hardly ate. During those rare times when we were able to share our meals, we did so in deafening silence. Sleeping did not come easily for either of us. We did just enough to make it from one day to the next. Sometimes not a word was shared between us all day long. Other times, I'd find Jason staring up at the ceiling, or worse, down at the floor. Somedays I woke up crying. Other days, I woke up to the sounds of Jason's soft weeping. But mostly, my son and I went about our bare existences, lost, haunted, and pained — by the ugly unknowns: *What had become of Lem? Was he still alive? And if so, where on earth was he?* Not knowing what had become of Lem was eating away at us. It was killing us. But the fact that his body had not been found, gave us a drop of hope that he might still be alive. *Somewhere.*

Other than Jason and I, Eugenia was the only person who had a set of emergency keys to our house. She showed up one day, unannounced, bearing a large box and a tote bag with some of our favorite foods. She had had enough of us not answering or returning her calls. What she found were two sick people — patients succumbing to the *dis-ease* of an unbearable tragedy.

Eugenia saw that we were being devoured by grief and self-pity. She refused to leave us alone, to be healed by the passing of time. Dropping by and visiting a few times a week wasn't enough. She moved into the house without even discussing it with us, and took over. Just like that. Like an almighty healer, she lured us away from the graves we were burying ourselves in, and slowly nursed us back to the land of the living.

It took her awhile getting used to our new security system. But Eugenia, being the person she is, came with a back-up plan. A practice brought over from when she owned the Jazzy Joint, she was the proud licensed owner of a concealed weapon. She called the Glock 43 gun she carried tucked inside her handbag, her "little peace of mind". Jason wanted to have no part of it, but she even convinced me to take shooting lessons — which I soon acquired a taste for. In no time at all, Eugenia had sublet her spacious Harlem apartment to a young Columbia University graduate student. With her Glock 43 in tote, she moved into our brownstone, and brought life back into our home.

Somewhere between Eugenia's delectable dishes and her funny as hell jokes, Jason and I started breathing again. He cleaned up the lab that had been left in disarray, and restored it to the way Lem had always kept it. Like Lem, he went back to spending most of his time downstairs in the lab, and did so with an abundance of determination and renewed energy.

I exhausted myself, and Eugenia, redecorating, moving furniture around, and redoing the house. This was my way of trying to erase what had happened there. When that did not work, I finally made a confession to myself, and announced my intentions to Jason and Eugenia. “I can’t live here any more. It’s just too painful. I’m going to put this house up for sale, and find a smaller place… maybe somewhere downtown.”

Jason was mortified. “No! I don’t want to move! We can’t move! Suppose Dad comes back! I’m staying here!” he shrieked.

Despite his initial pushback, I prayed, hoped, and thought that Jason would eventually come around. Reluctantly, I began house hunting, by surfing virtually, through various online listings. The glossy images and Hollywood-style-produced video tours were more distracting than they were helpful.

House hunting on a laptop did not sit well with Eugenia. “I don’t care how virtually real a place looks, it’s not the same as actually walking inside the house!” she exclaimed, throwing her hands into the air. “It’s impossible to know what a house really feels like from pictures and videos!, she huffed. “You have to walk on the floors… touch the walls… and feel the energy inside!”

“You’re right.” I responded, scrolling aimlessly through the listings that stared back at me from my screen, some of the 3-D photos almost hitting me in the face.

Eugenia came around, leaned over, and studied the listings on the screen.

"Hell's Kitchen has come a long way! It was still too gritty for me when I first came to New York. But look at it now!" she said, frowning at a list of old buildings that had been renovated and were now being offered as pricey co-ops and condominiums.

Annoyed by exorbitant prices of the small, boxy dwellings listed on the screen, Eugenia shook her head in disbelief. "Hum… it's so hard to see what the spaces actually look like on this screen," she said, squinting her eyes. "Listen… the only right way to do this is to make a list of your top choices, and see if we can get appointments with brokers," she added, waving off the listings on the laptop.

"That sounds like a plan!" I agreed, already jotting down names, locations, and numbers. "It's perfect weather for house hunting!"

We were out and about in no time at all. To Eugenia's surprise, Hell's Kitchen was no longer gritty. It was lively, colorful, and diverse, overflowing with an abundance of affordable restaurants, bars, and cafes! Equally plentiful were co-ops and condominiums in the area. They, however, were anything but affordable. We explored Hell's Kitchen, from West Fifty-Seventh Street, down to Forty-Fifth Street, traversing between Broadway and Twelfth Avenues. Some of the ultra-modern condos we saw were breathtaking. I loved the open, continuous floor plans and the numerous tempting amenities flaunted by the newer skyscrapers. So many of these towering structures were literally designed to be micro-communities. Some of them were designed so that dwellers never, or rarely have to go outside for anything.

Personally, the idea of living in a skyscraper that jutted into, or above the clouds, felt unnatural. And the thought of firemen trying to extinguish an out-of-control fire in any of those towering skyscrapers, frightened me. On the other hand, although a less-expensive alternative to a condo, the shared ownership of a co-op made me nervous. Nothing we saw made me jump up and down with excitement. After several days, we were left exhausted, disappointed, and extremely discouraged. Needless to say, my search to find a new home slowed to a snail's pace. That Jason was so adamantly opposed to moving, only further dampened my efforts to aggressively look for a new place.

I was wrestling with my own personal dilemma. In my heart, I felt I owed it to Jason and to Lem's memory, to stay in our home and work through the pain. Lem, Jason, and I had shared so many good times here. But in my mind, I knew that, in order to start living again, I had to break away from this dreadful tomb. I needed to leave the worst memory of my life behind me--in the past. In order to do that, I would have to find a new place to call home.

One day, while going through the house, trying to assess which items and furniture should be transferred, in an eventual move, and which pieces would be better off sold, Eugenia made an enlightening observation. “Girrrrl! No matter how you cut it… slice it… or dice it, there’s no way on earth you’ll ever be able to fit all of your must-haves in some three-room apartment! Hell! You need one room for your clothes, alone!”

She was absolutely right. It suddenly struck me that what I actually wanted and needed, was not an apartment, a co-op, or a condominium. What I should have been looking for all along was another house. Not a big house. But a house, nevertheless. My search was, henceforth, narrowed to finding a smaller, safer house, somewhere on the island of Manhattan. After taking a little time off to regroup from our earlier expeditions, Eugenia and I made plans to look only at affordable brownstones and townhouses. Our target destinations were the West Village, and the Chelsea areas.

Chapter 15
A Purpose and a Place

Jason and I awoke to the wonderful aroma of homemade buttermilk biscuits, scrambled eggs, fried onions, and country cured ham. After devouring far more than his fair share, Jason made his way downstairs to the lab. Together, Eugenia and I quickly cleared the kitchen counter, pulled out my laptop, and began looking for affordable houses.

"I see we're both still madly in love with the Chelsea area," she said, glancing at the time. "Let's have a girls' day out on the town. Why don't you make a list of your favorite, say… five houses. Let's see if we can get some appointments lined up with the brokers and actually look inside those houses!"

The idea appealed to me, and in no time, we were headed downtown. Eugenia had succeeded in getting me all dressed up, and out of the house. Four appointments were confirmed with more than enough time in between.

The first two houses were somewhat disappointing. They looked nothing like their doctored photos and online videos. Those images had been so photoshopped, and so enhanced that Eugenia and I, upon entering the houses, and seeing what each actually looked like, began laughing hysterically. Moreover, they were both dark, gloomy, and uninviting. No sun ever shined through those windows! So much for the glossy, well-lit videos! The house that I really wanted to see, my favorite, was located on West Twenty-Second Street, between Eighth and Ninth Avenues. That appointment wasn't until 2.30 p.m. and it was just now a little after noon.

Eugenia looked at me, still amused by what we'd seen.

"That last house was some doozy!" she exclaimed, shaking her head in disbelief. "That tomb will be on the market for an eternity! Not even Count Dracula would want to live there!" she added, still laughing.

Laughter is indeed the best medicine for the soul. And it's a good thing that it truly is contagious. Eugenia's infectious laugh got the best of me. Before I knew it, we were in stitches, bent over, and laughing so hard that we were both brought to tears. It felt good to *really* laugh again. Somehow, the salty water flowing from my eyes seemed to purge the bitter pain and anger that had for months festered inside me. These were healing tears — cleansing my eyes, mind, and soul.

Digging inside her shoulder bag, Eugenia whipped out a small packet of tissues. She handed me one, then gently dabbed her moist face. She was smiling, her big brown eyes gleaming almost green in the bright sunlight.

“Miss Thang… it does me wonders to see you finally coming around again. Lem would have wanted you to be nothing less than happy.” She adjusted her bag and threw both arms around me.

“You’re right. Lem always went out of his way to make me laugh.”

Eugenia shook her head and let out a chuckle. “Bad jokes and all! Lem Johnson knew how to ruin a good joke! Sometimes his jokes were so bad that that is what made you laugh!”

I was still reeling from Eugenia’s last lines when she suddenly stopped in her tracks. Turning around, her eyes darted from one side of the street to the other, as she tried to figure out exactly where we were.

“We’ve got two and a half hours to kill”, Eugenia started. “We can grab something to eat or stroll and check out the neighborhood. It’s up to you. Your call.”

“Uhm… I’m in the mood for a little stroll… Let’s see… we are now on…”

“We’re on Eighth Avenue and Sixteenth Street… not far from our next appointment.” Eugenia said, her eyes wandering up and across the street. She moved closer to the curb, squinted her eyes, and searched until she found what she was looking for. “There it is… the building near the corner!” she shouted, pointing to a gloriously ornate building that looked as if it was hanging from the sky.

The sight of such a magnificent building took my breath away. A recessed mansion, it stood out from all of the other buildings in the area. I was awe-struck, and drawn to it, not only because of how it was situated, almost unseen from the Avenue. But there was a columned portico that led to its amazing entrance, and a temple-like facade that reminded me of a much smaller version of the Parthenon in Athens, on top of the Acropolis. Even more, it reminded me of the theatre where I'd performed so many times in Sounion, Greece. For a moment, my mind drifted back to Greece, and how I'd fallen in love with the people, its ancient temples, statues, architecture, its deliciously healthy food, and airy houses — bleached white by nature, the sun, and time.

For a moment, Eugenia stared pensively, across the street. "That's it! That's the place!" she exclaimed, her face lighting up, childlike, as she pointed to the white building. "That is one amazing restaurant and bar! A friend of mine… someone I knew from my days at the Culinary Institute of America, works there as a chef. About a year ago, he invited me to stop by and I was beyond impressed!" Eugenia gushed, her eyes set firmly across the street.

"Is it nearly as beautiful inside as it is outside?" I asked, already walking towards the building, as if I was being drawn there by some invisible magnetic force.

Eugenia hastened her steps and caught up to me. "Beautiful doesn't do it justice! It's the kind of place I'd open in a heartbeat… if I had the money and the right connections! We're talking about high society, here!"

"Do they serve lunch there, Eugenia?"

With a thoughtful look in her eyes, she turned and smiled. "I went there for dinner. But I think they do serve lunch! It's swanky! Like those glitzy European places you performed in."

Great! I'm starving! Let's stop by for a quick bite!"

As we crossed the street and approached the small portico, our pace was suddenly broken. Plastered haphazardly across the heavy, paneled door of this impressive Greek Revival House, was a notice from The City of New York. In big, bold red letters, it read: *Premises seized by The City of New York/ Property of The City of New York.* Eugenia and I stood frozen in our tracks.

"How on earth did this ever happen!" Eugenia gasped. "The owners must have invested a ton of money in this place!"

"What do you think happened?" I asked, taking in the decorative facade and the elaborate entrance and door surrounds.

Eugenia, still reeling from the shock of the place being closed and seized by the city, looked like a deer caught in the headlights. She just stood there, unable to move, with her mouth wide open. After a painful moment, she was finally able to utter a few words. "To be honest, Kitt… I don't know what to say. I mean… it could be anything — taxes, violations, criminal activities. Hell! It could even be a goddam messy divorce." she replied, a not-so-subtle reference to her own divorce, which had left her in financial dire straits.

I was drawn to this place for a reason. I was feverishly reading the small print, when my eyes came across Van Court Realties.

"My goodness! Van Court Realties is listed as one of the agencies showing this property! I yelled out. "The broker we're meeting on West Twenty-Second Street is with Van Court Realties!"

Eugenia let out a little smile. "I'd love for you to see what that place looks like inside! I wonder if the broker would be kind enough to give us a little guided tour of the place?"

"It wouldn't hurt to ask." I said, reaching inside my shoulder bag for my cell phone.

Eugenia smiled and eyed me, mischievously. "There are only two things she can say: yes or no… and neither one of those words has ever gotten in the way of any Southern woman I know!" she said, shaking her head and laughing.

The broker sounded really friendly this morning, and was quite excited when I told her who I was. She's French. Her name is Brigitte. It seems she's a fan from way back. Originally from Monte Carlo, she's married to an American businessman… and lives here now. She calls herself a diehard fan. She knows the lyrics to all of my songs, and said she'd seen me in concert several times! She wants my autograph. It's been a long time since anyone's asked me for an autograph. I hope I still know how to sign it!

I scrolled through the list of phone calls I'd made earlier, found the broker's number, and tapped it. To our surprise, not only did she say she'd be delighted to show us the commercial space, but she was actually en route there, as we spoke, to show the place to three businessmen who were very interested in it. She arrived within minutes of ending our phone call.

I was in love with the place, the moment I stepped foot inside. I immediately felt at home.

It was as if I'd been transported back in time… to some elegantly magnificent place in the past. Bold, spacious rooms with simple moldings, friezes, and heavy cornices defined the main room. Large, oversized, walk-in fireplaces with marble mantelpieces graced several walls. Heavy, tapestried drapes and matching overstuffed chairs, velvet covered settees and chaises were sprinkled throughout. Opalescent Marius Sabino chandeliers hung from the ceiling, while lovely little Tiffany lamps, and fluted wall sconces lit the room. The place was perfect. Eugenia was absolutely right. It reminded me of some of the magnificent European establishments I'd become accustomed to performing in. It all left me feeling dreadfully homesick!

We started on the main floor, went downstairs to the garden restaurant, then upstairs, to a room whose walls were tastefully covered in a beautiful shade of scarlet velvet. Eugenia and I separated from the others and found ourselves sitting at the oversized bar in the main room. I took in the room, my eyes traveling across the floor, along the walls, and up the elegantly winding stairs that reminded me of gentle waves on an ocean. Eventually, I brought my eyes and attention to Eugenia, who sat quietly, observing me.

"Snap out of it, Kitt! Girrrl…! Don't even think about it!" she warned, her eyes following mine, enjoying what she was seeing, almost as much as I was. "This mansion is too big for you to live in! Besides… there's no place left in here for my boy, Jason, to convert into a laboratory!" she joked.

I turned towards the bar. "Well now… it had crossed my mind that perhaps Jason could build his lab right behind this rambling bar!"

"This is one massive wet bar!" she agreed, stretching her arms out, in an exaggerated manner. "Jason would have one helluva time stirring his potions and brews back there!" With that, we high-fived and roared so loudly, our voices rang out across the room.

When our laughter subsided, my eyes met Eugenia's. "Don't you miss The Jazzy Joint? We had so much fun there! Everyone knew each other. Folks felt at home. It was like one great big family… everyone just sitting around in your cozy living room!"

When she spoke, it felt as if a veil of sadness had been thrown over her beautiful brown face.

"I do miss those days. But what I miss more than anything else, are the people… Frankie and his trio… the singing waiters and waitresses… their wild stories.

The times were so different back then, Kitt. The nightclub business isn't at all what it used to be. Everything about it has changed. Restaurants and clubs used to be owned and operated by people… people who knew their guests by name… and cared about them. Nightclubs and restaurants are huge franchises these days. They have no charm… no real personalities. They're cold and uninviting. Nightclubs are owned and operated by mega corporations now, not people."

I had always admired Eugenia's raw honesty. As gentle and loving as she was, she was a realist to the core. Nothing that fell from her lips was ever whitewashed or sugar-coated. Her words came from the heart, and they were as straight as arrows. Whatever she said to you was meant to help and heal… even if it meant hurting you, a little bit. As she always said: "*No matter how much icing you put on cornbread, it's still just plain old cornbread!*" Everything that had happened to me in life… had happened for a reason. Just like everything happening on this day, was happening for a reason. There was a good reason why I ended up here, in this place.

I studied Eugenia while she studied the room. She loved this place almost as much as I loved it. And like me, she belonged here, as well. "Do you know what I miss, Eugenia?

She tilted her head towards me, with a knowing smile. "What?"

"I really miss singing. I miss hearing the music... and moving to it. I miss going through the changes of getting all made-up and dressed up. I miss strutting across a big stage... the bright lights and the spotlight. I miss reaching for a microphone... holding it... and singing into it. But most of all, I miss the people... adoring audiences who blew me kisses... tossed roses onto the stage... and asked for my autograph."

Eugenia shifted and turned to face me. Her eyes were filled with tears. "When I came here last year... I immediately fell in love with the room... the ambience... And of course, the food was divine! But there was something else that was missing. Something that's just as important as food, drinks, and ambiance. Do you know what's missing here?" she asked, staring thoughtfully at me.

"Yes. A big, beautiful white concert piano, and a house full of happy people--eating, drinking, laughing, spending lots of money, and having the time of their lives!" I blurted out.

Eugenia laughed and waved her arm with a grand flair. "That's exactly what I told my friend, the chef, when I came here." Her eyes swept across the room. "All of this luxury and grandiose, and no one to enjoy it! What an awful waste!"

"Such a shame!" I agreed, turning my attention to the petite, reed thin woman who was sashaying towards us.

"Ciao! My name is Brigitte! I am the broker," she beamed. "Isn't this a magnificent place, ladies?" she continued, tossing her long, blonde mane to one side, and smiling as she turned, from me to Eugenia. With her hands on her hips, she planted her eyes squarely on me, and gushed. "I can't believe I'm actually in the same room with the legendary Kitt Kougar! Let's not forget my special autograph!" she exclaimed, promptly pulling a red ink pen and an old concert ticket from her briefcase. "You look fabulous! Better now than you did years ago!"

I jotted down a line from one of my hit songs, signed the ticket, and handed it back to her. "Thank you, Brigitte. You are very kind."

Her face brightened when she read what I had written. "Thank you! Thanks so much!"

"Now when I tell people that I had the pleasure of meeting you in person, I can show them your autograph as proof!"

"Listen… I'd still like to see the house on Twenty-Second Street. I need to find another place to live."

She lowered her head, slightly. "Yes… I understand. My sympathies to you and your son. It's so tragic what happened to your husband… and in your home… of all places." she whispered. "May I ask how you and your son are coping?

"They're coping better with each passing day." Eugenia interjected.

Brigitte shook her head, delicately. "For a while, I followed it on the news… hoping that your husband would be found alive. Then, the story just disappeared from the headlines."

"Thank you, for that. My son and I are managing much better now with Eugenia around." There was a brief moment of silence before I abruptly changed the subject. "I… I need to do something with my life. I want to start living again… for myself… and for my son," I said, walking, and looking around, as I spoke. "I don't know why… or what it is, but my gut tells me that this might be the perfect place for me to start. So… What do I have to do to get this place?"

Eugenia's eyes widened and her mouth flew open, as she nearly fell off of the barstool she was perched on. "Take it easy, Kitt! I thought we were house hunting… remember? You can't live here!"

"I know. I want to open a restaurant-nightclub-piano bar here. It's perfect! You will be the chef… and we'll get Santini to manage it. And I'll have a place where I can sing anytime I want to."

Eugenia swallowed and blinked her eyes several times, trying to come to grips with what was happening. "How ironic!" she said, shaking her head. "The night I visited my friend here, he asked if I'd be interested in taking over his position as the chef. He'd gotten another offer elsewhere. Life is strange!"

"Well… will you be *my* chef, Eugenia?"

Eugenia sighed, then smiled. "There's no use trying to talk you out of it. Your mind was made up the moment you stepped foot inside! Of course! I'd love to be your chef!"

The broker beamed, glanced at Eugenia, then turned to me. "This is just perfect!" she said, in a hushed voice, trying desperately to contain her excitement. Brigitte shot a quick glance at the three men standing behind her, near the entrance, leaned in closer towards us, and whispered, conspiratorially. "Please… give me a minute to say good-bye to these men," she said, with a friendly wink of an eye. "I must walk them outside to the street. I will be right back. I think you will like hearing what I have to tell you!" With that, she spun around and strutted quickly over to the three businessmen, chatting, as she quickly led them through the door, and outside, onto the sidewalk.

By now, I was standing, scanning the room, while my mind ran a million miles per second. I knew instinctively what to do with a place like this. I had, after all, spent more than half of my life performing in similar rooms. I desperately wanted this place! It had to be mine! I would take a chance with it. It might be a risk… but it was a risk worth taking. It would be my own leap of faith. Between Lem's various insurance policies and my own, sizable, personal wealth, I would be able to secure this place.

Eugenia and Santini had both endured huge financial losses in their lives. Either of them would have gladly shared in this business venture with me, willingly taking on the risks, even if it meant going out on a limb and borrowing money… from the wrong people. Knowing what they had been through, I would not… could not… ever dream of putting either of them in such a precarious position. I loved both of them too much! I would make this place work. And it would be on my own terms. But, in order for it to succeed, I would have to hire Eugenia and Santini. The best damn chef and best damn manager the world could offer--two people whom I could trust… with my life… my money… with my eyes closed. Together, we would be the perfect team! Eugenia was easy. She had rebounded from the shock quite well. Convincing Giancarlo Santini to participate in this madness of mine, was not going to be an easy task! As a matter-of-fact, it would be next to impossible!

When Brigitte returned, she cleared her throat, then dragged a barstool over so that she sat facing both of us. Bringing her thin hands together, her face lit up when she smiled. "This might be your lucky day, ladies," she said, crossing her slender legs. Her voice was friendly, but calculated, and businesslike.

I am so thrilled that we found each other. This is why I believe in divine intervention. The City is trying something new. For seized properties such as this, New York City now has a more politically-correct way of handling them. In an effort to achieve more diversity in commercial property ownership in the Chelsea area, the Mayor, the City Council, Small Business Alliances, and the City Planning Board, along with several women's equal rights groups, are working together to make sure that women, and specifically, women of color, are not left out, as has been the case in the past. This property has been earmarked as one of the places where the preferred buyer should be a woman of color. As I see it, you fit the bill perfectly. You are women, and you're Black. How do you Americans say it? Ahem… you're a shoo-in!

Eugenia and I looked at each other in total amazement, turned towards Brigitte, and bounced off of our barstools. We jumped up and down, laughing hysterically. Our laughter filled the empty room, bouncing and echoing from the floor, the walls, and the ceiling!

Brigitte even joined in on our excitement. We were like three little girls on Christmas morning!

"It looks as if you already have two of the most important ingredients," Brigitte observed, opening her arms wide enough to embrace both Eugenia and I. "You have each other. But running a place like this, successfully, will take more than great friendship. You'll have to fill it every night… with the right kind of customers… very rich people… with deep pockets."

Still elated, Eugenia and I shot each other a silent glance. Brigitte was absolutely right. To maintain a place of this magnitude would require a constant flow of money… a lot of money… other people's money. We left there and headed up to West Twenty-Second Street, where, upon first glance, I fell madly in love with the townhouse I now live in. Brigitte and I later took photographs together, which she printed and made sure I autographed. She made two hefty commissions--one from the sale of the brownstone, and the other, from the City of New York, for having properly brokered the sale of a seized commercial property, as well as securing financing from a community bank to help me purchase the property. By pairing me with the bank, I was able to save my cash and hold on to all of my personal wealth!

Talking Eugenia into allowing me to hire her as the chef was a breeze. The only thing we fought over was her adamantly insisting to work for free, or for far less money than she deserved. I included a generous salary for her in the business plan. But being Eugenia, she argued that she could hold off from being paid until after the place had started making money. To get over this hurdle, I had to be as stubborn as she was. I had to put her between a hard place and a brick wall, so to speak.

“Accept the salary, Eugenia, or I’ll find another chef!” I threatened, desperately praying and hoping that this hard-headed woman, whom I loved so much, would give in, come to her senses, and accept payment for her exceptional talent, time, and work. She finally gave in, however reluctantly, and agreed to be paid a salary. Besides, she needed the money. The divorce from her husband — The Right Reverend Raphael Prentiss — a popular, philandering, Harlem minister-turned-mega gambler, had taken more than a financial toll on her. It had cost her, her business, leaving her high and dry.

Subletting her spacious Harlem apartment to a Columbia University graduate student, and moving into the Riverside Drive brownstone with Jason and me, was, in a way, a blessing for all of us. Life has an interesting way of throwing people haphazardly together, at just the right moment. One down, one more difficult one to go.

Talking Giancarlo 'The Count' Santini into leaving his estate in Italy and relocating to another continent, was not going to be an easy task. As a matter-of-fact, it was going to be downright difficult… perhaps even next to impossible. I had more than my work cut out for me, and I needed Eugenia's help to persuade him.

After years of having successfully managed my singing career in Europe, and over-seeing numerous hospitality properties that had been in his family for generations, this wildly-spirited, fun-loving patrician had settled down into a quieter lifestyle, traveling occasionally, but residing mostly at the huge and ancient familial estate located just outside of Milan, Italy. A far cry from the frantically fast and furious lifestyle we had once shared.

How was I ever going to convince Santini to leave 'la dolce vita' in Italy, and move a continent away, to New York? I mean… he could return, periodically, for visits, right?

One thing was sure, I wanted, and needed Santini and Eugenia with me in this venture. I wanted both of them--one on either side of me. I also knew that wooing Santini to New York wasn't going to be a piece of *torta!*

Old habits are the worst to break. It's a good thing that I knew Santini's schedule. The best time to reach him would be somewhere between morning and afternoon--after he'd had his morning espresso, but before he was on his way to enjoy a two and a half-hour long lunch in some decadent ristorante. That way, he could mull over my proposal while savoring the best of Italian gastronomy! Milano is six hours ahead of New York. So, at 6 AM, I reached for my cell phone and called him. It was noontime in Milano.

Pronto! Santini's voice blared from the phone.

"Buongiorno! Come stai?" I replied.

Kitt, my dear, it is so nice to hear your voice!"

"It's great to hear your voice, as well."

Did they find Lem? Is he... is that why you're calling me?"

"No, not yet", I replied, feeling a sudden twinge of pain. "There's still no trace of him. It's as if he's vanished in thin air."

Well, as long as his body's not found, there's hope that he might still be alive... yes?"

"Yes. Jason and I are not giving up on finding him alive."

"To what do I owe this lovely call, my dear?"

The only way to deal with Santini is to be straightforward. So I got it all out at once.

"I want you to come to New York… to live here and work with me in a business I'm opening."

"My dear… I can't just pack a bag and move to New York! I mean… New York's a wonderful place to visit… but living there is something altogether different… and what would I do with my estate?"

"I know this is a lot to ask of you… but I need someone whom I can trust. I want you."

He let out a little chuckle.

You are kidding, aren't you?

" No. I'm not kidding. I am very serious."

What kind of business is it, Kitt?

"A restaurant-nightclub-piano bar… in an old Greek Revival Mansion!

"Mio Dio! That's going to cost you a fortune! You'll go bankrupt overnight!"

"It has three glorious levels! There's a romantic atrium restaurant downstairs… a private speakeasy upstairs… and on the main floor, a magnificent bar lounge, which Eugenia and I agree would make an amazing piano bar!"

Has Eugenia talked you into this madness?

"Quite the contrary. I talked her into being the chef. Now, if I can talk you into being the general manager, we'll have the perfect team." So eager to tell him how I'd gotten the place, the words all tumbled out at once.

No pun intended… but I actually got it for a song and a dance! It's as if it was sitting there waiting for me with open arms. It was seized property that New York

City had earmarked for under-represented people — people of color, women — who wanted to operate a business in certain communities. I've purchased it from the city. The lovely realtor who showed me the property, was kind enough to introduce me to a local banker. A community bank is financing it for me.

"Magnifico! You never cease to amaze me, Kitt! Seems you've already won half the battle! Listen... I don't want to discourage you... but... the nightclub business is risky and demanding. And as you already know, it can sometimes even be dangerous."

"I know that. But I need your expertise and experience. And I trust you. Please... think about it. It'll be good for you, too. With Eugenia as the chef, and you, the general manager, overseeing everything... I just know it would be wildly successful!"

"Eugenia is one of the best chef's I've ever known. She's perfect to run the kitchen. But... me, the general manager?"

"Yes! You'd make the perfect general manager!"

You have far more faith in me than I do myself!

"You're the only one I can trust... completely. Remember what you always said to me?"

"I've said many things to you over the years."

"That there was nothing the two of us couldn't do together!" I waited for him to say something. When he went silent on me, I continued: "I still believe that. Besides, I can't have Eugenia cooking and counting the money all at the same time!" I exclaimed, hoping to lighten the subject. The image of Eugenia stirring a pot with one hand while counting money with the other was a visual that made both of us laugh out loud. Anyone who knew her would swear that, if she had to, she'd do her damndest best to work both positions all at once!

Santini's laughing faded and was replaced with a serious business-like tone.

"What condition is this place in? If you bought it from the city… I would imagine it's somewhat dilapidated, if not falling apart. Si?"

"I've just texted you some photos of the place. You know what they say: A picture is worth a million words."

"Eccoli! They've just come through. I'm looking at some of the photos now!"

"So… what do you think?"

"Meraviglioso! This building reminds me of the place where you performed in Sounion, Greece!"

"And what does the room with the fireplaces and staircase remind you of?"

I don't believe my eyes! This room looks like a replica of the place I once owned on the French Riviera!

"Yes! That wonderful place in Cote d'Azur!"

"Stupendo! Where is this place located?"

"It's in the Chelsea area of Manhattan… near The West Village and the Meat Packing District."

"Yes… I'm familiar with that area. I rather like that part of the city."

"Santini… my vision of this place is similar to some of the wonderful places in Europe that you always booked me in… to perform. This would be the kind of place all of your jet-setting friends would love to visit!"

"I must say… the place is quite charming… with the right kind of appeal. It is definitely the kind of place my jet-hopping friends would enjoy!"

"Eugenia and I thought a place like this would be good for your spirit, as well. At the least, it would give you the chance to see your friends more often."

"Yes… yes… that would indeed, be nice! But still, leaving the estate… moving to New York… and overseeing a new establishment is a gigantic responsibility. It has to be the right move. I'll have to think about it. And… please… have Eugenia call me. I'd love to chat with her, as well."

"I will. She's excited about getting back into the food business!"

"I think this endeavor will be good for both of you. As for me… Let's see what happens."

"Is your cousin Vincenzo still living at the estate?"

"Yes… from the time we were children, this estate has always been his favorite place to live. He stays here more often than not."

"You're closer to him than you are to any of your other relatives, and you've always trusted him. Couldn't he keep an eye on things there for you? I mean… you have a full-time, trusted staff there… and it's not like you're moving to another world somewhere. You can always hop a flight back to Italy if you had to… to check in periodically."

"Uhm…! I suppose so. I need a day or so to consider everything."

"Of course. I understand."

"And what is this place called? Have you named it yet?"

"Eugenia and I have been tossing around a few names, but haven't settled on anything yet. We can't seem to find the right name… you know, one that makes us jump up and down."

"Well… it is located in the Chelsea area. How about Chelsea Place? That's catchy. It'll be easier to remember… and also make it easier for people to find."

"Hum… like New York, New York… Chelsea Place… I love that name! It's perfect! A place named after its location. You're right. No one will ever forget the name. And everyone will know that it's in Chelsea. I've always known you were a genius!"

Eugenia made the call to Santini, and in her words, they "chewed the fat" for over an hour. They both agreed that I should sing at least a couple of songs every night at Chelsea Place. A few weeks later, Eugenia and I were greeting Santini at JFK International Airport. Most of his necessary possessions were already shipped ahead of his arrival.

It took four weeks to get our license from the New York State Liquor Authority. During that time, Halo, a statuesque, multi-ethnic, multi-lingual, bartender, dropped by. The bar where she'd previously been employed, had suddenly closed, without notice. She was warm, friendly, and in need of work. Eugenia and I immediately liked her. After a rigorous interview with Santini, who happens to speak six different languages fluently, Halo was given the seal of approval, and we hired her. A waitstaff was stringently interviewed by Santini, and properly trained by Eugenia.

I auditioned pianist after pianist, ad nauseam. Almost every one of them was either good, great, or exceptional. Still, I hadn't found the right personality. One day, without a scheduled audition, Sam Smalls, a recent graduate of the Howard University Music Department, strode in. With a portable organ, saxophone, trumpet, and a harmonica in tow, he literally blew us all away! Handsome, charismatic, and engaging, he came dressed in a classic black tail tuxedo that reminded us of a young, present-day Liberace. His musical repertoire crossed every known genre, and included at least four times more songs than any of the other pianists I'd auditioned. We were mesmerized as he played, sang, and went smoothly from one instrument to another, at times, playing multiple instruments simultaneously. An extraordinarily gifted musician with an amazing voice, and tremendous stage presence, Sam also had an eloquent way with words. Having fervently entertained us with a nice mix of dance, pop, jazz, and Broadway favorites, he ended his audition with a rousing medley of popular Italian, French, Spanish, Calypso, and German songs. Sam Smalls was the perfect one-man-band for Chelsea Place!

On opening night, Chelsea Place was packed to the rafters with American A-listers, royalty, world leaders, celebrities, and international dignitaries and tycoons. Overnight — from New York to London, to Paris, to Milan, to Dubai--Chelsea Place became the talk-of-the-town in high-society social circles. Within days of opening its gilded doors, the press had appropriately designated Chelsea Place as Manhattan's "*preferred nighttime playground for the world's most powerful, most privileged, and most pampered people.*"

Chapter 16
By Invitation Only

Chelsea Place was closed to the public for the night. The event, by invitation only, included one hundred close friends and guests, giving the affair an added touch of exclusivity.

The room was stunning — filled with only black and white — accented with the soft glow of light flickering from scattered silver lanterns and candelabras. It was all about glamor and glitz. Eugenia and the staff had done a magnificent job transforming the room into an elegant Gothic lounge. Invitations, mailed out well in advance, told guests to wear only black or white evening suits, formal gowns, and either black, white, or silver Venetian style Baroque half-masks. Jason's mask, however, was different. Santini and Eugenia had agreed that everyone should wear half-masks so that they could eat, drink, and talk comfortably, unencumbered by the restrictions of full face masks. Not one balloon or streamer was found anywhere! Instead, twenty-one gigantic silver, metallic cutouts of the number '21' were suspended high above from the ceiling. With no visible strings attached to them, the glittery cutouts appeared to float, magically in the air. The effect took everyone's breath away! The tables were covered with black tablecloths and white satin runners. Placed at the center of every table, was a crystal vase, which contained a single black rose set against varying heights of white lisianthus, white snapdragons, and white larkspurs. Here and there, huge, floor-sized glass vases were filled with feathers and black and white beads.

Sam and Halo had been put in charge of the entertainment lineup for the evening. A repertoire of classical music and songs from *The Phantom Of The Opera* were creatively integrated into Sam's repertoire for the event. Exotic belly dancers, a sketch artist, a magician-illusionist, and mystical fortune tellers, hopped from table to table reading palms. Adding to the evening's enjoyment was a Fred Astaire and Ginger Rogers look-alike couple, who gave complimentary ballroom dancing lessons. But it was the contortionist, with his beyond flexible twists, folds, and bends, who stole the night. Everyone declared, hands-down, that he defied nature in every possible way!

Eugenia had spent days prepping and preparing Jason's favorite dishes, along with an elaborate feast of lavish finger foods. His birthday cake was a towering sculpture of German chocolate cake squares with extra layers of coconut and pecans. Champagne and Prosecco flowed endlessly. Sam and Halo assembled an amazing black and white montage of childhood photos of Jason. Throughout the evening, images, photos, and videos of him at various ages flashed silently on a large wall screen. When he arrived at Chelsea Place, he was met at the entrance by Santini and Big Joe, who promptly handed him a mask that was made to look exactly like him!

Jason studied the mask, intently. With every detail and feature of his face meticulously replicated, it was astonishingly too realistic! Even the texture felt like skin! Eerily, the mask brought his twin brother to mind. A thought he quickly dismissed. "I'm sure this was Aunt Genie's grand idea!" he remarked, heartily.

"One of many," Santini replied, enjoying the look of surprise on Jason's face. "You certainly know your godmother well."

Recovering, Jason placed the mask over his face.

"There's so much more to come!" Big Joe teased. "This is only the beginning!"

They tied a blindfold over his eyes and led him into the main room, where guests had been hushed into total silence. He was positioned on the stage next to Sam, who played a medley of his favorite songs. When Kitt removed the blindfold, the entire room erupted into loud roars, cheers, and shoutouts of HAPPY BIRTHDAY, JASON! Looking out at the room filled with elegantly-dressed men and women, in black and white gowns and formal suits, Jason was completely surprised. His eyes filled with tears, as he threw his arms around Kitt and Eugenia.

"Thank you for making this such a memorable birthday party!" he said, through tears. "I love you more than you will ever know!" As guests raised their glass in a toast to Jason, Sam struck up a rousing version of *He's A Jolly Good Fellow*.

The celebrations were well underway when Jason joined Kitt, Eugenia, Santini and Big Joe's little circle. "How did you guys ever pull this off?" he asked, incredulously.

Eugenia winked at Jason and tilted her head towards Kitt. "We kept your mom as far away as possible from all of the planning and organizing!" she exclaimed, roaring with laughter.

"We did everything we could to keep the plans under wraps!" Big Joe joined in.

Santini smiled and shook his head. "Imagine how difficult that must have been!"

"Almost impossible!" Jason added, laughing.

That they had succeeded in planning this fabulous affair without me, left me feeling somewhat naive and greatly out manipulated. "I'm shocked by just how sneaky and underhanded you guys are!" I huffed.

Pleased with her feat, and not yet done teasing me, Eugenia narrowed her eyes and spoke in a mysterious tone. "My dear… you have no idea what we are capable of doing!"

"Ouch! You're scaring me!" I responded, feigning shock.

Our little tit-for-tat brought another round of laughs. I noticed that Big Joe's eyes were fixed on the entrance. "Isn't Gallagher joining us tonight?"

His face lit up. "She most certainly is. She left the precinct and went home to shower and get fancied up," he said, glancing at his cell phone. " As a matter-of-fact, I'll go wait at the door. She'll be arriving any minute now."

Eugenia gave Jason an overly-dramatic once-over. "Honey… you're way too skinny! Looks like you've given up on eating!"

Embarrassed, Jason smiled and lowered his eyes. "Work has been so demanding these past few months. I really haven't had the time to eat properly," he said, sheepishly.

Santini turned to Jason. "Yes, you are a bit thinner than you were the last time I saw you. But you're also much taller. I must say that you look quite handsome and gentlemanly dressed in this tuxedo. You've definitely made the right impression on everyone here tonight."

Jason immediately regained his composure. "Thank you, sir," he said, tilting his head. "I have Aunt Genie to thank for the tuxedo, and you, for this exquisite tie and cummerbund set!"

"It all suits you very well." His eyes swept over the room. "I hate breaking away from our lovely little circle, but I think I'll excuse myself and mix and mingle a bit with our patrons."

Extending his right hand, he placed his left hand firmly on Jason's shoulder. "I'm so proud of how much you've matured, Jason! You're a remarkable young man. Don't be a stranger. We'd all love to see more of you."

Jason beamed. "Thank you, Santini. Seeing everyone tonight made me realize how much you all really mean to me. I've missed you. I will definitely make it a point to drop by on a regular basis."

"Great! *A dopo!*"

Eugenia flashed a big smile. "I'm taking my cues from Santini. I need to run downstairs to the kitchen, just to make sure everything is okay." Her voice softened. "But before I go, ditto everything he just said, and more. I'm especially proud of you. You barreled through two degrees concurrently, from Columbia University… landed a high-paying job… and you look like a Hollywood movie star! I'm so glad you're my godson!" She said, dabbing at her tears. She gave him a big bear hug, then headed to the kitchen.

Jason looked at me with big eyes. "It's just the two of us now."

"Said who?" I replied, linking my arm with his. "Come. I'd like to show you off to some of my favorite people. I want them all to know just how proud I am of you!"

Jason placed his hand over mine. "If only I could tell them all how proud I am of you!"

"There is no need to do that. Hearing it from you, is all that I need."

Jason shook hand after hand. He was hugged and kissed by well-wishers, and people whom he'd heard stories about. Until tonight, most of these people had only been faceless names to him. Seated across from me, his eyes surveyed the room. "Mom… you fit in so perfectly here with this crowd."

I glanced briefly out across the room. "Yes… I'm quite comfortable here. It's a safe place to be."

Nibbling from a plate of food Eugenia had personally prepared for him, he wiped his mouth, tilted his head, and looked directly at me. "The nightlife is your world. You belong here, the way I belong in a laboratory. We are both creatures and prisoners of our own chosen worlds."

I thought about what he said. Such simple, yet profound words. "I agree. We are all creatures and prisoners of one world or another." I looked up just as Big Joe and Gallagher were approaching. She looked so different, all dressed up in a slinky white sequined gown and matching half-face mask. This was a far cry from the bulky police uniform she wore when first we met.

Her voice was animated, but warm and friendly. "Kitt… thank you for inviting me tonight. You look fabulous in that gown!"

"The pleasure is all mine! I'm glad you could make it! You look smashing in white sequins!"

"Thank you! I see we already have a mutual admiration society!" she said, turning to look at Jason. "This handsome twenty-one-year-old must be the one-

and-only Jason, whom I've heard so many wonderful things about."

Jason blushed, wiped his mouth and hands, and was about to get up, when she stopped him.

"Don't you dare get up!" she ordered. "This is your night. Enjoy your food. Big Joe says you play a mean game of chess."

Jason shot Big Joe a look. "I think he plays an even meaner game of chess. He allows me to checkmate him."

Big Joe grinned and returned the look. "As I recall, the last time we played, it ended in a draw."

"Ahem… to be exact, the last three games ended in a draw." Jason pointed out, chuckling.

"Seems you two are long overdue for a game!" I chimed in, turning my attention to Gallagher, who was quite enjoying the guys' back and forth. "Big Joe, I'm sure Gallagher would like something to eat and drink. If my son will excuse me, I'll join the two of you for a while."

"Great idea! But remember… you ladies are my witnesses. Jason owes me a game! Call me when you're ready to play! Ok?"

"Scout's honor!" Jason called out.

Left alone, he finished eating, and wandered over to the screen. Taking in the montage of old photos and video clips of himself, Lem and Kitt, he began reminiscing. "Those were the best days!" he said, to himself.

Sam approached him, and watched, quietly. "You still miss your dad, don't you?"

Jason shook his head. "More than ever."

Sam's voice was colored with sadness. "I'm sorry about what happened to him. At least you have good memories. I never knew my father."

Not quite sure of what to say, Jason looked calmly at Sam. "I didn't know that. I knew you never talked about him. I just assumed you didn't have a close father-son relationship."

"We don't have any kind of relationship. He abandoned my mom and my older brother and sister shortly after I was born."

"I'm so sorry!"

"No need to be. He probably did us a favor. Ok... enough with the pity stories! I actually came over to tell you some good news."

"I'm always in the mood for good news!"

"Well... a couple of guys from Howard kept in touch with the genius kid... you know... your dead ringer. Someone forwarded his contact information to me."

"Are you kidding!" Jason shrieked. "This is the best news I've heard in a long time!"

"I'm as serious as taxes!" Sam glanced at his cellphone. "I have two different numbers for you, bro... where would you like me to send this information?"

"Please...! send it now! Text it to both of my numbers!" Jason reached for his phone. "Thanks! It just came through!"

"The exchange student's full name is Jakov Markovic," Sam said, reading from his cellphone.

Jason repeated the name several times. "Jakov Markovic… Jakov Markovic." *Jakov is a variation of Jacob,* he thought to himself.

"Hey! Another message just popped up! I'll forward that to you, as well!"

"This is fantastic, Sam! I don't know how to thank you!"

"No worries. I told your mom I'd do whatever I could do to help you connect with this guy. I hope you are related. After all of this, it would be a shame if you weren't."

Jason's eyes were glued to his cellphone as one text message after another popped up.

Jakov is currently living and working in Zurich, Switzerland…

Jakov's parents are diplomats. He lives in Zurich, Switzerland with them…

Here's the last phone number I have for Jakov…

See phone number, email, and mailing address for Jakov Markovic attached below…

"This is a treasure trove of messages!" Jason exclaimed, unable to contain his excitement. "Apparently, his parents are diplomats."

"Adoptive parents," Sam asserted. "I recall seeing family photos of them. He's definitely Black and they're definitely White. I believe they're Serbian."

Oh, God! There are too many coincidences! Jason thought. "Sam… What if I reach out to him, and he doesn't respond? Then what?"

Grasping Jason's excitement and concern, Sam suggested that he should initiate contact with Jakov, remind him of their time together at Howard, and then introduce him to Jason.

"That beats a cold call." Jason agreed. "For all he knows, I could be some cyber pervert trying to hack into his computer."

Sam glanced at the time. "I have a few minutes left before my break ends. Let's do this!" he said, already composing the text message. "Done deal! Hopefully Jakov will get back to me before the night ends. If he responds, I'll photograph you and send him some of your pictures."

The smile on Jason's face went from ear to ear. "Thanks a million, Sam. That should work. At least it's a good place to start."

"Gotta go hit the stage, bro!" Sam called out, hurrying back towards the piano.

Jason was scrolling through the long thread of text messages he'd gotten, when Halo sashayed over.

"Happy Birthday, handsome! Hope you're enjoying this fun masked event!"

"I am! You and Sam did a great job with this montage. Thanks!"

Her eyes went to the screen, then back to Jason. "It was our pleasure! Sam and I agree… you're a carbon copy of your dad. You look exactly like him!" She threw her arms around him and planted a kiss on each cheek. "Listen… the natives are thirsty… and they're getting restless!" she yelled out, turning and sprinting back towards the bar. "Drop by when you get a moment! I'd love to hear what our Columbia grad is up to these days!"

All was well. Santini and I had made our way through the room, stopping to speak briefly with everyone. No one had been left out, ignored, or forgotten. We finally got to sit… at a little table that had just been vacated. The young couple, members of the British Royal family, insisted that we rest, and had happily surrendered the table. Both of us thoroughly spent, we accepted, graciously. Jason came into view.

Santini raised his flute of Prosecco, and gestured in the direction of Jason. "You've done a great job with that young man."

"Thanks for taking him to museums and art galleries on all of those rainy days."

"It's a good thing we both liked being outdoors in the rain. I enjoyed those times as much as he did. Spending time with Jason made me feel useful."

"Useful? Jason loves and adores you! You are so much more to him than you think!"

"I hope so."

It was time to change the subject. "You guys did a fabulous job planning this black and white birthday bash for Jason. He will never get over this!"

"That's exactly what we were going for!"

"I'm still a bit ticked off that you did this behind my back. But I'm thrilled that Jason was really surprised and caught off guard! He needs to know what that feels like."

Sam ended his song and turned, searching the crowd. It was time to bring me up to sing Jason's favorite song: *What A Wonderful World.*

"Ladies and gentlemen... it is my pleasure to welcome to the stage... the heart and soul of Chelsea Place... the talented and gifted... Kitt Kougar!"

My eyes met Santin's. "If I'm the heart and soul of Chelsea Place... then you are definitely the blood that flows through it."

Santini smiled, leapt to his feet, and applauded. "It almost feels like the old days." he whispered, escorting me to the stage. "Don't you miss them?"

"More than you know."

By the time I ended my song, the entire dance area in front of the stage was packed with couples hugging and holding on to each other. Jason's towering birthday cake was finally rolled out and served by waiters who distributed sumptuous squares in a manner that was nothing short of theatrical. Eugenia had the honor of serving him the first piece along with the large '21' that sat on top. The guests were all given shiny little black boxes filled with samples of some of Eugenia's most popular sweets. I was busy saying good night to several stragglers, when I got a glimpse of Jason, seated alone at a table. His eyes were fixed on his cell phone, which was buzzing, non-stop. I watched as his fingers tapped hastily on his phone.

He waited for an incoming message. He responded with another battery of texting. The texting came to a full stop. He was reading now, slowly scrolling. Jason bounced out of his chair with so much force that he toppled his cake plate, and the phone flew out of his hand. His entire body was trembling, uncontrollably. The look in his eyes was as if he'd seen a ghost. Jason didn't utter a word. He didn't have to.

I saw it all in real time, and raced over to him. I stooped, picked his phone up off the floor and stared — stricken at the photos on the screen. I could hardly breathe as I scrolled through the photos. He looked and stood like a young Lem. The face, eyes, and smile were exactly like Jason's! My entire body went limp. Unable to stand any longer, I slumped down into a chair and read his message:

Hi Jason! Thanks for contacting me. Wow! My old suitemate from Howard University, Sam Smalls, reconnected with me. He said we looked like twins! I agree! We look so much alike it gives me goosebumps! I'm 21 years old, born 12-12-2000. How old are you? Can't get over how much we look alike!

My heart was pounding and I was having problems seeing, talking, and breathing. Fortunately, all of our guests had already left, and the last staff members were leaving. When I finally came to my senses, I took a long, hard look at Jason, and forced the words out of my mouth. "That's Jacob! I know it's him!"

Jason reached for his phone. "There are just too many coincidences for him not to be Jacob," he mumbled, scrolling through the photos. "His physique… his face. He looks more like dad than I do!"

"We've Got to speak to him right away, Jason!"

He nodded and glanced at the time on his phone.

"It's almost eight o'clock in the morning Geneva, Switzerland time.

"Geneva, Switzerland!"

"Yes. That's where he lives with his… adoptive parents."

"My guess is they're the same people who worked at the company's compound."

Jason's face tightened. "Yes… probably the couple who kidnapped Jacob."

I looked across the room and noticed that the last staff members had left. Remaining were Eugenia, Santini, Big Joe and Gallager — all totally engrossed in what appeared to be a rather animated and lively conversation. Luckily, we were far enough away that none of them paid any attention to what Jason and I were going through. "Let's leave now. I don't want to wait a minute longer. We'll take a cab to my house where we can speak more freely to him."

Jason began texting, feverishly. "I'll let him know that we'd like to FaceTime with him!"

I reached into my evening bag and handed Jason the keycard to my office. "Get our coats and meet me at the entrance. I'll tell them that the champagne finally got the best of you."

"That works! And… tell them that we have a very early morning," he added, dashing off.

I collected myself and began talking as I approached them. "I can't thank you enough for what you did. Jason had the time of his life! And… I'm afraid he drank more champagne than he should have!"

"Is he okay?" Eugenia asked, looking around for him.

Santini tilted his head to one side. "I thought he handled himself quite well."

"So did I," Big Joe chimed in.

Gallagher's hand met my shoulder. "You should be so proud of him. Jason is an extraordinary young man."

"Thank you," I returned. "Yes, I am very proud of him. And he is quite special."

Jason's voice was heard before he appeared. "Thanks, again, everyone for reminding me just how lucky I am to have you all in my life!"

"Jason came prepared to stay at my place. The two of us will be fine taking a taxi home. Besides, you guys don't need me here to secure and close the place," I said, smiling. "Chelsea Place is in good hands with you!"

Jason hugged and kissed Eugenia and Gallagher, then flung his coat around his shoulder.

"I'll see that you get into a cab," Santini said, helping me with my cape.

"I'll do the honors!" Big Joe boomed, leading the way to the door. Outside, A taxi was parked in anticipation of any late night stragglers, who might have been in need of a ride home.

“First house on the corner of Ninth Avenue and West Twenty-Second Street!” I yelled out. Jason and I were practically hopping out of the taxi even before he came to a complete stop. I fumbled with the security remote control as we hastily entered the house, and threw off our coats.

Jason’s phone buzzed. “It’s Jacob! He wants to FaceTime with us! Quickly mom… log into FaceTime on your Mac!” Jason ordered. “We’ll see him better on the big screen!”

I entered Jacob’s number and clicked the video button. Jason and I stood, watching anxiously as Jacob’s image appeared on the screen.

“Hallo. I’m Jakov. So… you wanted to see me in person,” he said. “Here I am.” His voice sounded so much like Jason’s that I did a double take.

“Thank you for allowing us to do this,” Jason said, unable to take his eyes off of Jacob.

“You are Kitt, Jason’s mom,” he said, smiling nervously.

I could no longer control myself. “I am also your mother!” I blurted out. “You and Jason are twins! I believe you are my son who was stolen from me at birth!”

Silence took over as everything came to a full stop, and the three of us stared at each other.

Jason moved in closer. "Where were you born, Jacob? Do you know who your natural parents are? Where are you from, originally?"

Jacob cast his eyes downward and sighed. "So many times I've asked my parents… I mean… my adoptive parents… the very same questions."

"And… what do they say?" Jason beckoned.

He hesitated. "They say that it doesn't matter where I was born… and that my birth parents are dead." He paused and raised his eyes. "Why do you call me Jacob?"

"Your parents are very much alive!" I said, unable to hold back tears. "Your father, Lem, named you Jason and Jacob."

"Why have you waited twenty-one years to look for me?"

"I didn't know I was carrying two babies. You were a hidden twin."

"When did you find out about me?"

"Yesterday."

"Yesterday?"

"She… our mom was in and out of consciousness the night she gave birth to us," Jason explained, tears flowing down his cheeks. "It was a stormy and harrowing night. After we were both delivered, dad took a nap. When he awoke, the lab assistant and the groundskeeper were gone… and so were you. He looked all over for you. When he didn't find you, he thought it was best not to let mom know what had happened."

Jacob wiped away tears from his eyes. "The lab assistant and the groundskeeper… were they…"

"They were Serbians." Jason answered.

"My adoptive mother is named Katarina. She is a biotechnician. My father…" He paused and cleared his voice. "My adoptive father is named Andrej. He has always worked as a zookeeper."

The hurt and pain in his voice destroyed me. I moved closer to the screen and looked into watery eyes. I wanted to reach out and grab him… to hold him. I wanted to make up for all of the years that we'd lost! So much precious time had been stolen from us! "Jacob… For god sake… look at me! Can't you see that I'm your mother! Look at Jason! You two are identical in every possible way!" My heart was pounding and I began hyperventilating. I desperately needed air. "Don't you see? They've lied to you all of this time! Those people took you away from us. They are criminals!" I yelled.

Jacob shook his head vigorously. "I know! I know! Two people could not look any more alike than Jason and I do!" he exclaimed, looking at Jason, and wiping away tears. "But I want to be one hundred percent sure that you are really my blood mother and brother!"

My eyes were fixed on Jacob. I studied his features, face, his body language, every inch and angle of him. I turned, and looked at Jason. It took my breath away, how much they looked alike. I was gripped by tension so enormous that I could not think clearly. Back and forth my eyes went, between them. I watched as they leaned in, silently, and studied each other. The slant of their heads, movements, and facial expressions perfectly mirrored each other. They seemed to breathe in unison.

"What is your blood type, Jacob? I asked, nervously.

"It is somewhat rare," he replied, glancing at Jason. "It's B-negative."

"So is mine!" Jason asserted, holding onto the screen and moving his face within inches of it. "Our birthmarks!" he cried out. "The night we were born, Dad noticed that we had identical birthmarks." He paused and took a breath. "They are identical birthmarks that mirror each other."

Over the years, Lem, Eugenia, and I had often teased Jason about his unusually shaped birthmark. I was suddenly gripped by terrifying fear. What if Jacob's birthmark did not look like Jason's? I was puzzled, but mustered up enough nerves. "What exactly do you mean by mirroring birthmarks?"

"That's a rare occurrence with identical twins. It means their birthmarks look alike but are located in opposite places on their bodies."

Jacob sniffed. "I do have a birthmark. But most people do."

"I think I know exactly what your birthmark looks like, and where it's located on your body," Jason said, intently.

I stared at Jacob and sighed. "What does your birthmark look like?"

"A starfish," they both said, in unison! The pitch and intonation of their voices were so perfectly matched that they blended and sounded like one voice! Relieved beyond words, I was left in a state of wonderment, rendered speechless, and in total awe.

"Mine is behind my right ear," Jacob said, smiling, broadly and turning to show us. "I'm willing to bet that yours is behind your…"

"Left ear," we all said together, bursting into laughter and tears!

"Do you need any more proof that we are twins?" Jason asked, crying so hard he could hardly get the words out.

"No. I don't need any more proof. From the moment I saw your photos, something deep down inside told me we were twins." He turned his tear-stained face towards me. "I'm convinced beyond a shadow of a doubt that you are my birth mother."

We cried and laughed… laughed and cried. Jason and I pressed our hands against the screen, wanting so much to touch Jacob's.

"When can I meet you?" Jacob pleaded, trying to contain his emotions.

I glanced at Jason, then back at Jacob. "As soon as possible! We'll book a flight today and let you know when we'll be arriving."

"What do I tell my… ahem… adoptive parents?"

"Tell them absolutely nothing!" Jason implored. "Please… Jacob… I beg you, do not tell them that we've found you! That would put the three of us in grave jeopardy! Be yourself. Act normal, as if nothing has changed." Jason paused and stared at Jacob. "Promise me you won't say a word to them!"

"I promise!" Jacob complied, both of them extending their pinkies at exactly the same time. That mirrored image evoked a fit of laughter.

I aimed one pinky at Jacob, and the other, towards Jason. "Once we meet up with you in Switzerland, the three of us will figure out how to safely, and best handle everything!" I said, trying to reassure him.

"Tell Lem… ahem… Dad… that I can't wait to meet him!"

Jason gazed silently at his brother and nodded. Unsure of what to say, he turned towards me.

This was a bittersweet moment. But I was determined not to have this happiness we were sharing snuffed out of us. We were so caught up in the excitement of finding Jacob that we'd neglected to tell him about what had happened to Lem. I managed a faint smile. "Nothing on earth would please your father more than to know that we've found you! We'll tell you more about him when we see you."

"What's the best time to reach you this evening?" Jason asked.

"Uhm… how's four p.m. your time? That'll be ten in the evening here."

"Great! Is there someplace safe, away from your parents, where you can speak freely?"

"Yes, the laboratory where I work. It's open twenty-four hours a day. There are several rooms there that I can use, privately. It's one of my favorite places. I'll tell my parents that I'm working late on a new project."

Jason looked up and grinned. "The laboratory is also my favorite place!"

"You're definitely twins!" I gushed, shaking my head. "Honey… I'm so happy that we've found you! For twenty-one years, I didn't even know you existed. If I had known, I would have searched the world for you! And now, I'm looking at you… and talking to you. I can't wait for the moment when I can hug you, and hold you!"

Jacob's eyes watered. "I can't wait either, Mom! I can't wait! Soon!"

"Yes, soon!" I sobbed. "As much as I'd like to just stay here and look at you all day long… we've got to get busy making flight and travel arrangements… and hotel reservations must be made!"

Jacob nodded his head. "I know." He glanced at Jason and smiled. "I love you, Jason!" Then turned to me. “I love you, Mom! Thanks for finding me!” He cuffed both hands over his mouth and blew us a kiss.

“We love you, too!” Jason and I cried out, returning a barrage of air kisses to him.

“We’ll FaceTime you at 10 p.m. sharp your time tonight. Right now we have to make plans to get to you, and bring you home!”

Chapter 17
Brothers For Life

As Jacob logged off, then disappeared, Jason and I held our gaze glued to the screen. We embraced, held on to each other, and cried, as hot, salty tears poured from our eyes.

"First, we will bring Jacob home," I whispered. "Then, we will find Lem!" I wiped the tears from Jason's face with my hand, spun around and leaned into my computer. "Bringing Jacob home will make this the best Christmas we've had in a long time! I need to book our flights now... and reserve a hotel room in Geneva..."

"Mom... I'm thrilled that we've found Jacob! This couldn't have happened at a better time. I want to bring my brother home more than anything. But, remember... we still have to deal with your condition!" Jason spoke in a low, heavy voice. "Before we do anything else, I'll need to draw some blood from you to get an analysis of your current biostatistics. I'll also need to check and monitor your vitals to see if there are any extreme changes." He paused. "And most importantly, we need to figure out how you can best harness, exploit, and utilize these powers you have. You need to know how to trigger as well as curb your new powers. You're at a point now where you can't allow them to pop up at random, inopportune times. You must always be in control. It is vitally important that you learn how to prompt them, how to activate your superhuman abilities."

"Can't that wait until after I've booked our…"

"No. It can't wait!" he snapped. "I definitely need to do your blood work and vitals now so that I can try to figure out why your transformation is happening so rapidly and so… so aggressively. I brought everything I needed to test you. They're in the big bag I dropped off yesterday evening."

I eyed him, curiously. "Okay… let's do that now. I understand why that can't wait. But… can we put off trying to figure out how to turn my powers on and off until after we return from Switzerland? I mean… if we could leave now, I would. But I'm definitely getting us on the first flight tomorrow, that's bound for Geneva, Switzerland."

A worried look covered his face. "I would prefer that we at least spend some time on studying your triggers, just so you know how to manage your powers. You never know. Things happen."

"Honey, what can possibly happen in two, or three days? Besides, if Jacob is also transgenic, and endowed with superhuman abilities, as Lem thought he might be, doesn't it make sense just to wait until we're back here and you can study both of us at the same time?"

Jason shot me a thoughtful look, and slowly shook his head. "Yes… perhaps you're right." He went to fetch the small suitcase, returned, and skillfully arranged a series of medical devices on the desk.

"What are these things, Jason?"

He pointed to a round machine that held a rotating container. "That is a portable centrifuge. It will spin and analyze your blood samples for me."

"My blood samples! Ouch! How much?"

"In order to do a biometry reading, I'll need a small amount of your blood. One vial will do," he replied, extending my arm. He swiped an alcohol pad over the area, and patted my arm until blue veins popped up. With expert precision, he inserted the hypodermic needle, attached the vial, and out flowed brownish red blood. That done, he quickly covered the injection site with gauze and placed a band-aid strip over it. "Great! I'll run this through the centrifuge now and see what's going on with your biometrics. Once that's done, while you're booking our reservations, I'll hop a cab and make a fast trip uptown to pick up a few items of clothing… and the gold watches Dad gave me on my thirteenth birthday."

"For the world I could not understand why Lem would buy two identical gold watches, both with the initials "JJ" engraved on them. Now it all makes sense. You and Jacob have the same initials."

Jason smiled broadly and shook his head. "When he gave me the watches, he told me to hold on to the second watch for Jacob. Dad always believed that I would one day find my twin brother. I want to surprise him, and let him know that dad was always thinking about him."

"Great idea, honey! Go, grab your things quickly. And when you return, be sure to give me both watches. I'll hold on to them for safe-keeping while we're traveling." I spun around to the computer, and began searching for non-stop flights to Geneva International Airport. I booked a flight for the following evening — a roundtrip for Jason and I, and a return flight for Jacob. A reservation for two days was made at a small boutique hotel in the center of Geneva's Old Town, near Saint Pierre's Cathedral.

Jason made it uptown to Riverside Drive and back in a little over an hour. He reached inside his carry-on size duffle bag, and promptly handed me two beautiful boxes that contained their watches. Then he crossed over to the side of the desk where his medical gadgets were set up, and pulled on a pair of gloves.

Our flights and hotel reservations made, I turned around to observe Jason. "We're at that bridge where we have to let people know about Jacob," I asserted. "Santini, Eugenia, and Big Joe will need to know why we're making this sudden trip to Switzerland. It's impossible to hide Jacob's existence."

Jason extracted several samples from the Centrifuge, deposited them on a small slide and peered into the microscope's lens. A worried look covered his face, as he looked up and nodded. "I know, Mom. We'll also have to thank Sam for making all of this happen."

I shook my head and stood up. "Yes, Sam! Thank God for him! We'll never be able to repay him for what he's done." I studied the frown on Jason's face. "What's wrong?"

He pulled away from the microscope and looked dead on at me. "The analysis shows hyperactive levels of transferred genetic activity in you," he said, clearly puzzled.

"How many times do I have to ask you to tell me this stuff in plain and simple English?"

He swallowed and took in a deep breath. "It means that your senses and powers are far greater than I had originally thought they were." He hesitated. "Your senses are so greatly enhanced, that if you don't learn how to harness them, they could possibly outpower you."

I breathed to still my trembling. "The look on your face tells me that there's nothing you can do to help me with that. I guess I'm on my own."

Jason shook his head. "What doesn't come to you instinctively, you'll learn through trial and error." He paused. "Based on the rapidity of this transformation, I can tell you that you'll need to learn how to harness your powers as soon as possible. I think we should at least get started tonight."

"We don't have time tonight. We'll have to deal with that when we return from Switzerland with Jacob. We're booked on the first flight out tomorrow morning."

Jason stroked his furrowed brow, shuffled through his large sack, and pulled out a small bottle with clear liquid. "I guess I could use a little of this suppressant drug dad gave you over the years to keep the transgenic manifestations chemically inactive."

"How long will that last?" I asked, hopefully.

"A small amount will render your powers inert for about a week. That'll give us more than enough time to get to Switzerland and back before anything extreme kicks in."

"Perfect!" I exclaimed, relieved, as I reached for the bottle.

Jason made a mad dash to the kitchen and returned with a bottle of water. He poured several drops of the substance into the water, and handed it to me. "It has to be mixed into water or some kind of liquid." He shook the bottle and handed it to me. "Here, drink this now. It takes several hours before it goes into effect."

I took down the entire bottle all at once. "We need to break the news about Jacob to family members and friends… before we bring him home. That will make things easier for him, and it will give everyone time to prepare themselves to welcome him."

"I want Jacob to be welcomed by everyone with open arms. It won't be easy for him. It will take time for him to adjust, and feel at home here. I'm going to do everything possible to make life easier for him." Jason sighed and looked away. "I wish I had told you about Jacob when dad first told me about him. I owe you and Jacob so much!"

"It's all in the past now. Stop beating up on yourself. Soon you'll be reunited with your twin brother, and I will have another son. That's all that matters now."

A smile lit up Jason's face. "But how do we break this wonderful news about Jacob to everyone? How do we tell people about him? This is all so incredibly unbelievable!"

I reached for my phone. "I'll call family members on Edisto later tonight.

Right now, I'm going to call Santini, Eugenia, Big Joe and Sam, and see if they'll come here as soon as possible. I'll tell them that we have some really important news to share that can't be told over the phone. We'll have to look them in the eye when we tell them about Jacob." I paused, paced, then turned to Jason. "We'll have to tell them the truth about Jacob without revealing what Lem did to me. Considering the hand we've been dealt, telling them a half-truth is the best we can do."

Jason shook his head, and began putting away his medical items. "I agree. Call them. Let's do this for Jacob!"

Eugenia arrived first, then Santini, followed by Big Joe and Sam. We sat in the living room, on the circular sectional, with everyone facing each other. This circle, here in my home, was the perfect place for the news I was about to share. Not knowing what to expect, they all stared at me silently and anxiously.

Eugenia's eyes shifted from Jason to me. "Kitt… you know that I am never in the mood for bad news. So please, tread lightly."

Santini stirred and sat upright. "I admit that this emergency meeting here at your home leaves me quite unsettled, as well."

"Whatever it is, as you can see, we're all here for you and Jason," Big Joe blurted out.

Sam was so uncomfortable that he just sat quietly, his eyes fixed on Jason.

Jason, the most uncomfortable person in the room, sat next to me, fiddling with his fingers.

I took a deep breath, exhaled, and stood up.. "Thanks, guys for dropping whatever you were doing and getting here so fast. I truly appreciate every single one of you… and I trust you… which is why I've gathered you here today." I smiled and glanced at Jason.

He looked up and begged, "Mom… please… let me…"

"No… I've got this!" I retorted. "First of all, let me put everyone's mind at ease. Neither Jason nor I am sick or dying."

A collective sigh of release filled my cozy little living room.

"That said, I'm going to get right to the point. Twenty-one years ago, when I gave birth to Jason, unbeknownst to me or Lem, I was actually carrying twins..."

"Twins!" Eugenia exclaimed. "How was that possible?"

"I was carrying a hidden twin — another little boy, who was undetected by the ultrasound. Long story short, I gave birth to two boys — Jason, and his twin brother Jacob." I paused and prepared myself for what followed. "Jacob was kidnapped, shortly after he was born, by a lab assistant who helped Lem deliver the babies."

Eugenia leapt up. "What? Why am I just..."

"But... you've never even mentioned this to me!" Santini scowled.

Big Joe held his hand up, and shouted. "Please! Everyone! Let her finish! Let her finish! This can't be easy!"

Jason sprung to his feet. "Mom didn't know anything about my twin brother! She was sick and unconscious when he was born. She and Dad were caught in a harrowing snow storm, in Vermont, and had to seek refuge at a place where dad occasionally worked. After we were both delivered, the lab assistant gave dad a cup of tea, laced with a sedative, and convinced him to take a desperately needed nap. When he awoke, he discovered that Jacob, the female lab assistant, and the groundskeeper, were gone." Jason paused, took a deep breath, and stared at Sam. "Dad never told mom about my twin brother. I was ten years old when he finally confided in me. He made me promise not to tell mom."

I looked at Sam, and smiled. "Jason told me about Jacob two days ago, Sam. That's why I was so intent on you tracking him down. I'm sorry I didn't level with you. But Jason and I had to be sure that he was, in fact, Jacob."

Sam's eyes widened with disbelief, as he rose, awkwardly, from the sofa, and crossed over to Jason. "Oh, my God!" he exclaimed. "My suitemate from Howard! That explains why you two look so much alike! He is truly your twin brother! Something always told me there was a connection!"

All heads swiveled towards Sam. Puzzled, Santini shook his head. Eugenia opened her mouth, and for once, in all of the years I've known her, not a single word came out. Big Joe sat, silently and thoughtfully.

Jason reached for Sam, who was still in so much shock that his legs almost gave way. Sam's entire body shook, as he made his way over to Jason and man-hugged him. "I knew it! I knew it!" he said, grinning from ear to ear.

Jason held on to Sam, and patted him on the back with both hands. "It's all because of you! You've always insisted that we looked like twins!"

Eugenia heaved herself up. "Okay! Okay! This is a lot to take in!" she shouted. "I can't help but think that I'm missing a big chunk of this incredible story!"

Sam turned to Eugenia. "When I first met Jason I told him how much he reminded me of an exchange student I knew briefly at Howard University. Yesterday, Kitt asked if I could contact him. I reached out on social media, and bam! Got all of his contact information. Just like that!"

By now, Santini and Big Joe were also standing, shocked speechless, and shaking their heads, slowly coming to terms with what they'd heard.

Santin's hand met my shoulder. "My dear... are you one hundred percent sure this is your son?" he asked softly.

All eyes turned and seemed to echo what he had asked.

"There's no doubt about it!" Jason interrupted. "We FaceTimed with him for almost two hours earlier today. We asked all of the right questions... and got all of the right answers." Jason chuckled. "We even finish each other's sentences!"

"We're positive," I asserted. "They look exactly alike. They're the same size. They have the same birthday. The same voice. The same blood type. And they even have the same birthmark," I said, looking directly at Eugenia.

"A starfish behind his ear?" she returned, incredulously, shaking her head. "You've got to be kidding! Okay... I'm convinced!"

Jason pulled out his cell phone and showed photos of Jacob. "He lives in Geneva, Switzerland now with his adoptive parents," he said, with an edge, staring at Sam.

"Would that be the Serbian couple who adopted him?"

Jason and I nodded. "We believe they are the same people who kidnapped him twenty-one years ago."

As she gazed at Jacob's photos, Eugenia's hand went to her mouth, then to her chest. For a moment, she was left speechless. Her eyes watered and filled, until big teardrops fell. "I guess now they'll be two of you to love," she said quietly, to Jason.

"He's a dead-ringer for you, Jason," Big Joe mused, studying each photo calmly, and intently. "For sure, he's your doppelganger."

Santini, clearly awe-stricken, stared silently at Jacob's photos. He examined each photo carefully, then held them next to Jason's face.

"It would be impossible to tell the two of you apart," he finally uttered. "You're identical in every conceivable way! Now what?"

"Our flight and hotel room are already booked. Jason and I fly out tomorrow morning. We will return in two days with Jacob. I will need you guys to hold down the fort while I'm gone."

Eugenia, Santini, Big Joe and Sam shook their heads. They looked like a family of deer caught in the headlights. It was clear that they were all still reeling from shock.

"Are you going to get any pushback from his adoptive parents?" Big Joe queried.

"Pushback!" Eugenia huffed. "If these are the same scumbag people who kidnapped Jacob, they need to have kidnapping charges brought against them!"

Sam shook his head in agreement. "They need to be pushed behind bars for what they did!"

Santini ran a hand over his face. "Why must you and Jason fly to Switzerland to retrieve Jacob? He's twenty-one. He's an adult. He can come and go as he pleases. His adoptive parents can't keep him there against his will. Just pay for his flight to New York."

"No! No! We're too close to reuniting with him! I don't want to leave anything to chance!" I turned and shot Jason a look. "We've got to get to him! You and I, together. We have to bring Jacob back home. Nothing will get in my way!"

"I gave mom my word. I promised her that if it's the last thing I do, we're bringing my brother home. We're his family. This is where he belongs. Full stop."

Big Joe stared at Jason, and nodded, approvingly. "Spoken like a real man, Jason." He turned to me. "Do you need a ride to JFK Airport tomorrow morning?"

"Thanks, but that's all been taken care of already. I've reserved a car service to the airport."

"That's ridiculous to take a car service!" Santini exclaimed. "Someone... one of us should accompany you to the airport!"

"Santini's right!" Eugenia chimed in. "And I think that person should be me!"

"Thank you all, but no thanks! The car service it will be. I don't want to get you up and out of your beds any earlier than necessary. Besides, you'll have a long night ahead of you at Chelsea Place!"

An amused expression brightened Santini's face. "Well, if you won't let us see you off, there is one big favor I'd like to ask of you."

"Ask and ye shall be given," I said, playfully.

"Would you please bring me an assortment of Zimtsterne and Brunsli cookies! They are simply the best Swiss cookies ever! They shouldn't be hard to find this time of the year!"

"I totally agree!" Jason yelled out. "Those cookies are addictive! Don't worry. I'll bring several boxes of them back for you!"

I gave everyone a big hug and ushered them towards the door. "I love you all much more than you'll ever know. Now, if you'll forgive my rudeness, I'm kicking you out. Jason and I have to pack our carry-ons and get ready for our early flight."

With hugs, cheek kisses, and "I love yous" returned, Eugenia, Santini, Big Joe, and Sam wished us safe travels, said their good-nights, and left.

While Jason packed and repacked his duffle bag, I called my parents… texted photos of Jason and Jacob to them… and told them about the grandson they never knew existed.

Chapter 18
Chaos and Carnage

Jason and I were so excited about seeing Jacob that we practically talked through the entire flight. With the exception of a few random catnaps, the only thing we could think and talk about was Jacob. Jacob! Jacob! Jacob! There was so much we wanted to say to him. So many questions we wanted to ask him. What kind of life had he lived? Were his adoptive parents good to him? Did he have a happy childhood? What were his favorite foods? His favorite things to do? What was his favorite color? His favorite book? Was he happy? There were twenty-one years of catching up to do. Twenty-one years of filling in the blank spaces of time that had been stolen from his life… twenty-one years of Jacob that had been snatched away from us.

The more I thought about it, the angrier I got. What drove them to doing something so indefensible, so cruel and amoral? What kind of human being steals a child from his family? Why would a woman do something so dreadfully wrong to another woman? Was she incapable of having her own child? Did she once have a baby whom she had lost? I hoped that they had been good, loving parents to him. I prayed that he had not been abused, and mistreated by them. They were going to pay for what they'd done to us. I would do everything possible to bring them to justice and hold them accountable for breaking up my family. Once Jacob was safely back in New York with me, my next move would be to bring the harshest kind of punishment on the Serbian couple.

And Lem. How could he not tell me about Jacob? The audacity of him dragging Jason into that unholy tangled web of deception! As far as I was concerned, Lem was damn near complicit in Jacob's kidnapping. Lem! Oh God! Lem! How do I even begin to tell Jacob about what had happened to his father? That won't be easy, but it has to be done. No more secrets! Ever! We'll cross that bridge when we get to it. Right now, the only thing that mattered was getting to Jacob and bringing him back home. That was the only thing I could focus on.

As the plane was approaching its final leg to Geneva Airport, Jason and I sat quietly, gazing through the window. Flying over Lake Geneva, to our right, along the French-Swiss border, sat the Jura Mountain range. Situated to the left of us were breathtaking views of snow-capped Alpine mountains — with Mont Blanc, the massive 'White Mountain' towering through the clouds. A bright, morning sun set against the beautiful Alps was exactly the kind of welcome we needed.

A testament to Swiss efficiency, our flight arrived a little ahead of the scheduled time. With soft, Christmas music playing in the background, the Swiss Airbus descended, and landed with a gentle touch down, braking smoothly, as its wheels glided along the runway. In a hearty Swiss-German accent, the pilot wished everyone a joyous Christmas season, his voice, outdone by the continuous sounds of cell phones, and ringtones that chimed throughout the cabin.

Jason received a text message from Jacob just as the plane came to a complete stop. "Jacob's less than ten minutes away. He'll meet us at the middle taxi stand in the arrivals section. We should look for a sky blue 2020 Skoda Octavia." A look of approval gleamed across Jason's tired face. "A Skoda Octavia is the perfect car. It's practical, reliable, spacious, and comfortable. That's the kind of car I would buy!"

"And sky blue is exactly the color you'd buy it in!" I added, returning a big smile.

With less than two weeks to the countdown of December 24th, the Geneva Airport was filled with the smells and sounds of Christmas. Passing through the international security checkpoint without incident, I automatically went into travel safety mode and flung my travel tote across my body, pressing it securely against my chest, and away from sticky fingers of would-be pocket thieves. With our carry-ons in tow, Jason and I talked, laughed, and marveled at the ornate fairy lights and sightings of jolly *Samichlaus* everywhere. Rows of magnificent *Adventskranz* fir wreaths, lit with enormous candles, hovered overhead, ran the entire length of the airport's atrium. Tempting fragrances radiated from perfumeries. Aromatic, chocolate-filled kiosks lined the concourse floor. And specialty bake shops flaunted towers of *Chrabbeli, Zimtsterne, Mailänderli, Brunsli,* and other assorted delectables in their windows.

Notwithstanding the cold Alpine air outside, it was the perfect day — crisp, clear, and festive.

Jason and I took it all in, and plowed through the crowded concourse — filled more than usual with throngs of weary travelers, all excited and geared up for the approaching Christmas holiday. Our pace was slowed when we noticed that there was some kind of commotion developing ahead of us in the main terminal.

In one hellacious moment, everything changed. Blood-curdling cries rang throughout the airport's massive corridors. Scream after frantic scream echoed from every which direction. In front of me, to my left and right, people were convulsing, asphyxiating, and gasping for air. They were falling, collapsing, and dropping to the floor like flies! I could not believe what was unfolding before me. There wasn't even time for me to process the thought: *What on God's earth is happening?* Were it not for my eyes seeing this, I might have dismissed the whole thing as some freakish nightmare. I watched in utter disbelief as writhing bodies fell to the floor, one after the other. Those who had not fallen to the floor, were running, trying to find a way out. Bodies were strewn all over the floor, on benches and chairs, puking, and spitting. Some were twisted and jerking, violently. Others laid so still that I believed them to be already dead!

"Jason! What the hell is happening!" I cried out, turning around to where I thought he was. I freaked out when I realized that he was no longer by my side. My eyes spun rapidly across the chaos and mayhem that had consumed the entire concourse. I finally got a glimpse of him trying to help a screaming mother with her children. Two of the little ones were in fetal positions on the floor, squirming, kicking, and crying. The third child's limp body dangled lifelessly from the mother's arms.

WARNING! WARNING! Evacuate the premises now! Everyone must exit the airport immediately! We are under attack! Please exit quickly and safely! Big red warning lights that pointed to exits flashed throughout the airport, as the announcements blared from the main public address system, over and over again, in French, German, Italian, and English.

"Jason! Jason! Run! We have to get out of here now!" I yelled, running towards him. I was determined to get to him and pull him away. "Come on!" I shrieked, watching in horror as he knelt on the floor, coughing and clutching his neck! "I'm coming to get you, Jason! Hold on! Please, hold on!" Trying desperately to get to him, I looked up and found myself running against the tide. I was confronted head-on by a sea of screaming, panic-stricken people. They flooded my path, rushed into me, and knocked me to the floor. I was trampled on, run over, and stomped on with feet from hordes of terrified people fleeing the airport. Unable to get up, and now, disoriented, I remained on my knees and hands. My crossbody tote dangled beneath me as I was pushed along in a wild, frenzied stampede of humans.

My powers! I thought. *Where are my super powers? How do I ignite them? How do I turn them on?* Then it dawned on me: *I can't ignite them! I can't!* Jason had purposely suppressed them as a precautionary measure to prevent them from surfacing while we were traveling! I had fought Jason, and argued that there wasn't enough time to evaluate my powers! He had pleaded with me to explore them! He tried to tell me how important it was to know how to turn them on and off. *Why was I so stubborn? Why didn't I listen to him? God help me! What have I done? What have I done!*

I was still crawling on my knees, bloodied, and knocked senselessly, when my tote bag hit the ground with a thud, pulling me down. I fell onto my back and stared up at the sky — a sign that I was somehow, miraculously, still alive! Lying there, I sensed the masses of casualties around me, the hordes of sickened, shocked people, scattered unmercifully, about. Faintly, I heard the sounds of emergency medical vehicles as they careened to the site. Fire engines and police arrived, their sirens blaring from every direction. There was nothing but mayhem, pandemonium, and confusion all around. Screams and cries of uncontrolled, uncontained mass hysteria flooded my mind, resounded, and bounced against my eardrums. My head pounded with unimaginable pain! There were dreadful sounds of people wailing, crying, and mourning. I felt the ugly cold of death and the dead surrounding me. I was sinking… deep into darkness.

I was in a stupor when a familiar face interrupted the blue above me, and leaned into my face, his eyes, piercing into me. I tried to lift my hand to touch him, but could not move at all, paralyzed by the bombardment of pain that had been inflicted upon me. My entire body was ravaged, broken, and damaged by an onslaught of frightened feet. I was still sinking into that deep, dark hole. Amidst all of the turmoil, his voice emerged. "Mom… it's me, Jacob. Please don't leave me! I need you to stay alive! You must stay alive! I can't lose you again!"

It was Jacob! Yes! It was Jacob! I thought. *In all of this madness, he had found me! And Jason. Where was Jason?* I was still capable of thinking. But I wanted to speak to him. I tried, but could not open my mouth. I felt him position the tote bag under my head, and watched as he quickly removed his heavy coat, and blanketed me with it. His eyes were pleading with me… begging me to live… to fight for dear life… to do whatever I had to do to live! He leaned in and planted a small kiss on my forehead.

Where's Jason? Where's Jason? The thought repeated over and over, inside my head.

I heard Jacob faintly, when he echoed "Where is Jason? Where is Jason?" It was as if he'd read my mind. He stood up, swiveled his body, and searched anxiously across the frenzied, chaotic scene.

Numb, and disoriented, I kept trying to lift my arm, until I was finally able to raise it just high enough to point in the direction of the airport. He understood what I was trying to say. He spun around, quickly and ran towards the entrance of the airport. I heard him calling out to his brother. "Jason…! Jason…! Jason…! It's Jacob! Can you hear me? Jason! Where are you?"

I was sinking deeper and deeper into that hole.

Then… BOOM…! BOOM…! BOOM! Screams erupted from the already traumatized crowd, creating more hysteria. Then came another round of explosions. BOOM…! BOOM!.. BOOM…! BOOM!

I laid there, helplessly, unable to move, and watched as the airport was swallowed up into a billowing blaze of red and orange flames — spiraling towards the sky — fire spewing, retching, and spitting more fire! I did not scream. I could not scream. Those miserable sounds of people sobbing and moaning, that had at first, pierced through my ears, were now beginning to sound dull and distant. My eyes, unable to blink, dimmed, with unheard of pain. I felt the weight of my eyelids, closing down on me, like two heavy curtains that were being drawn shut. I closed my eyes, knowing that I had finally reached the bottom of that deep, dark hole.

Was I dying? This isn't the way it was supposed to happen! This is not how I wanted it to end!

A week later, my eyes are still closed, but I am no longer asleep. I am also not yet fully awake. Somewhere in my mind, I am aware of a disastrous and calamitous event that took place. In my ears, I still hear the sirens, the screams, and the sounds of bombs exploding. Somewhere in my fractured memory, the bedlam and turmoil of that harrowing event, remain. A thin glimmer of light peeps through the waning darkness. Is this, then, twilight that I am caught up in? I am floating, hovering, in a dreamlike state, suspended in a cloud of violet haze.

Aah! The violet haze! That is where I am! But why? Why have I come back here?

The silence is lifting, and I am beginning to hear sounds again. I hear voices of people, not crying and wailing, mournfully, but of people talking to each other… with each other. There are three walls of curtains, dividing me from two women and a young girl. From behind one of them, I can clearly hear what is being said:

BEEP…! BEEP…! BEEE-E-E-E-E-E-E-EP!

"My daughter…! My precious daughter!" the man gasped. "Did she…"

"Yes, sir. I'm afraid she has flatlined," came the cold, unemotional reply.

"Time of death… 6:07 a.m." the cold voice continued.

The grief-stricken father sobbed, inconsolably. "She was only seventeen years old."

"Our condolences, Mr Scheuringer," came another, more sympathetic voice. "I am so sorry we were unable to save your daughter. Unfortunately, the extent of the injuries she sustained internally, along with the trauma inflicted to her head were insurmountable. There are clergymen here, if you'd like to have one console you during this time."

"Yes, thank you. A priest, please."

My body and head were still aching with unrelenting, agonizing pains. My eyelids, severely swollen, were glued together with crusted tears. It was quite the struggle, but eventually, I willed my eyelids apart, and thus, allowed my blurry-eyed vision to become crystal clear. Zeroing in on the figure and face that sat protectively at the foot of my bed, I was taken in by his eyes — dark, powerful, and mesmerizing. They looked exactly like Lem's eyes. Those eyes were the last thing I'd seen before I fell into that long, deep sleep.

"Welcome back to the land of the living," he said, getting up and moving closer to me. "Something told me you'd wake up today."

I strained to look up at the figure towering over me. "Please tell me that this has all been a terrifying nightmare!" I uttered, startled by the sound of my hoarse voice. I tried to clear my throat, but it hurt like hell. "Where am I?"

He knelt down near the head of the bed, brought his face closer to mine, and gently rubbed my forehead. "As much as I'd like to say to the contrary, this terrifying nightmare is, unfortunately, very real. And, as per your second question... well... you're in a hospital in Geneva, Switzerland... where you are truly baffling the medical staff."

"How so?" I asked, my voice sounding less scary.

"There's a team of doctors who come around every day around this time. They should be arriving any moment now. It seems your biometrics are... ahem... perplexing... in ways that they cannot explain."

I stared at him for a moment, then tried to hoist myself into a sitting position. *Oh, my! Was this Jason or Jacob,* I wondered. *How could I not know the difference between them?*

"Easy does it," he said, propping the pillow up and positioning it more comfortably against my back. "You're extremely lucky! None of the doctors expected you to pull through."

"They were preparing me for the worst."

"What happened to me?" I asked, holding my bandaged head and grimacing.

"You fell victim to a stampede of people fleeing the airport. You were trampled on, literally crushed by an avalanche of people. Most of the damage was inflicted on your head."

"That explains this nasty headache I have!"

"Ahem… calling it a headache would be putting it mildly. According to the medical team here, there was extensive brain damage… excessive bleeding and swelling of the left and right hemispheres… incapacitated blood vessels… and multiple widespread, penetrative concussions."

I eyed him and studied his face more closely, annoyed that not even I could tell if he was Jason or Jacob. "I guess it's a miracle then, that I survived!"

He returned my stare with a painfully shy look. "In case you're wondering which one I am… I am Jacob."

"Jacob!" I gasped, startled that he knew what I was thinking. "Oh, my poor, Jacob!" I cried, struggling as hard as I could to raise my arms so that I could embrace him.

He leaned over, held on to me, and wept like a baby. I wept like a mother who had finally found her lost child. He released himself, and stared, tearfully at me. "I haven't been able to find Jason. God knows I've looked everywhere for my brother! I've spent the last week dividing my time here, with you, and looking for Jason." He paused and wiped his eyes. I've searched every hospital… every pop-up medical campsite, and every…"

"Every morgue?" I asked, reluctantly. "Have you searched the morgues, Jacob?"

He shook his head and held my hands in his. "I started with the morgues first. No one who fits our… his description has turned up. Not finding him in a morgue gave me the strength to keep looking for him." Jacob's voice was broken and strained. "This isn't how it was supposed to be!" he moaned, fighting back tears. "We were supposed to spend endless hours, days, and weeks getting to know each other… bonding and doing things together! How could God play such a cruel trick on us!"

It killed me inside to see the agony that had gripped Jacob. Physically, I was suffering excruciating pains. But there was nowhere I ached than inside my heart. I felt Jacob's pain, more than I did my own.

The team of doctors arrived, just as Jacob and I were wiping away each other's tears. Instead of the usual team of four, there were seven.

The senior, head doctor introduced himself, and smiled. "How are you feeling today, madam?" he asked in a heavy Swiss accent. "You've had quite an amazing recovery in just one week's time!" he added, brazenly examining my features. His long, bushy eyebrows came together and formed a line of silver-gray hair across his forehead.

I intentionally avoided looking him in the eyes. "Have I?"

"Your recovery madam, has actually been extraordinary!" a younger, French doctor weighed in. "Most people would have succumbed to the kinds of injuries you've endured."

My eyes went to the only female doctor in the group, who politely elbowed her way in to get closer to my bed. She was definitely on a mission.

“It seems my fellow physicians are having a difficult time believing the biometrical numbers I’ve retrieved from you. Please, madam, if you don’t mind, I’d like to check your vitals now while the entire team is present.” With that, she took my temperature, heart, blood rates, and drew two vials of blood from me. The bandage around my head was carefully unwrapped, and each took his turn examining my wounded head.

“I’ve never seen such severe head wounds heal so rapidly,” the elder doctor commented, rubbing his chin.

Another member of the team chimed in. “Please madam… ahem… prior to these injuries… were you taking any special type of supplements… or…”

“There are no known supplements capable of producing tissue repair and renewal at such a rapid rate, young man! It just doesn’t exist!” exclaimed the head doctor.

Pleased that my vitals were exactly what she had told them, the female doctor held her head up and proudly presented my biometrics.

Außergewöhnlich! the head doctor responded.

Extraordinaire! another declared.

“This simply can’t be!” the others agreed. “There must be something wrong with the equipment you’re using! These numbers are humanly impossible!”

Jacob maneuvered his way inside the circle, stood next to my bed, and draped his arm gently around my shoulder. “When can my mother be discharged?” he demanded. "How soon will she be well enough to leave this hospital?"

The head doctor cleared his throat, and surveyed the other physicians, before directing his attention to me. "Well… actually… madam… my team and I would like to have you stay on here at our hospital for a little while longer." He shot Jacob a daring glance and turned towards me. "There are some very ah… unusual and ah… unexplainable issues with you that we would like to… ahem… further examine."

Jacob dug his hand slightly into my shoulder. "My mother wants to leave the hospital right away. You see… my twin brother is among the people who are still missing… or have not yet been positively identified. She wants to help me try and find him."

"I can't stay here any longer than necessary. My son Jacob and I must find out what has happened to my son Jason. This is something we have to do as a family."

"I sympathize with you, madam. This terrorist attack has been the worst thing to happen in modern history. It has devastated Switzerland and destroyed so many families. But please… consider staying for just a while… until we can figure out what is going on with you."

I placed my hand over Jacob's and gazed at the team of doctors. "Ok. I'll think about it," I said, nodding. "But, if you don't mind, I'd like to get some rest now."

"Of course not. We don't mind at all," the French doctor replied. "You must get as much rest as possible."

He smiled and turned his attention to Jacob. "I hope you find your brother. I have twin daughters, so I know how attached you are to him."

The head doctor nodded. "So… we will see you tomorrow around the same time." With that they all bowed, politely and exited, military-style.

Jacob followed them to the door and watched as the doctors made their way down the long corridor, to the very end. They stopped in front of a bank of elevators and waited until they were alone.

"There are too many abnormalities with that woman," the elder doctor whispered. "There is no way she could have possibly survived those injuries! No one could have! Not one chance in a million!"

The female doctor drew in a long breath and exhaled. "I've been observing her sleep patterns and the way her wounds have been healing. Quite frankly, I don't think she is all human."

Several of the doctors chuckled, nervously. "Come on! You can't be serious about that!" one of them chided. "Just what do you think the woman is? An alien from Mars?"

Another joined in teasing. "No! No! No! You must remember now, *men* are from Mars! Which means that woman must be from Venus!"

She shot her colleagues a hard, 'fuck you' condescending glance. "Quite frankly, I hadn't given Mars or Venus the slightest thought. I'll leave that for you boys to debate. I'm thinking more along the lines or some kind of hybrid, created right here on planet earth."

The elder doctor smiled at his female colleague and nodded approvingly. "Now, that is the kind of thinking I admire!" he asserted. "This is precisely what has crossed my mind. That is why she mustn't be allowed to leave. Do whatever has to be done to keep that woman here… even if it is against her will."

The French doctor shook his head. "Consider it done. I'll send out an email blast at once, alerting the medical staff of her status."

Jacob quickly closed the door and rushed over to Kitt. "Did you hear what they just said?"

"I did hear them! They were whispering. But I heard them as clearly as if they were right here in this room!"

"Good!" Jacob sighed. "They're all the way at the end of the hallway… and they were whispering, yet we both heard them… clearly. That means your sense of hearing is as keen as mine is."

"Jacob! I've got to get out of here asap! There's something I have to tell you… something your father did to me… and you… just before you were born! I'm afraid that if I stay here… those doctors will discover what my condition really is…! Please! We've gotta get out of here now!"

Jacob turned to me with a knowing look on his face. "I think I know what the condition is that you're referring to. Those doctors are too far away for any normal human being to hear what they're saying. But you and I heard them." He sighed and turned away. "My adoptive parents said I was born with a very rare genetic disorder. They've had me on meds my entire life. Deep down in my gut, I've always suspected that they were lying to me." He took a deep breath and exhaled. "Several times this past year, I was brave enough not to take the meds for a while. When I saw how that affected me, I started doing my own research. I discovered that the meds were suppressants used specifically for controlling certain genetic manifestations."

"So… you are aware of our condition… of the powers we have?"

"Not only am I aware of them. Secretly, I've been studying and monitoring those special powers. I'm finally coming to grips with how to control them. But there is so much more I need to learn." He paused. "Luckily, this past week, while you were in a coma, whenever I came by to visit you, I somehow managed to get inside your head."

"Did you really get inside my head, even while I was in a coma?"

"Yes. I did Mom."

"How did it happen, Jacob?"

"I don't really know how to explain it. But, there's this strange, twisting tunnel… a sudden flash of light… and…"

"Go on… tell me! What else happens to you, Jacob?"

"There is always this veil of violet haze... and then...

SWOOSH!

WHISH!

THUMP!

I was inside your head. I could read your mind, and your thoughts. I even tapped into your vast memory bank. It took very little effort to get inside your head," he said, with a look of embarrassment on his face. "I hope you don't mind that I did that."

"Not at all. That's a damn good start! You probably know more about these special powers than I do. Right now, we have to find a way to get out of here unnoticed. But where do we go?"

"A friend of mine was visiting relatives in Spain when the terrorists attacked. Before he left, he gave me spare keys to his flat, to water his plants. He can't get back inside the country now. We'll hide out there until we can figure out what to do. You and I will figure it all out, mom. We'll get through this together."

"Yes... we will get through this together. That is what Jason would have wanted."

Jacob looked around and sniffed. "Give me a moment! I'll be right back." In no time at all, he returned, dressed from head to toe in emerald-green scrubs. He handed me a similar set, and within minutes, we strolled down the crowded hall and safely outside. That was when I realized that I did not have my tote bag.

"My travel tote bag!" I cried out. "My shoulder bag!"

"Don't worry. It's safely locked inside my car trunk," he said calmly. "There was so much confusion, and so many people being treated in the emergency room on the evening you were admitted to the hospital. I didn't think it would be safe there. Here's my car," he added, unlocking the doors and trunk with the remote to his sky blue Skoda Octavia. "How do women carry these heavy bags!" he teased. "I'll hand it to you once you're settled inside the car."

"Thanks! My arms are still hurting. There's a gift inside for you, and one for Jason. Jason gave them to me for safe-keeping. He wanted to surprise you with it."

Jacob smiled. "I'm pretty sure I know what the surprise is."

"How would you know? Did you peek inside my bag?"

"I didn't have to. I'll explain once we're settled in at the chalet."

Chapter 19
My Son, Jacob

Nothing could have prepared me for the devastation and destruction the terrorist bombings had wreaked upon Geneva. Geneva, Switzerland was home to the Red Cross. It was Headquarters of Europe's United Nations, a global hub for world diplomacy and international banking. Looking around, I gasped, in awe, at how quickly, the onslaught of terrorist bombings had reduced such a beautiful city to piles of ruin.

With so many widespread explosions inflicted upon Geneva's infrastructure, access to major roads — heavily damaged by a series of strategically planned bombings — was severely limited. There were military checkpoints, roadblocks, and mandatory detours in place throughout the Canton of Geneva. On our way to Pregny-Chambesy, I got a firsthand view of the extent of destruction and mayhem the terrorist attacks had wreaked upon daily life, in this once vibrant metropolis.

Considering that I had finally awakened from my deep, week-long sleep, and had essentially slept through most of the aftermath of the terrorist incident, Jacob made good use of our drive out to the chalet. He gave me a detailed, blow by blow recounting of everything that had transpired since the attacks. He left no area uncovered.

Looking around, I gasped, in awe, at building, after bombed out building that had crumbled and collapsed into mounds of scattered debris. Geneva — with its breathtakingly beautiful landscape — a booming service metropolis, the seat of unmatched financial importance, and home to headquarters of many major private and public international organizations — now decimated and reduced to rubble. The devastation made Geneva look like a war-torn zone. To make matters worse, in addition to the numerous attacks in Geneva, there was a series of more than eighty heinous bombings — explosions in airports, railroad stations, shopping districts, banks, and at major bus stations in Zurich, Basel, Bern, Lausanne, and Interlaken — Switzerland's most heavily populated cantons.

As organized, well-trained, and heavily equipped as Switzerland is, the country's overall preparedness fell short when faced with terrorist attacks on the scale of which it had come under. Thousands of people were killed, maimed, and injured. There were sporadic explosions at The World Trade Organization (WTO), The World Health Organization (WHO), and The International Labor Organization (ILO). Switzerland's iconic International Red Cross and Red Crescent

Movement, was overburdened with thousands of dying and severely injured people.

Across the borders, there were bombings in Domodossola, in the Piedmont region in Italy, at its main railway junction. Improvised explosive devices (IEDs) were detonated in France, in Chillon, Lyons, Ferney-Voltaire, Divonne, and Gex. In Germany, banks in Lorrach and Frieburg were bombed. The Basel Badischer Bahnhof, located on Swiss territory, but operated as a German station, was leveled from explosions of multiple bombings. God only knew what the rest of Switzerland and its neighboring countries must have looked like. What I saw in Geneva left me completely depressed and speechless. Jacob gave a blow-by-blow account of the brutality and atrocities of the unparalleled terrorist attacks.

Switzerland is bordered by Italy to the South, France to the West, Germany to the North, and Austria and Liechtenstein to the East. The terrorists were obviously militarily-trained members of cells that were entrenched inside Switzerland and its neighboring countries. Highly trained in unconventional operations, they respected no borders. The terrorist teams utilized a combination of deadly nerve gases, conventional military explosives, and IEDs in multiple coordinated attacks. They inflicted large-scale carnage, displaced thousands, and disrupted civil society activities on a scale unseen in modern times. Airports, markets, schools, banks, public transportation systems, and densely populated commercial hubs were deliberately targeted throughout Switzerland and in parts of Italy, France, Germany and Austria.

Homemade IEDs were detonated along the highways and roadsides. Bombs, loaded with shrapnel, were emplaced randomly around the city to kill as many people as possible, and inflict massive destruction on the population. The bombs came in many different forms, and ranged from small, pipe bombs, to more sophisticated devices that caused widespread damage and unimaginable casualties. Bombs were concealed in packages, food containers, and disguised as deliverable goods. Explosions inside transportation stations, banks, offices and residential buildings, destroyed the walls, floors, and ceilings, and blew out glass windows, causing death and severe injuries.

The attacks strategically targeted Geneva's infrastructure, critically damaging electrical power sources, public transportation, water and sewage systems, and all communication systems. Its key industries — banking and finance — were greatly impacted. There were extensive disruptions in municipal services and public facilities. Apartment buildings were so greatly damaged that thousands were left either dead, missing, or misplaced. Hospitals and morgues, severely understaffed, were filled beyond capacity.

The terrorists obtained vast amounts of Novichok — advanced nerve agents developed by the Soviet

Union in the 1970s and 1980s. At least eight times more toxic than other nerve agents, and harder to identify, Novichok is classified as a military grade chemical weapon. It takes effect in less than thirty seconds, and causes death by asphyxiation and cardiac arrest. The reason it was able to do so much damage, and kill so many people is because little is known about Novichok. What is known, however, is that it is a swift and silent killer — odorless, tasteless, and invisible.

The response to the undetectable nerve gas attacks did not come fast enough to prevent thousands of people from dying, or becoming permanently afflicted. The gas attacks and bomb explosions inflicted immeasurable deaths and grievous injuries. It interrupted every aspect of everyday life, and spread fear, tension, and mass hysteria across international communities. This was the worst international terrorist attack in modern history. The unprecedented damage, destruction, and death tolls were on a scale so massive, that even 911 paled in comparison.

Geneva, Switzerland, headquarters of Europe's United Nations, and a global hub for world diplomacy and international banking and finance — was brought to a screeching halt. Fortunately, Switzerland's response to the attacks, when it came to coordinating, and managing personnel, equipment, services, and supplies, was fast and broad. During the past week, the country had gone seamlessly through rescue, recovery, and relief efforts. The Swiss government, in collaboration with the International Red Cross and Red Crescent Movement; The Global Counterterrorism Forum (GCTF); which includes 29 countries and the European Union, The International Relief Teams (IRT), the International Rescue Committee (IRC), and the UN Central Emergency Response Fund (CERF), were among the many international organizations that had boots on the ground in Switzerland, immediately after the attacks.

Although not a member state of the European Union (EU), Switzerland is associated with the EU through numerous treaties, and maintains strong trade agreements. The neutral nation has a network of intellectual and economic relationships with the rest of Europe, The United States, Canada, as well as other countries overseas. The attacks shocked Europe and rocked the rest of the world, causing overwhelming harm to international travel, trade and commerce. All of Europe was thrown into turmoil, with member countries of the EU wondering if they would be targeted next. Because international terrorism is one of the most serious threats to global peace, within hours of the bombings and nerve gas attacks, members of Europol, the European Police Office, and Interpol, the International Criminal Police Organization (ICPO), along with other international partners and policing organizations, were briefed and equipped.

Interpol and ICPO experts and specialized personnel were immediately deployed to Switzerland, to assist in investigating criminal and terrorist related issues. The General Secretariat of Interpol ordered a shutdown of all borders, and notices were issued for fugitives and known terrorists, wanted for arrest. A database of possible suspects was accessed. Experts in explosives and biometrics, as well as digital forensics and operational data analysis personnel were dispatched to Switzerland. Everyone was focused on finding those who were responsible for the attacks, and bringing them swiftly to justice.

Swiss investigators and Interpol agents concluded that the attacks were designed to disrupt Switzerland's strong economy and destabilize the Swiss franc, by inflicting as much internal damage on the country as possible. They also believed that the masterminds behind the well-planned and orchestrated attacks were several terrorist fugitives included on America's Most Wanted Terrorists List. In the aftermath of the attacks, suspicion fell on a string of Russian terrorist cells, financed, supported, and backed by the Kremlin.

We finally arrived at the chalet — a small, modest stucco and brick house, with a sloping gabled roof, and broad overhanging eaves. It was clean, cozy, and comfortable. Fortunately for us, the pantry and freezer were stocked like a bunker or a fallout shelter, with canned and boxed goods neatly shelved and alphabetized. Between the pantry, refrigerator, and freezer, I quickly pulled together a sumptuous dinner — the first meal I'd ever made for my son, Jacob. I observed him as he went about setting the table. He did everything so much like Jason, it gave me goosebumps. It came as no surprise to me, when he made a big pot of bubbling hot cocoa for us.

Not knowing Jason's whereabouts, or what had happened to him, weighed so heavily on me, I thought that at any given moment, I might spontaneously self-combust. Preparing dinner was a distraction, and brought me an ounce of calm.

After dinner was eaten, and the table cleared, I removed the gold watches from my bag and placed them on the table. I took Jason's toiletry pouch from the side compartment of my tote and placed it on the table, next to the boxes containing the gold watches.

Jacob's eyes went from Jason's toiletry pouch to the watches. A shadow of sadness swept across his face. "They're the two identical gold watches Dad gave Jason on his twelfth birthday. Our initials are engraved on them. That was also when he told Jason about me."

"Yes. How did you know that? Neither Jason nor I've mentioned that to you. Are you sure you didn't peek inside my bag?"

He smiled, mischievously. "No, I didn't have to peek inside your bag. I had already peeked inside both of your minds."

"But… how? When did you have the chance to get inside Jason's head?"

"Last week, before you left New York. I entered his mind while the three of us were FaceTiming."

"While we were FaceTiming?"

"Yes, it happened suddenly and so naturally. Honestly, I hadn't planned on doing that. But Jason's mind and my mind were automatically drawn together… like a magnet. The gold watches were at the forefront of his mind."

I eyed him, curiously. "What else was on Jason's mind?"

Jacob took in a deep breath and sighed. "First of all, make no mistake, Jason's brain is filled with a lot of gray matter. You wouldn't believe how much information is stored in his head!"

"Oh, I think I have a good idea. Quite a lot!"

"Facts, figures, dreams, ideas, thoughts, fears! To describe it as information overload would be a vast understatement! Compared to other heads I've explored, his mind is vast!"

"Why do you speak as if his brain and mind are separate?"

"Because they are. The brain and mind are two different but interconnected entities. The brain is an organ, whereas the mind is energy, manifested through thinking, feeling, dreaming, emotions, perceptions, determinations, and even memories. I tapped into all of those things and acquired a wealth of information from Jason's brain and mind."

"Were you really able to tap into all of those things while you were inside Jason's head?"

"Yes. It happened quite effortlessly. Getting inside Jason's head was very different from when I got inside other people's heads."

"Different in what way?"

Jacob tilted his head to one side and squinted his eyes, exactly the way Jason did when he wanted to explain something. He sighed. "To begin, getting inside other people's heads takes more focused concentration and some degree of effort. But getting inside Jason's head was different." He paused, thoughtfully. "With Jason, it felt more like walking through a door that was wide open."

"I see. So, getting inside your brother's head was much easier?"

"Much easier and very different. I believe what happened between Jason and I was more like a transfer of energy and mental data, wherein every piece of information stored inside his brain and mind, was somehow transferred directly to me… to my brain and mind."

"Ok. I am not the smartest person in the room when it comes to computer talk. But what you're describing sounds a lot to me like when information or data has been uploaded from one computer to another."

"Precisely, Mom! That is exactly what it felt like. But considering that Jason and I are two humans and not two computers, it felt as if all of the information I absorbed from him was transferred through osmosis. All of the data inside his head flowed rapidly and freely into mine, with our combined information being synchronized. It certainly felt as if I was absorbing all of his knowledge, intelligence, personality, thoughts, and even his own self-awareness, and he, mine. Our minds definitely merged that day, and all of the contents were automatically assimilated." He sighed, then continued. "I must admit that my favorite place was when I stumbled into what I believe was Jason's hippocampus region."

"The hippocampus region? Ok. You've just lost me. I was good up until now. You'll have to explain how we went from thoughts and personality to hippocampus."

"The hippocampus is the inner region located in the temporal lobe. It is the central nervous system, the center of emotion and memory. You have no idea how much I enjoyed Jason's memories!" he said, closing his eyes and smiling.

The smile on his face made me smile. "Even if you did not grow up together, side-by-side, you are so much alike in every way. You are almost the same person! Jacob… I think we're onto something here."

"I agree mom," he said, shaking his head. "Do you remember what the French doctor said about twins?"

"Yes. He said that twins have an extraordinary connection, and that their minds are linked together, telepathically."

"That's exactly how I felt the day we were FaceTiming. Jason and I were thinking as one.

Therefore, whatever was inside his mind, is now also inside my mind." He shook his head and exhaled. "That explains why I'm having memories of people I don't know, and of places I've never been to. That day, after our conversation ended, and I hung up, I was so emotionally drained I could barely stay awake. I was completely spent!"

"So was Jason! He told me so! He also said that he felt emotionally drained. He kept yawning!"

"I guess transferring all of that information from one to the other took a toll on both of us. It was meant to happen. If our minds hadn't synced then, it might never have happened."

"We now have all of the information we need to move forward, together. It will take some time and a lot of work. But we can and will get through this."

Jacob smiled and nodded. "Shouldn't you give Santini, Aunt Eugenia, and Big Joe a call and let them know what's going on?"

I gasped at how easily he had called their names — three people whom he'd never met, yet knew — proof that he had, in fact, absorbed their names from his twin brother. "Yes, I'll call them tomorrow after we've looked for Jason. Drink up!" I said, filling his mug with hot cocoa. "We've got a lot of work to do, and a long night ahead of us!"

Jacob intentionally avoided bringing up any discussion of his adoptive parents. As such, I took his cue and steered clear of the subject. It was apparent that like I, he wanted to focus only on finding Jason. We spent the night going over information he had collected from Jason's mind that was pertinent to our superhuman abilities. He went over all of the superpowers Jason had spoken to me about, sometimes using Jason's words verbatim. When I didn't completely understand something, he took his time and explained it to me in full detail. There were things which Jason had casually mentioned that Jacob was now expounding on, in-depth. We went back and forth, observed and studied each other. During the course of the night, we experimented, tried, and tested each other's abilities. Telepathically, I was as sharp as Jacob was, if not sharper.

We went over everything enough times that our actions were thoroughly embedded into the memory banks of our minds. The last thing we did was make sure Jason's toothbrush and hairbrush were packed inside my tote. Jacob warned that, based on his previous experience, there would be long lines at the Digital Forensic Lab annex. We'd have to make an early start and be prepared to wait hours, in a long line. I didn't care how long it took. The only thing that mattered was getting some of Jason's DNA to the people who would use it to help find him.

Chapter 20
The Aftermath

When morning arrived, neither Jacob nor I felt the least bit sleepy or tired. It was as if our energy and stamina had self-rejuvenated during the night. It was 5.30 a.m. when we hopped into Jacob's car, bound to Interpol's Digital Forensic Lab. Jacob's last call to the Red Cross and Red Crescent Help Hotline gave instructions to go directly to the Disaster Victim Identification (DVI) annex, a division of Interpol's Forensic Lab that collects biometric data, fingerprints, DNA samples, and personal effects of missing individuals, to assist in confirming positive identification.

Jacob had compiled a list of Family Reunification Centers, hospitals, and morgues. The reunification centers, set up to help facilitate the process of finding and reconnecting family members who were separated during the terrorist incident, were numerous, and spread out. Days earlier, Jacob had visited and registered with all of the sites, listing Jason Johnson among the thousands of missing people. He had been issued a unique missing person ID number for Jason, which could be used to obtain information from a centralized source.

We wanted to make every minute of our search for Jason count. We were, literally on the same page, with plans meticulously laid out for the day. Luckily, cell phones were up and working again. While Jacob drove, I would make calls to the various reunification sites, the hospitals, and finally, the morgues. Call after painful call returned the same discouraging response: *"At this time, there is no new information attached to the person matching this missing person ID number. Please check back later for updates on Jason Johnson."*

With the last phone call made, I was so disheartened, I couldn't bear to look at Jacob. I gazed out at the long line of cars, SUVs, and motorcycles in front of us. The line was longer than we'd anticipated — a depressing indication of just how many people were still missing, unaccounted for, or dead.

Jacob queued into the line, sighed, and turned towards me. "No luck, I gather. Don't worry. There's always tomorrow." His voice was heavy, weighed down with the same kind of disappointment I was feeling. "Jason's toothbrush and hairbrush will give DVI enough DNA to work with. Remember, we can't give up hope. You and Jason found me. Together, you and I will find Jason."

Jacob's words brought me back on course. I perked up and nodded. "You're right. I needed to hear that from you."

He smiled and patted me on the shoulder. "Mom… we'll be waiting in this line for a while. This is the perfect time to call Santini, Aunt Eugenia, and Big Joe."

Santini picked up on the first ring. Kitt! Kitt! Finally! I've been trying for days to reach you, but the phones weren't working! Are you guys okay?

I took a deep breath and got everything out at once. "Jacob and I are okay. We're together. But Jason is missing. We were separated at the airport during the attack. It all happened too fast! There was just so much pandemonium and confusion!"

Mio Dio! Do you have any idea where he might be? I mean… from what I see on the news, it still looks very chaotic there. He could be anywhere!

"Jacob and I have checked out all of the family reunification centers, hospitals, and morgues. So far, there is no sign of Jason."

I wish I could be there to help you through this, but Switzerland is still in lockdown… and all US airports have been ordered to freeze flights, indefinitely. I'm so sorry! Where are you staying? What else can be done to find Jason?

"Jacob and I are staying at his friend's chalet in Pregny-Chambesy. It's a working-class residential area, on the southwest shore of Lake Geneva. The place is very comfortable, and we're safe there. Right now, we're in a line, waiting to give Jason's toothbrush and hairbrush to a forensic office called DVI — Disaster Victim Identification."

DVI… of course! They're the DNA experts under Interpol. Those guys are brilliant! If anyone can find Jason, it will definitely be them! He paused. Eugenia is trying to reach me. Please call her. She's been worried sick about you!

"Yes, I will call her now. But, do me a favor. Call Big Joe and let him know what's going on. Tell him I'll call him tomorrow afternoon, 1p.m. New York time."

"Consider it done. And Kitt… businesses all over have closed temporarily. People are terrified that there might be similar attacks here in the US. Eugenia, Big Joe and I agreed that it was in everyone's best interest to close Chelsea Place until things get back to normal."

"Good move. Thanks, Santini. That's exactly what I would have done. I'll be in touch. You can reach me on my cell phone." I ended the call and speed-dialed Eugenia's number. Her voice was filled with relief, anxiety and excitement.

"Thank God! Kitt! I've been praying morning and night that you all were safe! What a relief! How are Jason and Jacob doing?"

"Jacob and I are okay, Eugenia, but… Jason is missing. Jacob and I are doing everything we can to find him."

Nothing at all came from Eugenia. Nothing but a long, deafening silence. It was more than I could bear. I turned, weakly, towards Jacob, shook my head, and dropped the phone into his hand.

Jacob picked up from where I had lost it. “I’m Jacob, Aunt Eugenia! Are you okay? Listen… pull yourself together. We won’t give up trying to find Jason! I promise you. Scout’s honor!”

“Oh, my God! That’s what Jason always said when he wanted to put my mind to ease! You sound exactly like him! How’s your mom handling this?”

“Mom’s a real trooper. I see that I get my strength from her. We’ll be fine… We’re staying at my friend’s chalet just outside Geneva… Yes, you can reach her on her cell. Take care Aunt Eugenia.” Jacob ended the call, and handed me my phone.

I don’t know when, but at some point, it started snowing. I looked up and saw that there were finally only four cars in front of us. Ahead, a large sign was perched next to a beautiful white building that sat perfectly between two smaller buildings. In at least twenty different languages, the sign read: “Disaster Victim Identification (DVI).” Jacob pointed out that, before the attacks, this particular site was actually an exclusive all-girls school.

As we neared the main building, we were approached by two people dressed in bright red pants and matching red down-filled coats. A cross, a crescent, and the word ‘VOLUNTEER’ were emblazoned on the back of their coats. An appropriate uniform for the cold weather outside, the volunteers’ faces, tucked deep inside hoods, were partially hidden. Both held I-pads.

“*Bun di!*” They greeted us, in unison. “Are you Christian or Muslim?” one asked, swiping her I-pad screen.

I glanced briefly at Jacob, then answered: “Christian.”

“*Danke!* Please, may I see the name and ID number of the missing person.”

I held up the registration page, carefully spelled Jason’s full name, and read the number twice, as the volunteer tapped away on her I-pad.

“What items have you brought for DNA collection?”

Jacob held up the plastic bags that contained Jason’s toothbrush and hairbrush. “These belonged to my twin brother, our missing loved one. He used them shortly before the attack.”

Danke dir!” the other volunteer said. “Please, park your car in space number 27,” he added, pointing to the next available spot.

Once inside, we were offered hot chocolate and immediately ushered into a small, private office, where we met with four officials. “Good morning. My name is Doctor Talbot. I am the supervising DNA forensic expert,” a tall, gawky man announced, in an unmistakably British accent. Outwardly reserved, with a formal stature, oversized, thick-rimmed glasses covered most of his face. “I will be responsible for collecting and processing DNA from…” His eyes went to the I-pad he held in his hand. “Jason Johnson, a 21-year-old African American man. Is that correct?”

“Yes. That is correct,” I said, looking straight into his eyes. “My name is Kitt Kougar. I am Jason Johnson’s mother. This is Jacob, Jason’s identical twin.”

“I see,” Dr Talbot said, rubbing his chin. “I am deeply sorry for your misfortune, as I am for everyone who is in your situation. We’ll have to draw blood from you and collect whatever other personal items belonging to Jason that you’ve brought. It would also help if you can briefly tell us a little about your son and brother.”

Jacob and I exchanged sad looks. The big lump in my throat prevented me from saying anything.

Jacob cleared his throat, placed an arm protectively around me, and drew me closer to his side.

“My adoptive parents, the Serbian couple who reared me, kidnapped me twenty-one years ago, shortly after my twin brother, Jason and I were born. Our natural father named us Jason and Jacob. We were separated at birth. My adoptive parents brought me to Europe and named me Jakov Markovic. This woman, Kitt Kougar, is my natural mother. She did not know that she was pregnant with twins. I was hidden in her womb, and delivered while she was unconscious. She knew nothing of me until nine days ago, when she and Jason discovered that I was living here in Geneva. They dropped everything and flew here to meet me. Unfortunately, they arrived at the airport in Geneva at the worst possible time. They were separated during the attack, amidst all of the confusion. My brother found me and came to Switzerland to reconnect with me. Now he's missing. What I feel is worse than any pain I can describe. It hurts more than losing an arm or a leg. I feel utterly incomplete without him. I am begging you, please… help me find my twin brother."

Jacob's words were followed by a lingering moment of heavy, solemn silence. Two of the forensic experts hung their heads and wept quietly, while their comrade cried, openly. Dr Talbot lifted his chin and cleared his throat. When he spoke, his voice was filled with genuine compassion. "This is perhaps, one of the saddest stories I've heard," he uttered, clearly shaken. He removed his eyeglasses and regained his composure. "I am usually too busy with my work to consider other people's grief. But your story has touched me profoundly. You've reminded me of how brutally unfair life can sometimes be. My team and I will do all we possibly can to return Jason to you. On that, I'll give you my word."

Jacob and I took to Dr Talbot immediately. A good sign, considering what we had encountered the previous day with the team of doctors at University Hospital. He had a curious, goodhearted nature. Pure honesty radiated from him, even when he was left feeling confused, and could not understand why Jacob and I had so adamantly refused to give blood. We were determined not to. We couldn't. Leaving samples of our blood would surely have revealed that, not only was our blood of an extremely rare type, but even more so, not entirely human. We were also convinced that Jason's toothbrush and hairbrush would provide enough of his DNA.

There were numerous documents to be read, and a lot of paperwork to be completed. When Jacob and I signed off on the last document, Dr Talbot accompanied us to the door.

Jacob turned to face the doctor. "Realistically, what can we expect? How long will this process take?"

He retrieved a small packet of lens wipes from his lab coat, cleaned, and replaced his glasses. "Once all of the biometric data is collected from the airport site, we will preserve those finds with as much dignity as possible. We will then use DNA extracted from Jason's toothbrush and hairbrush to make direct comparisons, and reconcile the various data." He paused and sighed. "You should know that it can take a long time to accurately identify victims, especially when there has been a large number of casualties and so many missing people."

There was still hope. Jacob and I exchanged looks, but neither of us said anything.

Dr Talbot reached inside his pocket and handed a card to Jacob, and one to me. "This is my private contact information. Feel free to use it whenever you need to," he said, nodding with sincerity. "As you can see, Hunter is my first name. I always say that I have the right name for my business," he added, with a slight smile. "I said that, to say this: I will definitely hunt for Jason, very long, and very hard. I promise, I will leave no stone unturned."

Something told me that this was not the last time we'd be seeing Dr Talbot. I knew that our paths would somehow cross again... if not here, at DVI, it would certainly be somewhere else. I was finally beginning to feel hopeful. "Thank you so much for your kindness. We greatly appreciate your efforts."

Dr Talbot threw two long arms around us and gathered us into a gentle embrace. "In the meantime, my advice to you is to leave the searching and hunting to us. We're known for being thorough and quite adroit at that. You should be about getting back to the matters of life and living. I am sure that that is what Jason would have wanted. The sooner you do that, the better off you'll both be."

Jacob dipped his head and smiled weakly. "Thank you, Dr Talbot. So long."

Dr Talbot returned the smile and handed us off to a pair of volunteers who led us to an exit, on the opposite side of the building from where we had entered. Pointing us in a roundabout way back to the parking area, the volunteers explained that the separate entrance and exit were used to expedite the enormous flow of intake. It was snowing heavier by now. But that did nothing to discourage the hordes of people who were still lining up, armed with various personal effects that belonged to their missing loved ones, and hoping against all hope, to be reunited with them, in one way or another.

As we made our way back to the car, a large, rambling tent caught our eyes. Clearly recently erected, the structure was window-less, save for several small see-through plexi-windows at the very top. They were too high up for anyone on the ground level to see inside. The entire area was under surveillance, every inch guarded by huge German Shepherd K9 dogs and their handlers. The tent was surrounded by members of the Swiss Armed Forces, Interpol's Incident Response Teams, and special operatives from the ICPO. Whatever was going on inside the tent was high security and definitely off limits.

Without missing a beat, Jacob and I stopped in our tracks. Pretending to adjust our coats and scarves, we zeroed in on what was going on inside the tent. With pointed, well-focused wills, a moment was all it took. Our heightened senses activated, in no time at all, we could plainly see and accurately hear everything. I was astonished at how expeditiously and seamlessly we'd accomplished this undertaking. Zooming in was already beginning to feel like second nature.

One area inside the tent was completely occupied by a unit composed of an international team of specialized criminal police. Nearby, a group of Interpol's elite counter-terrorism and tactical officers were assembled. In that group, everyone was suited from head to toe in black military gear and survival equipment. In one quiet corner, away from all of the activities and chatter, several German shepherd K9s were housed in a series of extra-large vari-kennels. At the very back of the tent, sequestered behind a walled-off section, a group of high ranking military officers, environmental scientists, a team of anxious American bacteriologists from the Centers for Disease Control and Prevention (CDC), and the head of the Swiss Water Association (VSA) were gathered in a quiet, intense meeting.

Flanked by an Interpol officer and several environmental scientists, a decorated Swiss general stood near a round table and spoke firmly to the group. "It is with much disappointment that I inform you, that, as of today, only two of the culprits responsible for the massive terrorist attacks on our beloved country and neighboring nations, have been captured…"

An Interpol officer with a French accent jumped up and interrupted the general. "Sir, is it true that some of the suspects who committed these atrocious attacks were members of the same terrorist cell who escaped after the 2015 Paris attacks?"

"Were these attacks sanctioned by the Russian government?" another officer asked.

The general did not blink an eye, as he continued. "This is all highly sensitive and extremely confidential. Thanks to a concerted collaboration among the Swiss government, and various international policing organizations, we have succeeded in keeping this information from leaking out to the news media." He paused and eyed the Interpol Commissioner to his right. "Commissioner Chalmers, I believe there's some recently-developed information you'd like to share with us."

The Commissioner bent his head slightly, and shifted to the center. "As General Brunner just mentioned, so far, only two of the terrorists are in our custody. Earlier today, after Interpol interrogators played a video of his pregnant wife and two young children, one of the culprits confessed to his role in these devastating attacks. Apparently, the sight of his crying wife and children was more than he could bear," he added, sarcastically. "In exchange for protecting his family, he has agreed to work with us in our efforts to bring all of the criminals responsible for these savage attacks to justice." The Commissioner shifted, then stood at attention. "On that note, as some of you have just learned, the terrorist-turned-informant has warned us of another pending attack — one that is scheduled for tonight."

With that, a loud round of gasps rose from the room, as people stirred, nervously, and shook their heads in disbelief.

Commissioner Chalmers took in a deep breath, stood erect, and continued. "If successful, the attack will be major, with long-term, catastrophic results. This time, there will be no bombs detonated… and no nerve gas released. The suspects plan to deploy bioterrorism… using water as a weapon.” He sucked in a deep breath, and exhaled. His sharp eyes surveyed everyone at the table before he continued. “The terrorists plan to contaminate the Rhône River with dangerously high concentrations of deadly, waterborne pathogenic microorganisms. This is a new kind of war in which our enemies’ ammunition will no longer be limited to bombs, bullets, and gasses. Their weapons will include invisible, microscopic killers — anthrax, smallpox, botulism, tularemia, brucellosis, Q Fever, monkeypox, Ebola, Lassa, Machupo, Marburg, cocktails of typhoid fever, Hepatitis A, and new, more lethal variants of the cholera bacteria.”

Everyone gasped and stirred, anxiously. This brought an even louder uproar from the room with outbursts from numerous people.

“That would be biological warfare at its worst!” the senior American bacteriologists from the CDC cried out. “This can’t be allowed to happen! Most of these diseases lack corresponding and effective vaccines! Even more frightful is the possibility that these germs and bacteria combined might produce a strange hybridization of some new, more virulent plague!”

“Mayhem! That would be our worst nightmare!” a German doctor interjected.

“The Rhône River flows directly to the Mediterranean Sea!” one of the environmental scientists erupted. “True… The Rhône is shared by Switzerland and France. But it is one of the most significant waterways in Europe! Bacteria and viruses of this nature would cause death, disease and unimaginable, long term damage to the environment for generations!"

"Something of that magnitude would kill and sicken millions of people! It would wreak havoc and cause biological malfunctions in humans, animals, and plants!" the head of the Swiss Water Association cried out.

"This is exactly why the Biological and Toxin Weapons Convention (BTWC) was formed back in 1975!" a Swiss medic shouted. "The BTWC was expressly created to bring an end to and prevent the development and production of bioweapons so that humanity would be spared the kind of devastation we are now facing!"

"Tell that to rogue nations like China, Iran, North Korea, Syria, and Russia!" Commissioner Chalmers grunted. "BTWC is an international agreement that the United States, Russia and more than 100 nations ratified. Yet Russia continues to produce and stockpile large quantities of smallpox virus, anthrax, and other deadly bacteria. The Russians currently corner the market in cultivating, weaponizing, and deploying a long list of biological agents."

The meeting dissolved into a loud frenzy of shock and horror. Breaking up into small groups, everyone in the room went frantically about doing what had to be done next. The scene was one of rigidly controlled chaos.

Stunned speechlessly, Jacob and I stared at each other and shook our heads. A low, guttural sound emanated from my throat, prompting the K9s to unleash a series of rapid-fire barks. Several of the guards motioned us to return to our car, and ordered us to leave the premises at once — which we did, but not until we had gotten all of the necessary details — the exact time and location of the planned attack. This was bioterrorism on a massive scale.

The killers were prepared to deliberately release bacteria, viruses, and fungi agents that would cause a variety of different diseases. They were going to use non-human life to disrupt and end human life. Released into the Rhône River, these biological weapons would be difficult to control because microscopic living organisms can be unpredictable and incredibly resilient. Transmitted from person to person, these germs and diseases would result in astronomically high immortality rates, widespread social disruption, and cause billions of euros worth of damage.

The attack would come from the sky, by means of nine, well-coordinated airdrops. The execution would be done by way of aerial application, similar to crop dusting and aerial topdressing. Utilizing small air vehicles disguised as friendly search helicopters, the perpetrators would use targeted, high-powered, high-precision spraying of bacteria to cover vast areas rapidly. In short, the vitally important Rhône River would essentially be rendered polluted with high concentrations of deadly waterborne bacteria. Like the bombings and nerve gas attacks, it would be swift, with far-reaching death, destruction, and devastation.

Chapter 21
Thirteen Leaps

"There is a time to think, a time to wait, and a time to pounce.

Stay grounded, balanced, and centered. Reach into your indomitable soul and seek the power and the strength of the jaguar. There are no lines drawn between us, and no amount of distance that can divide us.

I am always with you, and you are with me, always. We are one, united, and undivided. Mighty, fearless, and feared, you are stealth, swift, and all-powerful. You were not born to be caged. You cannot be tamed. The fire in your belly is an inextinguishable flame!

It will burn forever! You are SH+AGUAR, THE NIGHT HUNTRESS! The time to pounce is now!"

~The Black Jaguar

In the scheme of things, waking up from a week-long coma was the first step of my journey back to life and living. Coming to terms with exactly what had happened to Jason had taken an indescribable toll on Jacob and me. At this point, we just wanted to find

Jason, or whatever remained of him. We wanted him back — dead or alive. In this darkest of moments, both outcomes felt as distant as the moon.

Jacob and I, so consumed by our thoughts, said very little to each other on our ride back to the chalet. Sometimes silence speaks louder than words. This was definitely one of those times.

As if life hadn't beaten up on us enough already, we were now doubly weighed down with the added, unthinkable information of yet another, even more far-reaching terrorist attack — one with greater detriments than the previous attacks. I was on edge. I felt helpless and agitated, all at once. I shifted, anxiously. I was angry! Mad as hell! Life had dealt me two bad hands. First, Lem was abducted. Jason was now missing. God forbid, if anything were to happen to Jacob. No! Not if I could stop it! There would be no third strikes in my life! I'd had enough! I would get revenge!

Jacob eyed me cautiously, and spoke as calmly as possible. "Mom… I know how you feel. I'm also angry. I'm distraught that only two of those murderous perps have been captured. The search is still on for the masterminds behind these attacks." He paused, and sighed. "It's sad that this is what humanity has been reduced to. I'd do anything to get my hands on them!" he fumed.

"I'd like to sink my teeth directly into their evil heads!" I growled, gripping the car seat armrests with my fingers. "Nothing would give me more pleasure than to crack their skulls!"

"Mom... your jaguar-ness is clearly becoming more evident. Remember what we went over last night. You must always be in control. Losing control puts you at risk of being exposed and leaves you vulnerable."

"I'm losing it, Jacob! I can't help it! I have to do something! Now! I don't know how much longer I can control myself!" I studied the look on his face. He was as determined as I was to get to those murderers and exact revenge. He was just doing a much better job of containing his rage than I was.

"I know. I know. With our extraordinary capabilities and superhuman powers, we have the upper hand on everyone in that meeting," he blurted out.

"We also have the way, the means, and the will power!" I exclaimed. "Seven years ago... when those worthless gangsters entered our home, beat your father to a pulp, then abducted him, I felt so helpless... so defenseless. But that was then. Things are different now. I am different!" I sat back and exhaled, deeply, struggling to keep a lid on the fire raging inside me. "The people who took Lem away from us are no better than these killers who have already robbed so many people of their lives and loved ones. I couldn't protect Lem. But I can do something to stop these killers from striking again!"

Jacob glanced nervously at me, annoyed that I had figured out how to prevent him from entering my head.

"Okay. I see what you've done," he admitted. "Please, try to calm down. We'll figure something out. There must be ways that we can help bring these perps to justice." He swallowed, clearly unnerved by the fact that I had succeeded in blocking him from entering my head. "We're back!" he sighed, his eyes fastened on me. "I'll make you some hot soup and a pot of chamomile tea. You've had a long day. After the soup, you should go straight to bed and get some rest."

"Okay. You're right. I need to shower and get to bed right away. But I don't have an appetite, and I won't be needing any tea. I'm completely spent. I'll be asleep before my head hits the pillow."

No sooner than we were inside the house, I gave Jacob a big hug, and a little kiss on his forehead. "Make yourself some hot cocoa, and hit the bed, young man!" I ordered. "You've been burning the candles on both ends. We'll make an early start tomorrow."

"All right, mom. I'll make you a nice, hot breakfast tomorrow morning!" he called out.

"Promise?" I teased.

"Promise! Scout's honor!" he yelled, extending a pinky.

As I made my way to the bedroom at the back of the house, my mind drifted to the melanistic jaguar, caged in the basement lab on Riverside Drive. I saw her panting and pacing. She was as restless as I was. I was walking briskly. Then suddenly, I felt her energy rising rapidly inside me. I entered the darkness of the room, crouched down, and poised into a balanced position. Without a moment's warning, it happened.

SWISH! WHOOSH! THUMP!

Her compelling presence was overpowering. I was left in awe of her black fur, spotted with dark rosettes. It was there that I came face-to-face with the incredibly intense, bright golden glow of her eyeshine! She let out a low, growl. Then, with her omnipotent mind and thoughts, she spoke telepathically and majestically to me:

I have inhabited this world for millions of years more than humans have, and still, I survive. A supernatural being, I am of the earth, as you are. Although I am divine, and revered as goddess-like, I am not a deity. What distinguishes me is not my behavior, or what I appear to be. It is, rather, my inner self. I am one with nature, an entity who shapeshifts and mingles with humans. With me, you will recognize the powers and strengths within yourself — where the ancient secrets of all creations await. You will learn how to defeat the shadows of fears. You have the power to see light in the darkness, and calm in chaos. Remember, the journey to true enlightenment has endless paths. Pave your own road, and you will find your way. Remain confident while you engage in what life has given you. Pace carefully and thoughtfully. Treat all of your powers mindfully. Your life is a journey, not a destination. Prepare now for battle, and your journey to the underworld. Fear nothing and no one. You are

SH+AGUAR, THE NIGHT HUNTRESS! The time to kill is now!

She disappeared in one bound! Then came that sudden surge of energy! The bright flash of violet light! And finally, the spiraling tunnel!

SWISH! WHOOSH! THUMP!

I landed, softly, in an out-of-the-way area, near an old military airplane hangar. The building was not at all dilapidated or abandoned. The structure had obviously been renovated, upcycled, and now, repurposed for a deadly operation. It was an extraordinarily large hangar, beautifully detailed with multi-paned windows, brick walls, and years of history and rich patina. Cavernous, with a soaring bow-trussed ceiling, the runway appeared to have been recently paved with asphalt.

Outback, behind the hangar was a smaller, attached building with two separate sections. There were no windows in the room closer to the hangar. It was completely enclosed and secured. Hidden inside was an impressive cache of military-grade guns, automatic firearms, and an assortment of high-powered battlefield weapons. The outermost section was a garage-like structure. Three camouflaged jeeps were parked inside — all emblazoned with the red cross and red crescent. Situated in plain sight, at first glance, most people would have concluded that these premises were under the auspices of The International Federation of the Red Cross and Red Crescent Movement, or even the Swiss Red Cross.

The hangar housed nine aerial crop dusters — all decaled with red crosses and red crescents. They were brand new planes, designed especially for aerial application. Powered by turboprop engines, I deduced that each crop duster carried a price tag of at least a million euros. This was clearly a large-scale operation with blessings and financing from the upper echelons of money and power. I zoomed in and saw that each of the nine planes — lined up and set to go — was loaded with a minimum of eight hundred gallons of deadly bacteria, viruses, and fungi! With GPS guidance, the pilots would be able to accurately pinpoint their targeted areas along the Rhône River. The resulting death, devastation, and destruction would be unfathomable.

Present were thirteen people in total — nine pilots and four ground operations crew. Everyone was Russian. Of the thirteen, three were women. Zeroing in, I noticed that one of the female pilots bore a remarkable resemblance to the brilliant female doctor at University Hospital where I had been a patient. Delving deeper and utilizing extrasensory perception, I discovered that the taller, blonde female pilot was indeed closely related to the doctor. The two women were, in fact, blood sisters. How interesting, I thought! While one sister was in the business of healing the sick and saving lives, the other sister worked in the bloody business of maiming, incapacitating, and killing masses of innocent people!

The mood inside the hangar was filled with light laughter and controlled jubilant sounds. Several of the pilots boasted heartily about their daredevil aerial stunts, and how many hours of flying experience they'd acquired. Others told brutal stories about how, over the years, they had used crop dusters to destroy farms, settlements, and entire villages, dropping deadly poisons as, unwittingly, people on the ground cheered and waved up at them. They all reveled in knowing that, with full financing, support, and protection from the Kremlin, they had gotten away with genocidal and widespread mass murders, over and over, again. There was no reason to expect that tonight would be any different. Finally, a round of vodka was poured, and the men and women raised their glasses in a celebratory toast to their expected success!

I had had enough! Thirteen was always a lucky number for me. But for these evil-minded, hate-filled miscreants, tonight, the number thirteen would rain down unimaginable horror upon them, delivering the kind of terror, punishment, and finality they all deserved! From this moment on, I was out on the prowl. These heartless, subhuman vultures were my prey. This wicked party was about to come to a justifiable, violent, and bloody end.

Uncontrolled fury surged inside me. I leapt, swiftly, and landed stealthily. Then, with strong, padded paws, glided, silently and completely undetected, across the steep ceiling of the hangar. In the vaulted apex, I came to a sudden stop. My skin and muscles throbbed and pulsed, spasmodically. With rapid contortions, my extremities contracted and expanded until they extended to three times their normal size and length! My entire body stretched and shifted in a manner that was not at all painful, but rather pleasurable and euphoric. In its entirety, the metamorphosis was nothing short of exhilarating. Embodied in a curvaceous phantasmagorical outline, my image twisted and shifted into a new shape. When the transformation was done, what emerged was a creature that was neither woman nor jaguar, but something else — a gargantuan monster, one that was ferocious and agile, an utterly frightening and powerful supernatural being!

I had been transformed into a perversion of life, a grotesquely deformed chimeric creature, with severely misshapen features. My large, cleft head and neck were more animal than human. My arms, and legs, covered with a sheath of taut, leathery-looking skin, bulged with sculptured, overly developed, muscles. Little black on black rosettes were scattered randomly over my torso, hands, and feet. On the surface, my face, framed with wavy black hair, consisted of my eyes, my nose, and my lips. From my long clawed feet and hands, sharp, ten-inch razor-like, retractable claws protruded. My glowing eyes were filled with a piercing golden green. Hidden, surreptitiously, behind my face and lips were forty teeth, six killer canine fangs, and super powerful, jaw muscles.

I breathed quietly, and sprayed my musky scent, while wafting in the ceiling. This old hangar was now my territory. Lunging, I landed, on all fours, squarely in front of the planes. I wanted the party-revelers to get a good look at me. I wanted to frighten them to death. Shocked and awed, the men and women were terrorized by my sudden, ghastly appearance. They screamed and cried out, none wanting to believe what their eyes were seeing. The ground crew quickly drew handguns and fired bullets continuously at me. Seeing that I was uninjured, and their guns emptied, they ran for backup.

The pilots, all equipped with their own automatic firearms, drew them, aimed squarely at me, and simultaneously released a battery of fire. Here they were again — those annoying mosquito bites! Waving the bullets off, I made my first attack. As the petrified pilot tried to get inside his plane, I pounced on him!

CRA-AC-KKKK!

With one bite to the back of his skull, I pulverized his head. Another pilot, armed with a double barrel firearm, raced towards me. I stopped him in his tracks, bit straight through the barrels with my canines, and broke the weapon in half. Frozen with fright and fear, he stood there. In one motion, my mouth opened, then closed on his spine, snapping it instantly with my crushing jaw force!

CHOMP! CHOMP! CHOMP!

Six deadly fangs pierced his vertebrae in a quick and painless death. Two down, eleven more to go, I thought. This was truly going to be a test of my superhuman powers!

I was being attacked differently now. The mosquito bites were increasing, and I was beginning to feel the stinging far more intensely. Then came a sudden, burning sensation — one that tingled my nerves, and rose straight to the top of my spine. I had been shot in the back of my head! I spun around, angrily, and saw that three pilots — a woman and two men — were now behind a six-barrel rotary machine gun. They had dragged it out from the room outback, and were firing non-stop at me, gangster style. Powered by an electric motor, the Gatling-style rotating barrel had unleashed more than 4000 rounds of fire on me! Infuriated, and feeling what could only be likened to a migraine headache, I growled and readied myself for a bloody, triple kill.

Just as I was about to attack the three evil-doers who were busy firing at me, the hairs on my body stood up. I caught a whiff of a certain smell in the air. It was the smell of masculine musk. Looking clear across the room, my eyes were met with two orbs glowing from the ceiling. The creature released a nasally, snuffing sawing sound. He yawned and displayed an impressive jawline, and a mouthful of sharp, dagger-like teeth. The monster on the other side of the hangar looked almost as terrifying as I did!

A black, melanistic jaguar, he was slightly smaller than what I had shape shifted into. He was strong, stocky, and robust, with a deep chest, and a very large head. He had claws, fangs, and a pair of keen eyes —

vertically slit pupils — that were golden, sparkling, and dangerous. There was a shrewd awareness about him, a kind of preternatural consciousness that emanated from him. He embodied the same kind of 'fierce jaguarness' that I possessed.

Looking straight ahead, the blacker-than-black jaguar stood stealth-like behind the pilots, who were wholly unaware of his presence. I watched in amazement, as his muscled body stretched outward, and contracted. Then, in one swift leap, he pounced on the first pilot, and bit forcefully into his face and neck, immediately immobilizing him.

CRUNCH!

The second pilot was stunned to death when the angry felid plunged swordlike, retractable claws into his skull, spewing blood and brain!

SCRUNCH!

As the third pilot abandoned the weapon and opted to run for her life, she was stopped abruptly, when the jaguar roared, opened its mouth, and killed her with one solid bite to the head!

CRAAACCKK!

Our eyes locked. As Jacob's eyes met mine, he greeted me, telepathically:

Mom… did you really think that I would let you do this without me? Remember, we're doing this for Jason! We are in this together!

With that, Jacob, now transformed into an extraordinarily augmented jaguar, leapt towards me.

We stood side-by-side as the last eight culprits either squirmed, ran for cover, or tried desperately to escape inside their planes. Instead of fighting one horrifying monster, they were now staring hopelessly at two hideously appalling, super powerful beings! Four pilots ran for cover in their planes as the last crewmen continued firing round after useless rounds of ammunition at us.

They all watched, open-mouthed, in disbelief, as my leathery skin, lacerated and shredded by bullets, quickly healed itself. They shuddered when Jacob's severely wounded, almost detached limbs were immediately regenerated and made whole. Reality had finally hit them. They had run out of weapons and hope. They were now running for dear life! They knew that even their most powerful automatic weapons were of little or no use against us. The last rats were trapped!

BATA-BATA-BATA-BATA! BATA!-BATA-BATA-BATA!

Several of the pilots had gotten inside their crop dusters and were trying desperately to escape. Jacob and I took them on with very little effort. I leapt onto the first plane, opened my mouth, shifted my jaws, then bit through the steel frame of the small plane.

CLANG! CLANK! CLANG!

The pilot squirmed as I opened my mouth, shifted my jaw, and gave him a single, fatal bite to the head.

CHOMP!

Another pilot struggled and waved a long machete at Jacob, who had already chewed a hole wide enough to get inside the plane. When the machete accidentally fell from the pilot's hand, Jacob wasted no time. With the full force of his jaws and bite strength, he crushed the pilot's skull bones!

CRACK!

As the last pilots were trying to lift off, I sprung into the air, shattered the window with my ten-inch retractable claws, reached inside, and grabbed him by the neck. With robust, canine teeth, I tore into his skull and chomped down to make the kill.

SPLASH! Brain matter splattered everywhere!

Heading towards my next prey, I caught sight of Jacob, in violent action.

Springing from wing to wing, he tore, effortlessly, through the window, with his claws. Inside the plane, the panic-stricken pilot yielded and raised his hands. One look around would have told him what he had just surrendered to. You see, Jacob was clearly not in a forgiving mood. He proudly displayed forty sharp teeth, pierced the pilot's head, and destroyed his neck, with the full bite force of his jaw!

CHOMP! CHOMP!

With four more pilots disabled and dead, Jacob and I set our eyes on the remaining cowards — all piled into two jeeps.

VAROOM! VAROOM!

The jeeps careened from behind the hangar. I greeted the first one, driven by the doctor's sister, with great hostility. In one leap, I pounced onto the vehicle, causing it to veer off. The would-be getaway driver slammed on the brakes, causing her and her passengers to be vigorously ejected from the jeep. Their hapless bodies met the icy ground, with deleterious impact.

FA-THUD! FA-THUD! FA-THUD!

Leaping into the back seat of the second jeep, Jacob took full advantage of the situation. He took the passenger, swiftly, with a decisive jaw bite to the back of the head.

CRAUNCH! CRAUNCH! CRAUNCH!

Then, he turned to the driver, looked briefly into his eyes, and plunged a mouthful of teeth and six sharp fangs into his skull!

CRACCC-UNCH!

When it was all over, Jacob and I surveyed the scene. It was a bloodbath. Pools and streams of red blood flowed across the white, snow-covered ground. Here and there, pieces of brain matter were congealing, and beginning to freeze in the cold. The air smelled of iron from fresh, raw blood. Together, our eyes shifted to where the doctor's sister laid. Her blonde hair, soaked in a pool of red slush, framed her face. One eye hung loosely from the socket, the other, stiff, fixed, and frozen. We looked on, mercilessly, as her slender body writhed in agony, on the cold ground. She wasn't dead just yet. But the gates of hell were wide open and waiting for her!

Our work had been done. It was time to contact the Swiss authorities, the military, and Interpol. Utilizing extrasensory perception and superhuman telepathy, we decided which government officials and military officers needed to be contacted first. Not surprisingly, all of the culprits were in possession of disposable, burner cell phones, which we made good use of. While I communicated the events and location of the kill to various organizations, Jacob made a call to Dr Hunter Talbot, the chief DNA expert at the Disaster Victim Identification site. We agreed that Dr Talbot would be most interested in getting his hands on the DNA of these terrorists. Jacob called him on his private number. At an hour in the night when most people were fast asleep in their beds, Dr Talbot was wide awake and busy at work in his laboratory.

Good evening… Dr Hunter Talbot here. May I ask who is calling?

"Good evening, Dr Talbot. I'm afraid I must remain anonymous. I am calling to inform you of the location of thirteen people whose DNA you might be very interested in."

Who are you? And how did you get my… this number?

"The Swiss authorities, military brass, and Interpol have already been contacted. You can find the thirteen souls at the old military hangar, half a kilometer north of the French-Swiss border. I must warn you… it is quite a gruesome scene. Good-luck, and so long." With that, Jacob ended the call and turned his sad, felid eyes to meet mine. "This was for Jason. I did it for him. I did it for selfish reasons!"

"I know. But think about how many lives we've saved. We did what had to be done. And it was the right thing to do. No matter how you look at it. By stopping these killers, and intercepting their evil plans, we've saved millions of innocent lives. That is what Jason would have wanted us to do. That is how your father wanted these superhuman powers to be used — for the good of humanity."

Jacob smiled and his eyes lit up. "It's time for us to leave, mom. Swiss officials are fast-approaching."

"Yes, I know." I took a deep breath and exhaled. "We're done here. At least for now." With my claws fully extended, I dipped them into a pool of bad blood. And in big, capitalized letters, on one side of the hangar, I left my mark and name: *SH+AGUAR, THE NIGHT HUNTRESS!*

The surge came, suddenly.

SWISH! WHOOSH! THUMP!

I landed inside the chalet, on all fours, then quickly sprung to my feet.

Jacob arrived moments later, a bit disoriented, and landed on wobbly legs. He was shaken and somewhat unbalanced, as I helped him to his feet. "Wow! That was some trip!" he blurted out, looking around, still jittery and trying to pull himself together.

"Yes… this has been quite the trip. But, now, it's time for us to go home… where we belong… back to the good ol' US of A!"

With a shy smile, Jacob nodded in agreement.

"I have a feeling in my gut that our services might soon be needed in New York City!"

Neither Jacob nor I had much of an appetite when we returned to the chalet. There was no mention of what we'd done… no discussion at all about what had happened at the hangar. It was as if the events at the hangar had never taken place. Before retiring for the night, I wrapped my arms around Jacob and planted two motherly kisses on both sides of his face — one for him, and one for Jason. It had been one hellish Friday night!

Jacob was quite the chef. I awoke Saturday morning to a most appetizing *Zmorge!* The robust aromas of kaffee creme, potato pancakes, fried bacon and eggs, braided Zopf bread, and a generous assortment of cheeses was just what my starving stomach needed.

"And a good morning to you!" I gushed, taking in the delicious smells wafting from the food-laden table. "This is quite a spread. It must have taken a while to pull this kind of breakfast together!"

Jacob smiled, proudly. "When in Switzerland, do as the Swiss do!" He poured me a long espresso and placed a small pitcher of hot, steamed milk next to my mug. "Saturday is officially the weekend, which means we get to enjoy a big, full breakfast!" He took a big gulp of his hot cocoa, and reached for the television remote. "I actually got up really early and made a list of all of the things I need to do before we leave for New York. I've already taken care of most of them online. I even found a buyer for my car." He paused and channel surfed until he found his favorite English language news channel. "Did you sleep well last night?"

"I slept like a rock!" was all I could get out, eagerly downing some of the strong kaffee before diving into my breakfast. This was a moment that felt eerily like déjà vu to me. Perhaps the setting was different, but everything else about it had the makings of a morning I had shared with Jason, not very long ago. So much had happened between then and now.

Our eyes were glued to the screen as the news reporter, with her crisp British accent, began with the caption: *THIS JUST IN!*

A good Saturday morning. I'm Christine Vance reporting to you live from the French-Swiss border in Geneva, Switzerland, where I've just learned that a planned bioterrorist attack targeting the Rhône River was intercepted late last night and foiled by… well… mysterious crime fighters. According to my sources, government officials, along with a team of bacteriologists, and the Swiss Coroner's chief magistrate have converged on the gruesome crime scene. The premises, under high-security, and off-limits to reporters and the public, are heavily guarded by members of Interpol and the military. Using small, crop duster airplanes, the would-be terrorist — believed to be connected to the recent string of devastating bombings and gas attacks — had planned to drop tons of deadly bacteria, virus, and fungi in the Rhône River, potentially incapacitating and killing millions of people. Anonymous calls were made to authorities with disposable burner phones to report the foiled attack. At this time, however, authorities still do not know who the courageous vigilantes were. Twelve souls have been recovered. The only surviving culprit, a female pilot, is clinging to life. She is not expected to survive her injuries. A source close to the investigation did reveal that unusually large feline-like paw prints were found near the scene. Even more baffling was what investigators found inscribed in blood, on an outside wall of the hangar — SH+AGUAR, THE NIGHT HUNTRESS! In other developing news… amidst continued cleanup efforts, Swiss Air Lines have announced that it will resume making domestic and international flights as early as Monday of this coming week…"

For a moment, neither Jacob nor I said anything. Jacob cleared his throat and turned to face me. "Mysterious crime fighters and vigilantes have a certain kind of ring to it," he said, thoughtfully. "But what will keep them all wondering is your name inscribed in blood."

I smiled and nodded. "Yes… my signature gives the deed a certain personalized touch. Don't you agree?"

"Most certainly!"

Less than a week after Jacob and I had put Lem and Jason's work to the test, we were organized, packed, and ready to depart from Geneva, Switzerland. Not knowing what had become of Jason was immensely painful. I would never get used to living with that kind of grief. Deep down inside I knew that it wasn't going to be easy for us. But I also knew that Jacob and I were going to have to learn to live with the pain. We were left with our own personal wounds — the kind that time could not and would not ever heal. Losing Lem, and now, Jason, had become a part of my newly altered life. Lem's abduction had shattered my world. And although he had never been declared dead, I still mourned him, every, single day.

The pain of losing a child is incomparable. There are no words that can articulate the loss of an offspring. That kind of grief is unfathomable, deeply personal, and complicated. Losing Jason left a bleeding, gaping hole in my entire being. The overwhelming pain and suffering I feel is indefinable. There are moments when I want to stop the world, for a while, to give me time — time to process everything that has happened, time to catch my breath and breathe. As for Jacob, my whole heart goes out to him. I can only imagine the torment he feels each day — having found his brother after so many years, only to lose him, and in such an horrific way. Grief is the saddest, most powerful emotion one can go through. His grief is different from mine. We will have to find our own way to get through this.

Jacob and I were greeted at JFK Airport by Eugenia, Santini, Big Joe, and Sam. I returned to New York the way I had left — with a beloved son by my side.

THE END

CPSIA information can be obtained
at www.ICGtesting.com
Printed in the USA
BVHW080010180323
660664BV00006B/169

9 781800 166660